I0654433

Sometimes Ya Gotta Laugh

Timothe Davis

To Brandi, for the gift of feedback, to Ricky for the gift of encouragement, and to Sha for the gift of faith. I wouldn't have finished this book without any of the three. Thank you.

And to all the other friends and family who read a word, a paragraph, or a few pages, who offered a kind word or expressed interest, to April, and Gina, and AJ, and Jason, and Jennifer, and Caleb, and Ric, and Wendy and Pablo, and Kevin, and Carmisha, I thank you. This is for you.

To my mother, who has a wonderful imagination- but doesn't need to read this book, my father, who loves to write, and to Phyllis, the only women patient enough to put up with my father. I love you all.

And Ryan Merrill for the art work.

Http://www.facebook.com/SometimesYaGottaLaugh

Chapter 1

Breaking The Girl

January 1(Tuesday)

New Year's Day. 5:00 am. My eyes are closed but I am wide awake. I open them to find my alarm clock mocking me with its metallic red neon numbers. The clock knows I am the only man in the universe waking up this early on New Year's.

She purrs peacefully in the bed behind me. *At least one of us is sleeping.*

I reach down, grab my boxers off the floor, toss them on top of the clock, and close my eyes again. Doesn't help. The red neon still flashes, she still purrs, and sleep still escapes me. I give the clock the finger.

What is her name? Alison? Alisa? What time did I go to bed last night? Three am? And was I too drunk to close the shades when I came home? The outside streetlamp floods my loft, conspiring malevolently with the alarm clock to deny me any additional REM.

Nights like these are the ones that Tivo was created for. Those nights when Mr. Sandman has abandoned you at the orphanage for wayward sleepers, your sheep have found a knoll with better grass and a better shepherd, and your friend who works as a pharmaceutical rep just got put on final warning for giving out free samples of Ambien to his friends.

I toss my legs slowly over the side of the bed, trying to move quietly and not wake what's-her-name. I snatch my boxers off the clock and turn the clock toward the wall. *That will teach it.* And I walk toward the bedroom door.

Unfortunately, my door cannot be passed through without a quick study of my reflection in the cheval. When this ritual began, who knows? I'd guess somewhere around my thirty-fifth birthday began my obsessive compulsive check for signs of middle age and belly fat. Middle age men with paunches and receding hairlines don't get *the girl. Whoever the girl is.*

I look at my stomach – four pack not a six pack but good enough for the beach. And I battle the onslaught of gray hairs by plucking six from my goatee.

She rolls over and sighs. What is her name? And why do I care? I've been butt-ass naked with several girls I've met in Uptown and haven't known their name – at least not their last name. So why *her* name?

Our sex wasn't mind blowing. But that wasn't her fault. Sex rarely is mind blowing these days. At eighteen, horniness is only a wind-blow away and any sex is good sex. At thirty-six, the horniness still persists. But the sex isn't as consistently good. Crazy thing is, she was earnest. She was making all the appropriate sounds … almost but not quite … a little over-the-top. Which was good because I prefer the more natural sounds to the wanna-be-Jenna-Jamison sounds. But I digress … she's making the appropriate sex sounds and I'm obliging her with the appropriate pelvic thrusts. The headboard is knocking against the wall and the springs of my too old Posturepedic are creaking rhythmically to Maxwell's falsetto crooning out my iPod speakers. Almost all the ingredients were present for a toe-curling descent into jizz paradise. Yet, no dice. I'd give it a six on the one to ten scale. Long story short, and it's much too late for that now, exactly eighty-three minutes after we walked in the door and twenty-two minutes after she says, "I'm about to cum …" she was sound asleep. (She came four times. She was tired).

My friend Gabrielle says that fuck buddies never spend the night. An interesting statement coming from Gabrielle as she doesn't believe in fuck buddies or one night stands. Nevertheless, she says once both of you get what you want, you go your separate ways. Why this is the case, I'm not sure. Perhaps staying overnight implies some level of emotional intimacy that isn't there.

Her statement is probably truer when the fuck is neither good nor your buddy. But asking a girl to leave after sex requires more cajones than I have. Besides, Ally or Andrea is sleeping peacefully. Her shoulder length brown hair falls loosely on the pillow, her pouty lips are slightly parted, and she purrs quietly as if in the midst of a good dream. I stare at her. She is as pretty now as she was at the party. (At least the alcohol didn't lower my standards.) More importantly, in spite of the fog in my head, I know I enjoyed her company last night.

Screw TIVO. I need to learn her name.

I take a quick look to make sure she is still sleeping, and then I pick up her pocketbook and begin rummaging. Let's see. Her name is Alicia Farmer. Nice enough name. More rummaging. Parkland hospital badge. Okay, she told the truth about her work. She is an attractive professional. I can dig it. I put the purse down and go to the bathroom to take a leak.

By Gabrielle's account, this non-sleeping over is a universal rule that all women are aware of. If that's the case, Alicia Farmer is in violation.

Last night about 300 people ushered in the New Year at Glenn Michaels' house. Glenn Michaels buys a new CLK in the fall prior to the year the car debuts. Every time the newest condo goes up in Dallas, he is the first to move - which means he moved to Victory Park about six months ago and is paying four dollars per square foot for his place or some other insane number. Plus he knows a host of B and C-list celebrities. Pretentious, smug, and self-absorbed are three of the kinder words I've heard used to describe him. General consensus is he is an all-around-asshole. Yet everybody flocks to his parties.

Dallas revels in its "scene-and-be-seen" mentality. And there is no telling who you might see and be seen with at Glenn's place. Two years ago I thought I saw Perez Hilton engrossed in conversation with T.O. Doesn't make much sense, but I thought I saw it.

While I have no desire to be an intricate part of the Dallas social party club scene, I do agree that the parties are a must. If nothing else, they provide great fodder for conversation. Last year, me, Chris, and Gabby counted six Dallas Cowboy cheerleaders, four Mav players, three former boy-band members, two reality stars, and one porn star.

This year, though, we were surprisingly bored. Glenn had the usual host of celebrities but too many Entertainment Tonight D-listers – children of former Celebs or girls (and boys) who made six minute sex tapes stretch into fifteen minutes of stardom. 300 guests, thirty servers, five valets, and yet the room felt oddly soul-less and disconnected. My boredom was so overwhelming, I had every intention of calling the night early – right after the clock struck midnight and not before one more drink.

I was scanning the room when my eyes met Glenn's. He smiled and held up his glass. I lifted my drink in response. When I did, he tapped his glass and that's when I noticed mine was empty. I flashed him a smile and turned to find a server who could rectify this travesty. Who I found was Alicia Farmer.

Alicia Farmer was pinned in the corner of the room, looking more than a little bored. A smile sat on her face but clearly had not reached her Hershey eyes. Her head was tilted in what was meant to convey interest but everything else about her body language was disinterested. Her blue-eyed blond suitor might have seen it had he not been blinded by the sexiness that seemed to ooze from her pores. Her black Cavelli dress clung to her every curve as if it was stitched on her. The neckline plunged seductively; her Jimmy Choo stilettos flattered her toned calves and legs.

I watched until her suitor walked away befuddled and dejected. For my part, I grabbed two glasses of wine off the server's tray and strolled toward her.

Thirty minutes later I had all but forgotten Gabby and Chris, entranced in a conversation and seduced by the night. Or by Alicia, I'm not sure. We slipped onto Glenn's patio in search of a quiet space only to find several couples who were seeking the same. Already buzzing from wine, we were having that semi-personal conversation that's somewhere between what you have with your bartender and your therapist. It moves from intimate to casual to flirting and then back again. I have a vague recollection of some talk about EHarmony or Match.com or some other internet dating site. She recounted tales of guys who were a bit too metro, guys who were a bit too short ("he came up to my left breast, I'm not kidding"), and guys who were a bit too desperate.

"Your left breast?"

"Yes, my left."

"Why your left?"

"Because it hangs a bit lower than the right."

"Really?"

"Really. Maybe I'll show you some time," she grinned. I grinned back. A waiter stepped onto the patio to refill our glasses. "The truth is," she continued, turning her statement clinical as the waiter poured our wine, "most bodies are not symmetrical."

"Uh-huh," I nodded. "But didn't you know he was short? Don't they tell you how tall they are?"

"He lied."

"Ouch."

She shrugged.

"Well, it's not all about the physical," I replied casually.

"Oh, it isn't?" Her eyebrows furrowed as if she had detected a lie.

I was lying. I mean, I know it's not ALL about physical. But how much isn't? Where does physical end and spiritual and emotional begin? I have passed up some pussy that's been attached to some ugly faces. But that's okay, right? I mean, fucking is supposed to be all about the physical.

But I've also passed up some great ladies because they weren't attached to pretty faces. Is that okay? And do I really care right now? It's New Year's.

"It isn't?"

It isn't? I can't let an introspective question lie. So it continued to tumble through my head.

I was lying. I think. In part. For some reason I felt compelled to make the answer legit. Unfortunately, I needed time to think through my response. "That's an excellent question," I said as I shifted from one foot to the other.

I like words - when I have the right ones to use. Responding when I'm not prepared is not my thing. Granted, I was putting the pressure on myself. But still ...

"What are you two doing?" My friend Chris had stumbled onto the patio. Vodka and cranberry splashed out his drink and onto my shirt as he clumsily wrapped his arm around my shoulder. He took the napkin I was holding under my drink and attempted to pat my shirt dry. "I'm sorry."

Another place, another time, I would've been slightly irritated at my inebriated friend who had just stained a perfectly good white shirt maroon in front of a woman who was sexy enough for me to drink her bath water. Tonight, though, he had saved me from a question I couldn't answer. I could only feign irritation.

"Fuck you, Chris. We were almost on the brink of world peace. And you screwed it up." I grabbed the napkin out his hand and attended to my own shirt. Alicia smirked in amusement.

"I'm sorry," he slurred. "All those poor children in Afghanistan." He looked genuinely worried. *He was drunk and it wasn't even midnight. O but it was midnight.* I had been so enthralled with Alicia, I hadn't notice the confetti, the toasts, and the congratulations.

"I'm sorry," he repeated. "You want another drink?"

"Please." I said the word as if penance was required. "Alicia, you want anything?"

"An apple Martini."

"Make it two, Chris. Thanks." He stumbled off to get the drinks.

She spoke. "Friend of yours?"

"Best friend actually." I smiled.

She nodded. "So where were we?"

"Desperation on EHarmony."

"Oh yes, so I met this guy ..."

Thank you, Chris.

She was talking again. But I was still distracted with her question. *Am I lying?* If I meet a girl who isn't my type physically but is a wonderful person, should I pursue her?

What good does it do me to be involved with some chick I'm not sexually attracted to? How is it that such a small organ controls such a large piece of my life? And just to be clear, that isn't a comment on the size of my manhood. I come from a rich heritage. When I say small, I mean relative to other body parts: arm, leg, foot ...

Three hours later my large organ has me in bed with some chick whose name wasn't quite clear to me, having sex that is just marginally above average, and uncomfortable in my own apartment.

I throw on jeans and a t-shirt and decide to go for a cup of coffee but second guess myself when I reach the door. A strange woman is laying in my bed. Is leaving wise? What does gut say? Gut says she is naked, you know her first, her last name, and where she works. Besides if she is comfortable leaving her Louis Vuitton purse on my floor, I should be comfortable leaving her alone with my valuables. I close the door gently behind me.

Starbucks is about eight blocks from me – a decent walk, especially when I wanna clear my head. The street is empty, no one else having been cursed with the inability to sleep off a hangover on New Year's day. I shove my hands in my pocket, wish I had thrown on a windbreaker, and walk briskly.

I hit Starbucks' front door about fifteen minutes after the store opens. I come here so often they know my name, know I despise the taste of Americana, and are the root cause of my annual teeth whitening trips to the dentist. I have got to stop drinking this shit.

The cashier is a dowdy woman with a warm demeanor. She calls me, "Hun." I like that. She is supported by a barista who is short and chunky with … one … two … three … four earrings in his ear. He also calls me "Hun." It's cool.

I pour half the coffee in the trash, refill it with half-and-half and six packs of Splenda, and walk back to my loft.

I'm a processor – always analyzing information, reshaping, reformatting. I weigh words before I speak and if I don't have an immediate answer … well I mull. My ex-girlfriend, Chloe, called me retarded once. Her exact words, "Is my boyfriend retarded? Can't he answer a single question without taking thirty minutes to think about it?"

The quality drives some people to distraction and sometimes makes me feel like an observer of life not a participant in it.

The other thing is, sometimes I'm processing but I'm not sure what I'm processing. Something will be bothering me; I'll be feeling unsettled. Yet, I will be hard pressed to put my finger on exactly what's the cause. That sensation seems to be occurring more often these days.

I pick up yesterday's *USA Today* on the way home and take the stairs up to my loft. As I go to open the door I suddenly realize I have only one cup of coffee in my hand. I hope Alicia Farmer is awake. I hope she's gone. But say she hasn't left? Say she is awake and she wants some coffee? Argh! I take a huge sip of coffee and then sit the cup in front of my neighbor's door. I have a guest in my bed and I have come home with one cup of coffee. Am I a nimrod or what?

I can't see her when I open the door but I can smell her. At least, I can smell what she is doing. She is cooking. I walk into the kitchen and fight to keep my mouth and eye from twitching like a Tourette syndrome patient. Before I can speak she says, "I hope you don't mind. I was starving.

"I hope I'm not overstaying my welcome," she adds. I take two beats to respond – one beat too long. She winces and adds, "Sorry! I'll be outta your hair momentarily. Besides, my eggs are delicious."

She slips a plate of eggs scrambled with cheese in front of me. I pause before taking a bite. Good thing I didn't meet this chick off Craigslist. Or I'd be scraping this into the trash when she wasn't looking. But gut says she is cool. So I take a bite. She is damn skippy. These eggs are the bomb. I wonder if she has made enough for seconds.

Chapter 2

January 7 (Monday)

"She spent the night," Christopher Beauchamp asked, more intrigued by the three SMU females that had just walked into the bar than any comment I might be making. Blue eyes, blond hair, cleft chin, he claimed he was part Norwegian, which was fitting as he deemed himself a Nordic god. In truth, his ancestry was rooted somewhere in the backwoods of Baton Rouge. While he would want to deny it, his thick gumbo accent would betray him every time. He removed his tie, unbuttoned the first three buttons of his Geoffrey Beene, and put his suit coat on the chair beside him. When he did so, his concealed weapon flashed unconcealed.

"Seriously," I asked, "do you think you really need that?" nodding toward the gun.

"Absolutely," Gabby said, sarcasm dripping from her every word. "With all the gang violence in the West Village, I'm sure he'll need it to defend us."

"It's my constitutional right," Chris replied simply. I shook my head, Gabby rolled her eyes.

Over the years, we had had the gun conversation too many times to count. By the end of every debate, Gabby was the liberal undermining the country, I was the know-it-all-New Yorker, and Chris was the gun-toting-what-our-forefathers-died-for Republican.

Nowadays debates on the subject amounted to well placed sarcasm and smug retorts - none of which phased Chris. "You were saying," he said.

"I was saying, she spent the night."

"She spent the night," Gabrielle's emerald eyes sparkled

with curiosity.

I repeated my words for the third time. "She spent the night. And for God's sake, would you button your shirt, Chris?"

Chris winked at me and grinned.

We sat at Cosmo, a sushi bar in uptown Dallas, just on the edge of "the gayborhood". Gabby had been invited to a business lunch at the restaurant about eighteen months ago and had introduced Chris and I to it the following week. It wasn't nearly as popular as the other sushi places in Dallas – Sushi Zushi or Steele – but Cosmo had a Temptation roll that was out of this world. The three of us were weekly happy hour guests.

Great sushi and great location didn't give Cosmo a great deal of other customers, though. It wasn't the place to be "seen". To the contrary, if there was a spot that was off-the-beaten-path in the most popular area of the city, then Cosmo was it. The sparseness of the crowd all but guaranteed the bar a short lifespan.

"No big deal," Chris said. "I have girls stay overnight all the time."

"That's cause you're a man whore," Gabby, which she prefers to Gabrielle, offered as she waved a waitress over for another round. Chris believed every woman who he was reasonably attracted to deserved a roll in the hay. Gabrielle was totally and completely a one-man kinda woman.

"What the? I am not a whore." His look of offense read almost sincere.

"Dude," I interrupted. "You had more sex last year than Gabby, myself, and," I scanned the room, "the ten other people sitting in here have had in the last three years. You're like a fuckin' John Holmes."

"Hey, I'm single," he grinned.

"Dude," Gabby said flatly, "you're almost forty."

Chris is thirty-six and sensitive about his age.

Tension at the table. I took a swig of my martini.

Sometimes the tension between Chris and Gabby was palpable. Chris would say the tension was lust inspired. Gabby would say it was disgust inspired. If I was a better poet, I would write a limerick about the two.

There once was a boy full of lust ...

Instead I waited it out. These moments only lasted a second or two, coming to a conclusion when one of them said "whatever."

Chris said, "Whatever," and clumsily picked up a piece of the Temptation roll with his chopsticks. When half the roll fell back to his plate, he opted for a fork.

"I'm just saying." Gabby wasn't letting him off the hook. "You guys act like you can't get any satisfaction. Isn't there a time when a man stops chasing ass?"

"No." Chris nudged me and laughed. I took another swig of my drink.

"I'm being serious. How fulfilling can it be, chasing ass all day and night?"

"Very," Chris answered.

Gabby rolled her eyes and turned to me. "What do you think?"

I shrugged my shoulders.

"He's a man. He thinks ..." Chris began.

Gabby threw him daggers. "I'm asking him. What do you think? Isn't there a time when a man needs to stop chasing ass all day?"

"Gabby, baby," Chris interrupted again. "It's how we are wired."

She did one of those talk-to-the-hand moves and continued to stare at me.

"Great question," I began. "I think everyone has to decide what's right for them. It's not up to me to make that judgment call for anyone else."

Chris slapped me on the back with a smile. "Bravo!"

"Tell me," Gabby asked. "Does your ass hurt? Because it should, sitting on the fuckin' fence all the time."

I flipped her off and she returned the favor. "Anyway," she said with exaggerated frustration, "back to the original topic. So how did you feel about this overnight stay?"

"Ah … I'm not sure. Conflicted, I guess."

"Why," Chris wanted to know. "Bad sex?"

"No, it wasn't that. It's … I dunno. Something didn't seem quite right."

"Empty sex," Gabby offered.

"Actually, it felt more real when she was making breakfast in the morning."

"She made you breakfast?" Had their timing been better, they would have sounded like the harmony line in a Broadway musical. But they were a few seconds off. They sounded more like a chorus sung in a round. Chris looked incredulous. He rubbed the weekend face scruff he had refused to shave before going into work that morning.

"None of my over-nighters have ever made me breakfast," he said half to himself.

"More skills with the dick," I said. I did a faux grasp of my crotch. Chris punched me on the arm. Hard. Unwritten rule: Never question Chris's lovemaking skills. I rubbed my arm.

"Well I don't quite know what to say about that," Gabby said. "I mean … it sounds kinda odd. But by all accounts, she is relatively well adjusted."

"Relatively?" I asked.

"Well adjusted and maladjusted are brothers. Twins actually. The distance between the two is always relative to the next person," she responded.

"I don't get it," Chris said. I wasn't sure if he was talking about Gabby's previous statement or the pretty girl who had been in my breakfast nook. "Some pretty girl spends the night and then makes you breakfast in the morning. What's not to like about this?"

"You know he's got space issues," Gabby said to Chris.

"Oh yea, that's right," he chimed in. "Kinda like that funky thing you have about not riding in a two door car."

"Well," Gabby interrupted, "that's a physical space issue. He has that, too. But we are talking about emotional space here."

"Guys, I am here."

"Why don't you like riding in the backseat of a two door car? I never understood that," Chris said.

"It's just too cramped," I explained. "And if there's ever an accident ..."

"He doesn't even like to be touched," Gabby continued. She reached out and rubbed my arm. "Look at how he stiffens." I tried to relax my arm. It stiffened.

"I get stiff every time you touch me," Chris grinned. Gabby paid him no mind.

"It just takes me a while to get to know people," I answered.

"You've been in this city for almost six years and you've never had a relationship that's lasted more than six months," Gabby said sounding like an attorney.

"I've also never had a relationship that's ended badly. Thank you."

"What's that supposed to mean? Maybe you haven't been emotionally invested enough for it to end badly," she countered.

"Like ending badly is the sign of a good relationship. Maybe I've dated people who were mature and we realized early on that it wasn't meant to be."

"Or maybe, you're inability to connect ..."

"Guys, guys." Chris threw up a referee's time-out. "You are killing my buzz. Geez. Does every happy hour have to end up in some psycho-babble?" We both looked at Gabby.

"Yes," she affirmed. "If as friends, we can't help each other peel back our issues ..."

"If as friends, we can't mind our business ..." I began.

"If as friends, we can't have a good time," Chris interjected.

"What's the point?"

"What's the point?"

"What's the friggin point," Chris said as he raised his glass. He gulped the drink down and added, "Gotta go drain the main vein."

As soon as he was outta ear reach, Gabby smiled at me slyly. "I met someone," she said.

"What?"

"I met someone. His name is Brad. He's a doctor."

"Oh really? And when did this happen young lady?"

"At the party. When you were over there looking all starry-eyed at breakfast-girl. He called me the next day. We've talked for almost three hours on the phone every day this week."

"I see. And when will we get to meet him?"

"Oh ..." she fidgeted a little. "I don't know. I mean, I need to get to know him before I begin introducing him to my friends."

I stifled an eye-roll. *Time to change the subject.*

"Look at your boy Chris." I nodded toward Chris, who stood across the room, talking to a red-haired very non-Dallas looking chick.

Gabby uncrossed her long legs and stood. She is a beautiful girl – full lips, bone straight hair with a rich black hue, olive skin that spoke of her Argentinean Italian legacy.

"What is he doing?" Gabby asked.

"What do you think?"

"Ugh," she looked at her watch. "It's almost seven. Are

you ready to go?"

"Undoubtedly. He won't miss us."

"Do you think he'll take her home?" I can't believe she asked that question. She already knew the answer.

"The question isn't whether he will take her home," I replied. "The question is whether he will work it well enough to get scrambled eggs in the morning."

We left side-by-side and that was the last time I saw either of them for almost three weeks.

Chapter 3

January 7 (Monday)

Chris sat still on the large leather brown couch. But the room spun like a merry-go-round.

"So you're a virgin?" The lilt of the voice was somewhere between disbelief and coyish mocking. It came from a femme fatale with auburn hair, luscious red lips, and blue eyes. She leaned over, planted her cherry lips on Chris's ear, and gently blew. "You've never tried? Never?"

Chris placed both his hands on the couch and fought to focus. He peered at the blond guy on his left, whose presence made him uncomfortable. When he did, the guy grinned and winked.

"I can't believe he's never tried." The guy spoke to the auburn-haired girl.

She licked her lips and agreed. "Me either." She moved closer to Chris, put her hand on his groin, and flicked her tongue across his ear. He let out a low moan as he turned his attention back to the girl. "Don't be scared, baby. You should try it."

Chris? Scared? Never. What he was was fucked up; that much he knew. And he was getting wood. He wanted to shift so that his hard-on wasn't so clear but he feared he'd lose his balance.

She massaged his dick through his pants. "Mmmm ... you have a gun in your pocket? Or are you just happy to see me?"

His dick pushed against the zipper of his pants.

The blond guy spoke. "He's happy," he said. "Very happy." The guy stood up and wandered over to the bar. "I think this may call for another drink."

"You aren't shy are you?" Auburn girl asked.

"Hell … no." Chris enunciated slowly, distracted by the clink of the ice in Blond guy's glass. When was this guy gonna leave?

"Then take off your shirt. You have a great body." She ran her hand across Chris chest.

Chris hesitated.

"Well, I'm going to take mine off," she said. She stood, took off her blouse, and in one deft move, removed her bra. Titties sprung from everywhere. Chris's mouth fell open. "I take it you like what you see." She sat down on Chris's lap. "They could use a lick. Are you gonna lick them for me, baby?"

Chris obliged her.

"Here's your drink." Blond guy placed a Grey Goose tonic beside Chris.

Chris stopped, momentarily, mouth still full of tit.

"Honey, relax," she said.

"Have fun, dude." That's what the dude said. "Give in. Let go. Nobody needs to know. If you don't like it, then don't do it again. But you only go around once."

So while the room spun and the Grey Goose flowed, Chris licked and kissed and bit. Like some scene from a porn flick, Auburn girl never removed her heels. She stood and straddled his face on the couch and directed every motion. Deeper baby, deeper. Yeah, like that. Chris gazed down in the midst of the scene and saw his pants and boxers had been shimmied down to his ankles. Between his legs was Blond guy. Their eyes met, Blond guy winked again, and then deep-throated him. But all Chris could think of was scrambled eggs.

Scrambled eggs. Scrambled eggs! He threw his head back and began to laugh hysterically.

Chapter 4

January 25th (Sunday)

I was feeling guilty. Kelly (I-don't-know-her-last-name) had left my place and I was pretty confident that she was married, which meant leaving my bed wasn't the most irreprehensible thing that could've happened. Granted, I didn't know for sure. But she called at the oddest times, got distracted with incoming texts, tended to be anxious, and drove a 2007 Dodge Caravan.

I cared but I didn't ask. People should only ask questions when they want to know the answer and I wasn't sure if I wanted the truth. Particularly if it meant sharing her guilt. I grew up in a deeply religious household. I carried enough guilt at most of my own activities. I had no desire to share hers. So I played the ignorance card, which in fact, can be bliss. Just not this time.

She came over at eight but it was almost ten before clothes came off. That's because we never got right to "it". Instead we made small talk - building empty rapport on subjects that neither of us cared about. We had nothing in common. She was a fuck-buddy, in the truest sense of the word. But somehow the conversation added legitimacy to our union. She had laughed at everything I said, regardless of how witty, her laughter rising in her throat and sounding out in notes too sharp or too flat.

At twelve-thirty am, when I closed my front door behind her, I realized that for the past six months I had been having mediocre sex with someone I had met in the fresh produce section of Kroger's. Someone who I had every right to believe was married.

I walked to the fridge and pulled out a Corona. Why do I

do this shit?

Two Coronas later someone knocked on my door.

I meandered to the door, bottle in hand, and flung it open. Chris stood there; face red from the cold but jacket-less.

"You okay?" I asked.

He brushed past me without answering. I closed the door behind him and repeated myself. "You okay?" He responded by pacing across my living room.

"You been smoking?" Weed chills some folks, it fills Chris with nervous energy. He moved so frenetically, I thought he was high. I watched for a few minutes, flopped on the couch, and clicked on the TV. "Sit down, man. You are making me nervous and you are wearing a hole in the concrete."

He paced another sixty seconds before stopping in front of the television. "You remember that girl?" He said.

Chris had numerous girls and he wanted me to narrow it down to one. Was he serious? Is this why he had come over? Seriously?

"That girl," I repeated. I leaned to my left, trying to catch a repeat of *Samurai Jack.* I like that Samurai's moves.

"Yes, the girl from Cosmo."

"Oh yeah, that chica you were hemmed up in a corner with. She was hot. All that fiery red hair, I thought she was Irish or something."

"Her name was Julianna. Her father is Scottish and her mom is Greek …"

"Scottish. Greek. Whatever." I shooed him from the front of the TV.

"She has a boyfriend." He didn't move.

"Uh oh."

"No, uh oh. He's cool. I met him. His name is David. He was there at Cosmo with her."

"Okay."

"After you and Gabby left, the three of us sat at Cosmo

for a while. I dunno, until maybe nine or ten pm. Then we went back to David's place."

"Okay."

"Dude," he started pacing again, "you should fucking see this guy's place. It is awesome. The guy is, like, thirty-two, and he's a pharmacist. Incredible place in Oaklawn, not far from the Mexican restaurant Gabby likes. He's got the latest 3D TV and it's huge. I don't know. He's got this whole surround sound system, some shit he said he got from Germany. Incredible sound. He loves music like you do. He must have over three thousand CDs he's trying to add to iTunes. Super cool guy. You would really like him."

Smells like the oversell. But I knew Chris well enough to know this was going somewhere. Reluctantly, I turned off my favorite samurai and I waited.

"Anyway," he still paced, "we were shooting the shit for awhile. Talking about nothing really. He didn't have much to drink except some Kettle One. So we mixed it with some juice. I mean, we are just chilling and watching some vids. And then the guy decides he wants to get high. So he had some coke. And we started ..."

He said the coke comment like it should slide by me causally. "Chris, are you kidding me? I thought you didn't do that shit anymore. Are you serious? Do you remember what happened before?"

"I know, I know. I don't. At least, I hadn't. Not since … I dunno … college. I promise you. But anyway ..." he took a deep breath. "Anyway, we ended up having a threesome."

I almost missed that comment, lost in Chris's coke revelation. Don't get me wrong, I wasn't an innocent. When Chris and I were in college, we had gone to a party and had tried it. The feeling was good but my guilt was worse. But Chris had liked it, more than we both realized. Over the course of the school year, he descended into madness as he alienated his old friends, made pseudo new ones, and tried shit I'd never heard of. He ended up getting kicked outta school. It took him a hell-filled year to get his shit back together. When he did, he vowed he'd never go back.

"Did you hear what I said?"

"What? Threesome? Dude, seriously?" I was sitting straight up on the couch. "Is this why you've been missing for three weeks? The coke?"

"No."

"The threesome? Are you kidding me? Chris, you've had threesomes before. Who the hell cares? I can't believe that you ..."

"The guy gave me head,"

"What?"

"The guy gave me head."

"What?"

"The guy gave me head. He sucked my dick."

WHAT THE??? Did he just say? Oh hell no! Cardinal rule of the straight ménage a trois: The guys NEVER touch. Oh yeah, they may touch if the chick is giving them head at the same time or if there is some double penetration going on. But otherwise they NEVER touch. Hear me, they NEVER TOUCH DELIBERATELY.

"Okay, um, well ... was it the coke?"

"Yeah."

"Okay, cool ... so not your fault." *Argh? Fault? Blame? Fuck.* "It happened. Big deal." I tried to sound casual.

"Bro, I think I liked it."

"What?"

"I liked it, man. I fuckin' liked it."

"Okay," Clearly there was a scratch on this record because it kept repeating itself. What was he trying to tell me?

"Do you think I'm gay?" He blurted the words out as if I should have an an answer. I didn't. I'm a processor

I stood up and walked toward the kitchen. "Hey ... it was

head. What man doesn't like getting his dick sucked," I joked.

"Do you think I'm gay?"

"I don't think that getting head from a dude makes you gay," I called from my kitchen. I believed that. "You were aroused, you were doing coke … there were a lot of contributing factors."

I leaned into the fridge to get the lemonade. "Gay, bi, and straight aren't defined by one random sexual act. It's …" I was about to say "complicated and more complicated by drugs." But when I stood and turned around he was standing right behind me. Two words: weird and uncomfortable. Well three words but I'm only counting the adjectives. I ducked around him and moved to the counter.

"Sexuality isn't just about who we sleep with. It's about who we love." I poured the last drop of Smirnoff into the shaker.

"Do you believe that?" Chris stared at me hard. He knew my poker face.

Did I believe it? I wasn't sure. At least not sure if I believed it totally. "Totally, I do. Lemon drop."

"Huh?"

"Your martini …" I held out the glass.

He took it from my hand, placed it on the counter, and stared at me like he needed consoling. I stared back, confounded by my inability to be comforting. Awkward silence lumbered into the room.

I put my hand on his shoulder. "It's okay, man," I said. He clasped his hand over mine. I tried not to stiffen.

"Thanks, Jordan."

We drank our martinis in silence and then chased them down with a Heineken. I had had five drinks in ninety minutes. They left me a bit numb – thankfully.

"So what are you going to do next?" I asked.

He gave me a tentative smile. "Forget about it. Reclaim my manhood. Fuck a bitch."

We laughed nervously. "That's the Chris I know." I glanced over at the clock on the wall. "Man, it's almost two am. I'm gonna crash."

"You don't mind if I take the couch, do you?"

"Of course not." I got him a blanket and a pillow out the bedroom closet. "Sleep tight, my man."

At three-thirty am I was still staring at the ceiling. I decided to text Gabby although she was probably sound asleep.

Chris is here.

Three minutes later Gabby texted back. **Why?**

He's had some things on his mind.

Is he okay?

I was mulling how to respond when Chris knocked on the door. "You awake?" He asked.

"I'm up."

He walked in and sat on the edge of the bed.

"You think I'm gonna go to hell?" He asked.

"Huh?"

"You think I'm gonna go to hell?" He repeated.

"For doing coke?"

"No … for the other."

I sat up in bed. "Chris, are you kidding me? You're not even religious. Look, you had some little experimentation thing going on and … I don't even know if it was experimentation. It was a thing okay, it was a thing. It happens. You were drunk and high and shit happens. I've told you before not to fuck with that stuff."

He said nothing; I rambled on.

"Seriously dude. Heaven, hell, it's a state of mind. Besides, my Dad was Catholic and my mom was a Jehovah's Witness. Anything I'd tell you would give you guilt." More silence from him. He wanted an answer. "Chris, all I know is that I hope and pray that God is more interested in how we treat other people than what we do in bed."

"Guess I haven't been very successful at either one," he replied quietly.

I opened my mouth to say something else, but closed it instead. He walked back out the room.

My phone buzzed. It was Gabby again. **Is he okay?????** Five question marks followed. She didn't know that Chris had had a drug problem and she didn't need to know about the threesome. I turned off the phone, closed my eyes, and tried to go to sleep.

****

"Who was that?" Brad asked as Gabby put the phone down.

She rolled over in bed and beamed at him. "Jordan."

"What does he want at this time of night?" He looked concerned.

She moved closer to him. "It's Chris. I guess he was worried."

Gabby put her head on his chest and he wrapped his arm around. She never, NEVER, slept with a guy unless they had been dating for three months. But there was something about Brad that made her feel so safe. He was so unlike the guys she had dated in the past. Strong. Protective. Assertive.

She was being more passive than she had been in her past relationships. She was trying to identify why she had been unsuccessful in love and thought maybe she was too controlling. Which would make her the exact opposite of her Mom, far too weak, and her brother Luis, as laid back as they come. Speaking of which, she need to call Luis. Maybe even tell him about Brad.

"You're not thinking about Chris and Jordan?" Brad asked.

"No," she laughed. "Of course not."

"Then come closer," he said. "I have a gift for you."

"What is it?"

He grinned at her. "My tongue." Then he slid down

beneath the sheets.

Chapter 5

February 4 (Monday)

"If so many people are searching for love, then why are so many people single?" Gabby took the cherry out her drink and placed it on her napkin. Chris picked up the cherry, ate it, and winked at her. She ignored him.

"And," Chris asked, "if marriage is the union of two people in love, why are so many people unhappily married?"

"Thus," I added, "the reason I am single."

We were at happy hour again. But not at Cosmo - Cosmo had been written up in *D Magazine* as the best undiscovered bar in Dallas. Needless to say, it was no longer undiscovered. In a matter of two short weeks, it had gone from semi-busy on Mondays to being in danger of violating the fire code every damn day of the week. It's the type of shit that irritates me: *Somebody* somewhere in Dallas christens a place the "it" place and suddenly the masses are believing and following. That *somebody* has been opening and closing spots all over the city for years. The extra traffic was good for Cosmo. But not good for us. After having waited ninety minutes for a third round of drinks last Monday, we had opted to try another spot. This place was simply called Jim's. It sat on lower Greenville Avenue and like many of the bars on Greenville was dark, dank, and dingy. The club had a retro feel that was less about deliberate design and more about a lack of renovating. Nevertheless, the crowd was friendly, the appetizers were pretty good, and the drinks were strong.

"The reason you are single," Gabby began, "is that you don't take risks."

"I don't take risks? And what risks have you taken?"

"She dated a black guy once." Chris smiled. He only took friendly digs at Gabby when he thought he was inciting a battle he could win.

"Oh yeah, that's risky business." I laughed.

"Very," Chris added.

"Go screw yourself," Gabby said.

"For real, though," Chris said. "She went out with that black guy on one date and called it quits. That's not dating. That's satisfying a curiosity. She was curious and then she was uncomfortable."

"I was not uncomfortable," she said. "We just … we just didn't have much in common."

"You didn't have much in common?" Chris howled. "You two had tons in common. Both in oil and gas, both love to travel, both *habla espanol* and both are pompous." Chris was enjoying this.

"It was because he's black." I said. "Definitely."

"It wasn't because he was black. And I'm not pompous," she declared.

"Well it shouldn't have been because he's black. His dad's a dentist, he went to JMU, he plays golf …" Chris and the guy bowled on a league together. "He's the whitest black guy I know."

"Did you catch Gabby on the TMZ special, when they were profiling Tiger Woods?" I said to Chris. Gabby kicked me under the table. Why were my friends always hitting me?

"Just because his dad is a dentist and he went to JMU and he plays golf doesn't mean he's compatible with me."

"And just because he's black doesn't mean he isn't," Chris countered. "What about Raheem?" He asked. "You dated Raheem."

Gabby blushed. "It was three dates. Raheem is a player."

"Because he's black," Chris said.

"No … it had nothing to do with …," she shook her head.

Chris turned to me, "What do you think? And don't say great question either," he added.

I sighed. "I think people have the right to choose who they …"

"Don't sit on the fence," Gabby added.

"I'm not, I'm not. People are … we all are … so consumed with the physical, skin color, eyes, height, weight, whatever, for various reasons. I think maybe it blinds us to what lies beneath. Chris, you've never dated a fat girl. Is that preference or prejudice or both? And whatever it is, is it wrong? Gabby, you never date the blue collar type. What's up with that? When do our preferences become prejudices? And who's to blame for that?"

"Our parents," Gabby answered.

I shrugged.

"It's true," she continued. "We are a product of their upbringing, their mores, and their social indoctrination. They give us all their shit."

"Don't ya think they're doing the best they can? There is no handbook on parenting," I responded. "Parents make mistakes; we forgive them."

"No handbook? Is that an excuse? How many people have children for selfish reasons? He wants a junior. She wants someone to love her because he doesn't. Mom and Dad want grandchildren. The neighbors are on their second kid. If your reasons aren't altruistic in the first place, isn't doing the best you can empty?" Gabby was on the verge of a soliloquy but Chris cleared his throat. That was for my benefit; he was subtlety reminding her of *my* family situation. Gabby stopped.

"Ignore me." Her smile was remorseful and tender.

"Have you told Chris about the doctor?" I asked.

"What doctor?" Chris looked at Gabby.

"Oh, our little Gabby is hot and heavy with a doctor nowadays."

She popped out a mirror and reapplied plum lipstick that hadn't smudged in the first place. "His name is Brad."

"Did you just giggle?" I asked. She ignored me. "So tell us about this doctor," I said, "who, I might add has been taking my phone time. You don't call me anymore."

"We have been spending a lot of time together," she admitted.

"We've barely heard from you," Chris chimed in.

She waved us both off. "Sure, you have."

Sure we haven't.

"More importantly, when are we going to meet him?" Chris asked.

"Soon," Gabby assured him. "I want us to get to know each other a little first."

Chris and I exchanged looks. "Gabby," I said. "We are your best friends. The guy has to meet us."

"Yes, I know. But you two met Antonio, remember? And that was a fiasco."

"That's because Antonio had the personality of wet sandpaper," I said.

"True," she conceded.

"We will be on our best behavior this time," Chris said crossing his heart.

"I know, it's just, I'm trying to take this slow and we have to get to know each other first."

Chris paraded every date in front of us. Getting to know each other first was not in his vocabulary. Gabby, on the other hand, set up an "out to lunch" sign for her friends and disappeared. She called that taking it slow.

"Just bring the guy to happy hour," Chris said flatly.

The expletive Gabby was about to use was cut off when

someone called her name. The three of us looked over to see some guy waving from the other side of the bar.

"Who is that?" Chris asked. Jim needed to buy some lights for his dive.

"Is that Gary?" Gabby asked. "Oh my god, that's Gary." She waved back. Gary, for his part, rose from his stool and sauntered toward us. I'd met Gary once or twice while hanging out with Gabby at Northpark Mall. From what I knew, he did makeup at Nordstrom and drag on the weekends. I'd hate to see him in drag. He isn't a good looking guy. He is about six two - which makes him an inch taller than Chris and two inches taller than me – and looks like he weighs a buck forty five. He suffers from an enlarged Adam's apple and his vocal intonation is Wendy Williams-husky - not to imply that Adam's apples have anything to do with vocal intonation. I'd have to Wikipedia that later. And he walks like he is Rupaul.

"Hey honey," he embraced Gabby with a lavish hug and a kiss on the cheek. "I haven't seen you in ages. How are you?"

"I've been crazy with work. We just bought another small oil company. The work load has been unbelievable."

"Well you are looking as fierce as ever," Gary said.

"And so are you," Gabby responded. I didn't know Gabby to lie but she had to be. Gary's voice was good, but the skinny jeans and matching scarf had to go. "By the way, I have a coworker getting married in a few months. I recommended your services."

"Oh thank you, girl."

"And I may need you to do my makeup for the wedding too."

"Who's getting married?" I asked.

"I'll tell you about it later."

"You know you don't have to ask." Gary answered. "You have my number, right? Just call me. I'll come to your place."

"Gary, you know I love you."

"I know you do," he said while in a knee-deep assessment of me and Chris. "Now don't be rude. Who are your two friends?"

"Oh, I am sorry." Gabby turned to me. "You know my friend Jordan."

Gary appraised me positively. "Yes, I do."

"And this is another one of my closest friends. Chris."

Gary appraised Chris even longer. He stepped closer to Chris. "How do you do?"

Chris mumbled something in response.

"A shy one, isn't he?" Gary said to Gabby.

"Not usually," Gabby responded. "So what's going on with you?"

"Girl, I've got shows every other Friday through the end of April."

"What are you singing?" Gabby asked.

"You know I've got to change it up. But my favorite is "Single Ladies" … if you like it, then you shoulda put a ring on it, if you like it then you shoulda put a ring on it …" He proceeded to break into a partial booty shaking dance at the table. Beyonce would have sued for defamation of a dance routine, I was sure. "Com'on by and see it if you can."

"I definitely will," Gabby said. She was telling the truth. She would try to go if she could.

"Well let me get back to my table. I've got a date."

"A date?" Gabby inquired. "I thought you were dating …"

Gary waved her words away. "Oh he wasn't gay, honey. He was just lazy."

"Lazy?" Gabby grinned.

"Mmm hmm. Lazy. Too lazy to get a woman. You know boys are so easy. No, this is one of my fans. He fell in love with me at one of my shows and has been chasing me and sending me flowers ever since." He laughed giddily and then walked away singing, "Uh oh uh oh uh oh ..."

Once he was out of earshot I said, "Do you think he's happy?"

"What do you mean?" Gabby asked.

"Is he happy? At the core of his existence, is he happy with life, with where he is and what he's doing?"

"Why wouldn't he be?"

"Maybe because he's a fucking faggot," Chris said.

Gabby almost spilled her drink. "What did you just say? Where the hell did that come from?"

Chris shrugged his shoulders.

Gabby looked at me. "Where the hell did that come from?" She repeated the question to me as if I could speak for Chris.

I could speak for him because I knew where it came from. Chris wasn't at peace. Instead, I ordered another round of drinks and waited for one of us to say "Whatever."

Chapter 6

You Know I'm No Good

February 14th (Thursday)

I called Alicia on Tuesday and invited her out for
Valentine's. It was late and tacky. But I did it and, thankfully, she
accepted. I wanted to go to Hibiscus. It's one of the fifty best
restaurants in the city and the type that you reserve for special
occasions. The food and the service are so outstanding, though,
you find yourself inventing special occasions to go – *the Cowboys
won two in a row. Yeah! Let's go to Hibiscus.* But it was far too late
to get a reservation, *any reservation.* So we had Chinese at a dive
joint in East Dallas. The thing was, she didn't complain. She
didn't even look disappointed. We were laughing and joking and
having a great time, which made her more intriguing.

The evening did have two wrinkles. The first occurred
when Alicia looked up from her saki and asked, "So what made
you decide to call me?"

The question seemed to leap from nowhere and I
wondered if guilt flashed across my face. *Nothing like a question
unprepared for.* I took a slow sip of Reisling. "Call you?"

"Yes, what made you decide to call me?"

"Why wouldn't I have?"

She paused as the waiter sat down our entrees. "I don't
know. I felt something was off the first time we met."

"Off?"

"Off. I mean ... I felt like we connected really well at the
party. But by the time the next morning rolled around ... I don't
know. It felt different."

"No ... I thought ... we had a great time."

"Somehow I felt like we connected, then disconnected. Maybe I shouldn't have stayed over ..."

Her question was fair enough. We had connected then disconnected. Not her fault. Mine.

Why had I called her? I wanted to connect and out of every woman I had slept within the past year, ours felt the most authentic. And for some reason, I didn't want to be alone on Valentine's Day.

"No, that wasn't it at all," I lied. "I woke up and started thinking about a project that I had to complete for work. Sometimes I get distracted. Really. Blame it on my head. That's why I wanted to invite you out again. I sensed we were off-kilter and I wanted to make it up to you."

We resumed eating. A thirty-something pie-face girl on my left shrieked as her paunch-laden middle age boyfriend got down on one knee. *Maybe middle age dudes do get the girl.*

I hoped Gabby's and Chris's Valentine dates hadn't stumbled into the landmine of awkwardness.

"May I ask you something else?"

"Anything."

"Why did it take you so long to call?"

"Huh?"

"Why did it take you so long to call? You said you sensed something was off-kilter and you wanted to make it up to me. But you didn't call for almost four weeks." She had been looking at her plate as she spoke. When she finished the question, she looked up, her eyes met mine, and she pushed a tuft of hair behind her ear.

"I ..." I started. Why hadn't I called her? I didn't know. No, I did know. But the truth about loneliness seemed much too intimate in the moment. So I lied again, "I don't know why. I'm sorry."

"I almost didn't come," she said before she took a bite of her stir fry. "But then I thought, he's cute, it's Valentine's Day, you don't have a date and … he's paying. A girl likes a free meal sometimes." She laughed when she said it, and with that laughter, pulled me off the landmine. I laughed too, though I still felt guilty.

Wrinkle number two occurred after dinner while sitting outside her apartment.

"I had a great time tonight. Thanks for inviting me."

"No worries." I returned the smile. "I had a great time too."

She leaned over and pecked my cheek. I turned to repay her with a kiss on the lips. But she had slid out the car. I watched her as she walked into her house, hoped she would look back, and longed for a continued connection. *Can't I come in?*

I sat there long after she had closed the door. Then I called Nicole.

Nicole and I had met about three years ago in a club in South Dallas. I was walking out the club, Nicole – short tight skirt, deep V-blouse, curves for days – had been walking into the club. Think Janet Jackson. Stop, turn around, follow. What had developed was an intense connection that was light on words but heavy with eroticism. Like most of my connections, we met sporadically and arbitrarily through the year.

She told me she loved me once. Admittedly, we were fucking at the time. I think I said the words back. Good sex will make you say things. Afterward we had gotten up and gone our separate ways - like the words had never been exchanged.

Nicole would be home, she would connect. Not to mention, she abides strictly to the no overnight stay rule. I could come over and be in and out (no pun intended) within a couple hours – sleeping securely in my own bed.

She picked up the phone on the third ring; our conversation lasted twenty seconds. When I arrived, she opened the door wearing a hard-on inducing Victoria's Secrets outfit.

In less than two hours I was getting back into my car to

drive home. I noticed the text message on my cell as I walked in my house.

Alicia had texted: **I had a great time. Give me a call when you get home.**

I froze: **Sorry, I fell asleep as soon as I got home. Just waking up to go to the bathroom. Will call you first thing in the morning.**

Sent. I waited. But she didn't respond. Was she asleep? Or had she figured out I was an asshole?

Yes, you know I'm no good. And my time with Nicole hadn't been that good either.

****

As Chris walked into his Lakewood townhouse, he remembered the game that he, Jordan, and a few other guys used to play in college. They would go to a club or a party and see who could get the most numbers. Chris never lost. Married or single, he could get any woman's number.

He had developed a bit of reputation for being a lady's man - a reputation that he liked. Of course, with that reputation came an expectation – that he was always willing to perform. And he was. At least, usually. For some reason, not tonight. He had banged Jessica more times than he could count. But tonight, he didn't even want to. She was cute and all. But he had simply dropped her off after dinner. He could tell she was disappointed. He'd take a few days to clear his head and then go over and fuck the hell out of her.

Chapter 7

February 14th (Thursday)

Gabby and Jordan had spent Valentine's together last year. Neither had had a date so they had decided to go as a duo. Chris had had one but opted to join them instead. The night had been a blast. The three had dressed up, gone to Hattie's in the Bishop Arts district, and had indulged in some of the best New American food that Dallas had to offer. Gabby remembered having one ... maybe two ... too many key lime martinis. It was one of her fondest memories. But as she stood in Times Square, whisked away for a weekend by Brad, she had to admit that this Valentine's surpassed it.

Brad hadn't told her where they were going, only that it was a surprise. The Gabby of the past would've pressed. But she was taking a different approach this time. Unfortunately, work had kept her longer than she anticipated. When Brad had gotten to her place, she hadn't been ready and he had been irritated. He had recovered quickly, though. Standing in Times Square in NYC, she understood his irritation. She had almost made them miss their flight. Besides, if he could make time, so could she. All her friends knew she needed a better sense of work-life balance.

"Are you happy?" He asked.

"Yes." She was breathless.

"I'm glad I make you happy. I love it when you smile."

Gabby couldn't stop smiling.

Chapter 8

February 25 (Monday)

Gabrielle Garcia, like every other Texan - from the weird of Austin, to the country of Lubbock, to the cosmopolitan of Houston - loved Mexican. And like the rest of her brethren, if she had her choice, she would feast on it every day. People here gorge on the food, like it's the last bit of manna to fall from the skies and bless their conservative Christian hearts. Someone among the ranks even invented a dish called Tex-mex: cheese, sauce, grease. Our Mexican neighbors probably thought the destruction and reconstruction of their food bordered on blasphemous. But you can find someone selling and buying a burrito on every other corner of the city. Tex-mex has an enormous fan base.

Being one of only a handful of people in the Great State of Texas who isn't a fan, I could have easily passed on it. But I wanted to see Gabby and Gabby wanted Mexican.

I got to Cyclone's in Uptown around five-twenty. Twenty minutes later, my second Bud Light was lukewarm (I swore off margaritas when I started boxing last fall although I hadn't sworn off chips and salsa) and Chris and Gabby still hadn't made it. Odd because Chris worked about three minutes away and Gabby was a stickler for time. I had to come all the way from my job in Addison, fifteen minutes north of the city.

After ten more minutes passed with no arrivals, I ordered a new light German beer that the bartender recommended. At six, Chris walked in with a damsel on his side. Blonde layered hair. Perky tits. Wide blue-eyes. She looked nineteen and definitely SMU.

"Hey man, sorry I'm late." Chris removed his tie and slid a casual arm around the blonde's waist as he introduced her. "This is Bethany. Bethany, meet my boy J."

Bethany stuck out her hand and gave me the dead fish handshake. "It's so nice to meet you. I've heard so much about you." Her voice was a sticky east Texas drawl.

I returned her dead mackerel to her. "I've heard a lot about you," I lied. She smiled appreciatively and moved closer to Chris.

"Where's Gabby?" Chris asked.

"I dunno. I thought maybe she called you."

"Is Gabby your other ..." Bethany began.

"Yeah," Chris answered. "She is my other friend I mentioned. We meet for happy hour every Monday. Or we used to ..."

"I'm sure she will be here," I said. "What do you guys want to drink?"

"What are you drinking?" Chris asked.

"Some new German beer they have here. Don't get it."

"Thanks for the heads-up. I'll have a margarita swirl. And Bethany wants ..."

"Umm ... I'll have whatever Chris is having," she smiled. Chris smiled. I sighed.

"Okay," I said. "I guess that's two margaritas."

"Please ..." She smiled more.

"Sure, no problem." I walked over to the bar to get the drinks. When I returned, Bethany had left for the ladies room.

"She looks nineteen," I said.

"She's twenty-one," Chris responded nonchalantly while scanning the room as if he didn't already have a date.

"Yeah, okay. What is up with you?" I asked.

"What do you mean?"

"I mean ... twenty-one? Two weeks ago you took Jessica

out. Two days ago, I don't know what her name was. Now Bethany? This parade of chicks is a lot for you, Mr. Ultra Stud."

"What's that supposed to mean?" He put his drink down.

"I'm just saying. Ever since …," I faltered.

"Ever since what?"

I decided to leave it alone. "Never mind. Forget it."

"No, let's not forget it," he said. "If you have something you want to say. Say it."

Before I could respond, Gabby walked through the door. Argument averted.

Gabby strolled in and sat on the stool between Chris and me. She placed her Birken on the table.

"Did you do something with your hair?" I asked.

She shrugged. "I cut it a little."

Chris wrinkled his nose. "A little? I've never seen it that short before. I liked it better the other way."

"I gotta agree," I said.

"When you two start paying for my salon visits, you can have some sway over my choice of haircut," she responded. "Besides, Brad likes it better this way."

"Ooh … mysterious Brad …" I said. I put my hands up and shook them and my head like I was Casper the friendly ghost.

"When are we going to officially meet your new boo anyway?" Chris asked with more than a touch of sarcasm.

"I don't know," she answered. "Soon I guess. You know he's a doctor. So he stays pretty busy."

"So, he's a doctor. What? He can't come to happy hour and meet your friends?" Chris asked.

"It's not just that," Gabby said. "He feels like since we are getting to know each other we should spend time together."

"So what does that mean?" Chris asked. "Is he busy or does he not want to meet your friends?"

"Chris …" I said.

"I think it's a fair question," Chris started up again. "Which is it?"

"Chris, let it alone, man. If they want to spend some time together, let them have a little time."

"Yeah, right," was all Chris said. He picked up his margarita.

I turned back to Gabby. "I think what Chris is saying is that we miss you and would like to see our friend again." I tried the more gentle approach. "We are glad things are going smoothly between you and Brad."

"And you know I miss you, too. I'm just trying to balance work with a ..." she hesitated at the word, "boyfriend that could be very special."

"When has work ever gotten in the way of a gathering of friends at happy hour?" Chris deliberately avoided the boyfriend word. "Shit. You tell us what you are going to do all the time. You can't tell Brad?" The words tumbled out harsher than intended, I was sure.

"Well let's enjoy you while we have you." I tried to run interference. "What would you like to drink?"

She hesitated. "Actually, I can't stay long."

"What?" Chris and I said in unison.

"I can't stay long. Brad has a special dinner planned for tonight and I need to get to his place. I wanted to stop by for a quick hello ... I've missed you guys."

"Argh ... are you kidding me?" I said. "You haven't been out in two weeks. Today you show up thirty minutes late and say you can only stay ten minutes. Seriously? We haven't even caught up on Valentine's day." Now I sounded frustrated.

"I'll make it up to you," she said quickly.

"Next Monday, perhaps?" Chris suggested. "A round of drinks on Gabby?"

"Actually," she winced. "I won't be here next Monday."

"What do you mean?" I asked.

"I ... uh ... well ... Brad feels like since we are getting to know each other we should spend more time ..." *Can you say broken record?*

"Come on, Gabby," I said. "Give us a break. We've been doing happy hour for over a year now ..."

"I know, I know ..." she kinda shrugged her shoulders. "It's just that ... we are connecting and ..." *Out to lunch sign for her friends...*

Bethany returned to the table.

"Who the fuck is Brad?" Chris's voice wasn't a yell. Somehow a yell would have sounded less ferocious. Bethany's eyes widened. Gabby and I jerked back.

"He's my boyfriend," Gabby snapped.

"I know who he is," he spat as if she had missed the point. "Brad, who we have never met, has you six damn days a week. I am sure he can spare you on the seventh. Even God rested on the seventh day."

"It's not that simple," Gabby said. "You know he's ..."

"I don't care if he works for the fucking C.I.A." Chris was yelling now. "How is he just gonna come and say ..."

"Look, there will be other happy hours," Gabby interrupted, composure on the brink of slipping.

"Com'on, give us a break, Gabby." I heard myself side with Chris. "He's a doctor but he's not the surgeon general."

"Oh so today you decide you can choose a side?" Gabby asked me. "You can't choose a side any other time."

"I'm not choosing a side. I'm just saying ... you can't meet a guy, know him for three or four weeks, and decide you can't spend time with your friends."

"You two need to get over yourself," she snapped. "Can't you just be happy for me? Isn't that what *friends* do?"

"It's got nothing to do with not being happy ..." I began. "Of course we are happy for you. It's just that ..."

"It's just that nothing," she said. "I've found Brad. Brad

found me. And we are going to spend some quality time together, whether you two like it or not. Do I need to be an emotional loner just because you two are?"

The question lingered in the air, snuffing out the conversation between us. "I ..." Gabby opened her mouth to say something. Instead she snatched her Birken off the table and stormed out the door.

"Gabby, wait ..." I called after her. But she didn't stop.

****

"And then what happened, babe?" Brad asked as he pulled Gabby into his arms.

A pang of regret clutched Gabby's chest at the thought that she had betrayed her friends. Why had she said anything? She had been so frustrated, and Brad's arms were so comforting. "Please don't think badly of them, Brad. They mean well. They're just used to our hanging out more often."

"If they cared about you," he countered, "they'd give you some room."

Gabby turned to him. "They do care. They care a lot."

He wasn't convinced. "Maybe. But it sounds more like jealousy to me. Gabby, I feel closer to you than I have to anyone else in a long time. I think you feel the same. Your friends can probably sense that. That's why they are reacting so badly."

Gabby didn't respond.

"This is the reason why I don't like you going to happy hour. You are beautiful, absolutely breathtaking. And those two ... I know they are your friends ... but I think they may be basking in your beauty. I mean, why don't they get their own girlfriend?"

"No, Brad, I promise you. It's not like that. Jordan is like a brother to me. We've had these tiffs before. I was probably being too sensitive. I shouldn't have even told you."

She felt Brad pull away a little. "I hope they won't come between us, Gabby."

"Oh they won't." She pulled him back towards her.

"They better not," he said with a devilish grin. And then he kissed her tenderly.

Chapter 9

February 28 (Thursday)

Eros, Philia, Storge, and Agape are four Greek words for love. *Eros* is erotic love, think Cupid, think porn, think lust. *Storge* is the love one feels for family members – Dad, Mom, Brother, Sister. *Agape* is a broad stretching love that people should have for all humanity in general – it moves us to give to people we don't know and saddens us at human tragedy. *Philia* is brotherly love, the kind of natural affection that close friends have for each other.

If love makes the world go round - as an esteemed poet once suggested - then my world was at a standstill.

I hadn't spoken to Gabby since Monday. I had texted her Tuesday to apologize. On Wednesday she texted back: **Don't worry about it**. But I was worried. I hadn't talked to Chris, either. *There goes Philia out the door.*

Alicia and I hadn't communicated since Valentine's Day. She hadn't responded to a single text. Maybe she sensed my inner asshole. Not to mention, I hadn't had any great sex this year and couldn't remember the last time I was in love. *Good bye Eros.*

My phone was packed full of numbers I had collected over the years. The numbers had amassed like pseudo-Facebook friends. Most of the people I never talked to and some I didn't care to talk to. *No agape was flowing through my veins.*

Three down, one to go. *Storge.* The one your parents provide.

My parents had been wonderful people, great humor,

great compassion, great values. Where my sister and I would go to church on Sunday and whether Jesus was born in December seemed to be their only cause of contention. Otherwise, the house was a place of peace. We were happy.

When I turned ten, we learned my six-year-old sister had leukemia. The news was delivered by a fifty-something doctor who had delivered similar news many times before but still hadn't gotten use to saying the words. My mother fell into my father's arms and everyone – including the doctor - in the room bawled. From that moment on, everything that happened in the house revolved around my little sis.

I wanted to help. But at some point, I realized that they – my Dad, my Mom, my sister – had a problem that was so big, my ten-year-old problems weren't worthy of attention.

That's where my processing started. It was then I learned that I had to work through things alone.

I thought it was the best thing at the time. It was how I was helping, by letting them focus on more important issues than me.

We were a loving family. But that love was ruptured when they were killed in a car accident on the way home from the hospital with my sister. *Storge over.*

I was twelve years old.

After their death, I moved in with my favorite aunt. She was a sweet lady and did her best to fill my parents' shoes but there was only so much she could do. I was disconnected.

Insurance money sat in a trust fund until I was twenty-one. The money made me feel guilty. My spending was an imperfect see-saw of stupid indulgences and generous charitable donations. One bled into the other with abandon.

My phone buzzed with a text. It was Kelly. I wasn't in the mood. But I wanted someone to connect with. So I texted her and said to come over.

Chapter 10

March 3rd (Monday)

Jim's and everything about lower Greenville are the antithesis of uptown Dallas. Lower Greenville is earthy grunge, uptown Dallas is trendy chic. Lower Greenville is tatts, pool tables, and beer. Uptown Dallas is tiny dresses, independent movies, and gelato. Separated by fewer than five miles, the two exist in perfect balance - aware of each other but completely ignoring the other's existence.

"Have you talked to Gabby?" I asked Chris.

"Naw, I haven't." He picked up some cashews from a bowl on the counter and tossed them in his mouth.

"Man, I don't get it ..." I started.

"What's not to get?" He snapped. "She's found a dude who likes her. And she likes him. Is there anything wrong with that?"

"What? Wait. Why are you biting my head off? I didn't say there was anything wrong with ..."

"Jordan, you have got to stop being so jealous." He spoke without looking in my direction. When he finished speaking, he popped more cashews in his mouth.

I almost said, "Me? Jealous? What about you?" But then I wondered: *Is he right? Am I jealous?* "Okay, okay, I need to stop being jealous," I conceded. I didn't want to argue.

"There you go," he said without satisfaction. We drank our beers without a word.

"So wassup with you?" I nudged him. "How's Bethany?"

"Bethany didn't work out."

I laughed. "Well, my friend, you should probably stop going to the High School to get your dates."

"Shut up, Jordan."

"Aw, com'on. I'm only saying ..."

"I said, shut up."

"Man, what is it wrong with you?"

"Nothing." He shrugged his shoulders.

"Nothing? Dude, this is the second time you've gotten in my ass since we got here. And you haven't looked at me once. What's your problem?"

He turned to me and stood. "Come here." We walked over to the far side of the bar. "You remember that guy?"

Chris with his "this girl" and "that guy". Ugh! "What guy, Chris? Do I remember what guy?"

"That guy?" The expression on his face gave it away.

"Yeah, of course, I remember. So what about him?"

He didn't answer.

"What? Is he causing you some bullshit?"

"He came over my house this weekend."

"He came over your house this weekend?"

"Yeah."

"What does that mean? He came over your house this weekend?"

"He came over my house."

"How did he even know where you live?"

"I guess we exchanged information when I met him before."

"You guess?"

"Well we must have. I mean, he came over. So I must've gave him my info."

"And?"

"And ... we didn't do anything. We ..." he paused then leaned into me and whispered almost inaudibly. "The coke thing."

Sometimes Ya Gotta Laugh 51

I stared at him blankly.

"I mean, I didn't invite him over to do it. But … I was chillin' at the crib and he asked if he could come over. He's kinda a party type of guy," he continued. "You understand."

"No Chris, as a matter-of-fact, I don't understand. I don't understand that you are supposed to be my best friend, I don't see and sometimes hear from you for a week at a time, and now you are telling me that you are doing coke again like … like …"

"Like what, Jordan?"

"I don't know … like …"

"You know what, Jordan? You say we are friends. But as soon as I share something with you, you pass judgment. I don't need your judgments. I'm a grown man. Everything isn't always about you and how you feel. No wonder Gabby is avoiding you."

He slammed his beer down and I stood with my mouth opened as he shoved past me and stormed out.

What happened to the days when arguments ended in "whatever"? I walked back to my bar stool and asked for another beer.

"Are you gonna drink that?" The guy beside me asked. I looked at him, my watch, and my beer. Thirty minutes had passed and I hadn't taken a sip. "Here." I slid the drink in his direction, put a twenty on the bar, grabbed my suit coat, and drove home.

Surprisingly and fortunately, Alicia texted me as I was leaving the bar. Good. She had been on my mind and I wanted to see her.

Chapter 11

Find The Way

March 8th (Saturday)

"Friend problems," Alicia said. We sat at Northpark mall, seeking shelter from the thirty-six degree temperature outside. Most of Dallas was doing the same. It took us twenty minutes to find side-by-side seats in the food court.

I shrugged. "Everybody has them."

"True," she agreed. Then she took a sip of her hot chocolate. "But yours are bothering you." She paused. "Don't be afraid to share."

I thought I had my game face on. Either I didn't or she could see through it. Those beautiful Hershey brown eyes bore into me. "And if they're bothering you as much as your face seems to suggest, then the question is what are you going to do about it?"

I blew into my vanilla chai to avoid her gaze.

"What are you going to do?"

I didn't have a ready response.

"I know this is going to sound like a platitude," she said. "But I do believe that some friends are for a season and others are for a lifetime. If these are for a lifetime, then you need to breathe life back into the relationship. If they are for a season, then it may be time to let them go. Only you know the answer to that."

"What if I'm the problem?"

"When things go wrong in a relationship, rarely is one person one hundred percent to blame. But even if you are the problem, you still need to find a way. You need to own it and make amends."

So here we were, straddling the conversation between bartender and therapist. How is it that we can have intimate conversations with people we barely know and intimate sex with people we've just met? And how is it that every now and then you get the feeling that one of those intimate encounters might turn meaningful?

I changed the subject. "You want some ice cream?" I asked. "I could use some strawberry. Maybe a double cone."

She gave me a big beautiful grin. "I could use some ice cream. Some double mint chocolate." She let me off the hook for more introspection.

"Your wish is my command." I stood and bowed chivalrously. "Come go with me, my lady," I said as I extended my arm.

"Gladly." She curtsied and then slid her arm around mine.

Chapter 12

March 9 (Sunday)

Make amends. Alicia's words floated through my head long after we had parted company Saturday evening. They were the first words to pop into my head when I opened my eyes Sunday morning.

Make amends. I picked up my cell phone, looked at the clock blinking nine am, and punched in Gabby's number. She is an early riser; she would be up. But I got no answer. I called again an hour later. By four pm, she had received eight phone calls. I should have left a message.

Make amends. We never had to make amends before. Yet, Gabby and I hadn't had a real conversation in two weeks.

Make amends. I punched in her number for the ninth time. A male voice answered the phone. "Hello?"

I hesitated. "Can I speak to Gabby?"

"Is this Jordan? This is Brad."

A very weak "Oh hey, Brad," was all I could muster. *Why is he answering Gabby's phone?*

"Nice to finally talk to you," he said. "Gabrielle has told me a lot about you."

A clumsy and forced thank you stumbled out my mouth.

He continued, "I'm really really looking forward to meeting in person."

Had I imagined his voice, this was how I would have thought it - relaxed, strong bass, with a hint of North Carolina flowing through it. Sarcasm tempted me to invite him to happy hour; he was *so* looking forward to meeting. But Alicia's words rolled through my head. I needed to make amends. "Let's plan on that soon."

He lingered without speaking, as if he didn't know why I had called. The thought flashed that he lingered deliberately, that he enjoyed my discomfort. But I dismissed the idea.

"May I speak to Gabby?"

"I'm sorry, man. Gabrielle isn't here right now." The accent was a bit stronger.

"Isn't there?"

"She had to go to the store. We are about to cook and she went to pick up a few things."

"Without her phone?"

He laughed. "You know Gabrielle. Always forgetting stuff."

Yeah buddy, I know Gabrielle. Better than you. And the Gabrielle I know doesn't forget stuff. Instead I said, "I know what you mean."

Make amends.

"Will you tell her that I called?"

"Of course," he assured me.

"And have her call me back?"

"As soon as she gets in." I could tell he was smiling.

"When do you expect her?" I was trying to extend the conversation, hoping she might walk in while we were talking and that I wouldn't have to rely on Brad's ability to convey a message.

"Oh, I'd say ..." He paused and I imagined him looking at his Rolex. "I'd say in an half hour or so."

"Okay great. Thanks for letting her know."

"Anytime, Jordan," he said. "And thanks for calling. I gotta tell ya, you mean a lot to Gabrielle."

Coming from Gabby, those words would've meant the world.

I hung up the phone and waited. But by nine pm I hadn't heard anything from Gabby. I was tempted to call her again. Instead, I texted Alicia. No response.

At ten-thirty I called Chris.

He answered right before the phone went to voicemail.

"Hello?"

"Hey Chris, it's Jordan."

"Hey man." Chris is a night owl but his voice was groggy.

"Did I wake you?"

"No, no … I was just sitting here." He cleared his throat.

"I just wanted to make amends and say I'm …" I began.

He interrupted. "Don't worry about it. It's no big."

"But I," I started again.

"Seriously, it's no big."

Why didn't I feel like this was no big? I changed the subject. "So are you coming to happy hour tomorrow?"

"Of course," he said. "Aren't I always there?"

"Good. I'll see you then. By the way, have you spoken to Gabby?"

"Look Jordan, I'd really like to talk. But I have some things I have to get done for tomorrow. I'm glad you called though. Let's talk tomorrow. Cool?"

"Cool," I said. Things were definitely not cool.

He hung up the phone without saying anything else.

I walked into the kitchen to make a sandwich and pour a glass of wine. This whole situation was bullshit. I was trying to make amends – for what I did not know. Gabby and Chris were acting like they couldn't care less.

The Kraft salad dressing slipped out of my hand as I went to put it on the counter. The glass shattered into a zillion pieces on the floor. "Fuck." As I bent over to clean it up, my phone buzzed with a text. I dropped the glass into the trashcan and stubbed my toe rushing through the living room back to my phone.

I snatched it up.

Not Gabby.

Not Chris.

Not Alicia.

Sender: Nicole. **Do you want to come over?**

Nicole wanted to connect. I needed to connect.

I typed back: **See you in twenty minutes.**

I pressed send.

Unfortunately, the whole time I was with Nicole, I kept thinking about Alicia.

Chapter 13

March 15th (Saturday)

    I-35 stretches 200 miles between Dallas and Austin. Gabby hated the drive. There was nothing to see on I-35 – no interesting scenery, no exotic specialty shops, no ma and pa diners. What made the drive worse was that she disliked Austin with its eccentricities and its desire to stay weird. While her friends loved it, to her Austin's eccentricities were an exercise. Though her friends would often tease her with their "Keep Dallas Pretentious" t-shirts, she preferred Dallas.

    Dallasites believed their values, their heritage, their resources, their constitution, set them apart. Did the beliefs make them smug? Perhaps. But what city didn't love itself? Not to mention, embracing or at least respecting Dallas's paradigm of thought went a long way in developing relationships there. People outside Texas, sometimes outside Dallas, just didn't get that. Not that Gabby agreed with everything Texan but she loved and understood her city.

    She wished she could say the same for her life. She and Brad were outside Waco – halfway between Dallas and Austin – and something inside her nagged her about the wisdom of this trip. She was meeting his parents, for God's sake. In her past, meeting the parents meant putting some type of stake in the ground. She wasn't sure if she was quite ready for that because … well that was the problem. She couldn't quite put her finger on it. But something nagged her. Brad had made no attempt to meet Chris or Jordan, although, he knew they were her closest friends. And when she disagreed with him, or even if she was a little late for something, she could feel him pull away – only to return later as if nothing had ever happened between them. He had the ability to make her wonderfully happy one second and off-kilter and insecure the next.

Should she speak up? Chris had been right when he said she had no problem telling him and Jordan what to do. But this was a relationship.

She adjusted the air conditioner vent so it would blow on her.

Truth was, even on his best days Brad wasn't as fun loving and as easygoing as Chris and Jordan. Brad could make her laugh until her stomach hurt or surprise her with the most thoughtful of gifts. But those times came much less often than they did with Chris and Jordan.

Brad caught her restlessness out the corner of his eye and briefly glanced at her. She reached out and grabbed his hand. Maybe she was over-analyzing. Was it fair to compare your boyfriend to your best friend? She had never had a truly successful relationship. Maybe this was all part of the learning process.

She took out her Blackberry and texted Jordan. **Miss you. What's going on?**

Jordan texted back: **Where have you been? I called you.**

Gabby: **When?**

Jordan: **What do you mean when? Last Sunday. I called you.**

Gabby: **I ran to the store. Brad had my phone.**

Jordan: **I know. I spoke with him. He said he would tell you that I'd call. Didn't he?**

Brad hadn't told her.

Gabby lied. **Of course he did. I'm sorry, I've been busy.**

Jordan: **You know what Gabby? You haven't been much of a friend lately.** He sent the words before he could think and immediately regretted sending them.

He was about to send another text message when Gabby texted back: **I know. Sorry.**

Brad looked over at Gabby. "Who are you texting?"

"My admin ... he's a scatterbrain." The lie was concealed by a forced laugh. "He has a lot of questions."

Brad nodded and looked back to the road.

Jordan waited for another text message. But he didn't get one.

Gabby wondered why Brad hadn't told her Jordan had called.

She also wondered when she had started lying to her friends.

Sixty minutes later they pulled up to Brad's parent's house in Round Rock, ten minutes outside Austin. Brad's Mom answered the door of the modest home. She was a petite woman, standing not quite five feet tall, with short black hair salted with gray. She swept Gabby up in a warm but disconcerting hug, planted a kiss on Brad's cheek, and then led them by the hand inside.

His Dad, an older but still handsome version of his son, met them in the foyer. He greeted her with the same warm hug his wife had. Behind him stood Brad's nineteen year old sister Hailey, sparkling blue eyes, shoulder length brown hair, Uggs, iPod, smart phone. They were a very attractive family.

As Gabby sat on their back porch, peppered with questions from Hailey, smothered with attention from Brad's mom, eating a fantastically grilled steak prepared by his dad, she couldn't help but think how different these people were from what she had expected. They were salt-of-the-earth, humble, sweet, unassuming. Everyday people. Brad was a lot of things, everyday wasn't one of them. Maybe that's why he was so distant from them and, Gabby hated to admit, a bit condescending. They, on the other hand, catered to him -

changing topics based upon Brad's response, eagerly trying to make him happy but clearly weary from the effort. Hailey was the only one who challenged him.

"Obviously they don't teach doctors manners," she said as she texted on her phone.

"Hailey." Their mother sounded mortified.

"It's true. He thinks he is so much better than we are."

"You need to show some respect," Brad snarled.

Gabby's mouth fell open. Brad was moody. But she had never heard him snap so harshly. "Brad," she heard herself say. He threw her a withering look.

"And you need a personality," Hailey snapped back.

"Hailey, that's enough," their Dad interrupted.

"And you two," Hailey would not be stopped, "need to stop enabling him." She made a display of leaving the table. She gathered seconds from the bowl of macaroni salad and poured herself another glass of sweet tea. Right before she opened the door to go back inside, she turned to Gabby and mouthed "I'm sorry". Then she exited into the house.

No one moved until Brad said, "Well this has been fun … as usual." His father looked at his wife and she stood and began clearing the table. Gabby felt compelled to follow her as she walked into the house.

She washed dishes, Gabby dried. Brad's mother broke the silence.

"I'm so glad Brad has met you." She looked down and carefully selected her next words. "He needs … he needs peace. And I think you may be able to help him."

"Peace?"

"Yes peace … Brad has always been a bit … awkward with us. I think …" she paused again and then almost winced as she said the words. "I think he was a bit embarrassed of us growing up." Her discomfort was unsettling.

"Why would he be embarrassed of you?"

A rueful laugh escaped his mother. "Oh we have always struggled. We never had the means of Brad's friends, the resources, the money. My husband ... a good man ... but so many businesses that started and failed. Paycheck to paycheck too often. We've only gotten comfortable financially in the last few years." She waved a soap-covered hand as she spoke. A bubble rose into the air, hovered above them, and burst. "We were barely middle class." She laughed another bitter laugh. "I called it upper poor. I think ... he was embarrassed because he had so much less than his friends.

"But Hailey is a good girl," she added as if somehow Hailey's good behavior made up for Brad's.

"Gabby, are you ready to go?" Brad called from the living room. His voice startled both of them and the plate Gabby held almost slipped from her hands.

"Be right there," she yelled back.

She gave Brad's mother a quick hug. The older woman quickly dried her hands and together they walked back to the kitchen.

Brad's family's goodbye hugs were as authentic as their hello hugs. As Gabby and Brad traveled back up I-35, she squeezed his hand and held it tightly.

I'll talk to him, Gabby thought. The time for being passive had passed. Now it was time to speak.

Chapter 14

March 22 (Saturday)

Gabby and Brad sat at her place eating brunch. The day was extraordinarily beautiful for March and a cool gentle breeze blew through her dining room window.

She had done her best to set the mood. Incredible love making last night and homemade waffles and bacon – Brad's favorite breakfast - this morning.

The time to talk was perfect.

She had practiced in her head how she would say the words. She had thought about her phrasing, chosen her words carefully, role-played with herself. She had picked up a self-help book, designed to help learn to control anger, and a book on managing a relationship.

She had even called a therapist. She couldn't make an appointment for Brad. But she could make an appointment for them both. She was sure that if she agreed to go with him, he would go.

She could fix this.

So she took a deep breath and she began to speak. Ten words into her statement, she realized the conversation would go badly.

As she spoke, Brad stopped smiling. His fork was suspended somewhere between his mouth and the plate. Syrup dripped unnoticed onto his lap. His faced molted from affection to anger as he slowly put the fork down.

Should she continue? Should she stop? But he said

nothing. So she stumbled on, rushing through words she had meant to enunciate clearly and jumbling thoughts she had meant to express succinctly.

She did manage to slow her pace and regain her composure as she got to the end of her plea. When she told the part about the therapist, she expressed her deep support, her care, and her commitment.

She stopped.

"You want me to fucking see a therapist?" Brad exploded out his chair. His plate hurtled to the floor, and strawberry waffles and Log Cabin syrup splattered onto Gabby's bare arms and legs.

"I just thought ..." Gabby began.

"Thought? You thought? You didn't fucking think anything." Embarrassment drove heat into Gabby's face and she couldn't help but think that the neighbors could hear every word. "What would it look like for me to go to a therapist?"

"Brad ... calm down, please ..."

"Are you telling me what to do?" He planted his hands on the arms of her chair and touched his face to hers. He repeated himself. "Are you fucking telling me what to do, Gabrielle?"

"Brad, honey, no ... I ... I want what's best. Your mother wants what's ..."

He pushed her chair back violently as he stood. Gabby gasped as her chair rocked.

"And who gave you the right to talk to my mother?"

"Brad, you hurt her feelings. She's your mother."

"I don't see you talking to your mother every day, Gabrielle." She didn't respond.

"That's what I thought."

"Brad, it's not just that. It's ... it's you've been tense a lot lately and ..."

"I'm a fucking doctor. I have shit on my plate."

The neighbors could hear. There was no doubt about that.

"Brad." She lowered her voice an octave.

"I'm a fucking doctor," he yelled. "I'm a fucking doctor and I thought I was dating someone intelligent enough to understand that."

Gabby eyes widened.

"But clearly, I am not. I'm leaving."

"What?"

"Leaving. Going home. You're smart enough to understand that, right?"

"Brad, let's ..." He ignored her. He walked into the bedroom, snatched up his bag, and slammed the door behind him as he left.

Gabby jumped at the noise. She sat for a moment, then grabbed up her keys and headed toward Jordan's. But a mile before she got there, she had to pull the car over and vomit. There was no seeing Jordan after that, she had to go home and shower.

Besides, her tears kept her from seeing the road clearly.

Chapter 15

March 22 (Saturday)

The music blaring from Chris's Sony surround system compelled him to move. Its ingratiating beat penetrated his skin and he swayed across the room, blissfully unaware of whether he was thrusting his body in or out of sync with the rhythm.

The house beat faded into another beat, as urgent and insistent as the previous. And Chris continued to thrust, even though he wasn't a dancer. He stripped to the waist because the music told him to do so and laughed giddily as he glided across the room.

A collision with the equally shirtless David only caused Chris to laugh hard. They both laughed, and Chris wished the auburn-haired girl had hung around longer. He wanted to fuck her again and he really didn't care if David watched. But no fucking was going to happen tonight. Chris would've been irritated had it not been for the X. The X had him feeling so good - horny but hella good.

David didn't dance any better than Chris. He kept bumping into Chris. The last time they bumped, David stumbled and fell on the floor. Chris burst into unbridled giggles. He wasn't sure about David's staying once auburn-girl left. But now Chris was glad David had.

Chapter 16

March 23 (Sunday)

Every muscle in Chris's body ached. There was no way he was going to the gym. He didn't even have the strength to summon last night's details. The throbbing in his head was too intense.

He willed his eyes open and saw bright light streaming across the bedroom. What time was it? And why was he so thirsty? The mornings after were always the same – memories were hazy and guilt was fresh. He wasn't sure whether he felt guiltier about the X or the fact that he and Jordan were drifting apart.

He knew what he needed to do. He needed to call Jordan and hash things out. Call Gabby too. Take them both out to dinner, maybe Hibisicus, and get back to a good place with them.

Yeah, as soon as his head stopped pounding he'd call. Shit, he'd do it now. He reached for his cell phone and hit the key for Gabby's number, while his guilt was still fresh. Before the phone finished its first ring, he jumped, startled by movement in his bed.

He looked to his left. David lay beside him. Naked.

Chris slammed the phone shut.

****

The ring of the phone woke Gabby up. Although, she

knew she hadn't been sleeping well. She had tossed and turned all night. She picked up the phone and saw Chris's name flash across the screen. His was one of eleven missed calls. The other ten were from Brad. Ten calls. Ten messages. She turned her phone off and walked to the bathroom. Mascara ran down her cheeks and her eyes were swollen and red. She took a warm damp cloth and washed her face.

Times like these, she wished she had more female friends.

She checked her image in the mirror one more time before turning off the light and walking back into the bedroom. She slipped off her clothes, pulled on some pajamas, crawled back into bed, and pulled the covers over her head.

Chapter 17

March 29th (Friday)

     The knot in Gabby's stomach constricted and released, emotional pain manifesting itself as physical pain. But she resolved not to cry. At least, not again. What she would do is filter the emotion into work. As a teenager, when life wasn't good, she threw herself into her studies. As an adult, she threw herself into her work. That pattern hadn't led to many successes in the field of love but had brought her plenty of success on the job.

     On the front seat beside her sat development plans for mid-level managers at the company, she planned on working on those this weekend. On the back seat sat a few groceries from Whole Food – a salmon feta burger, a bottle of Dr. Loosens Reisling, some pita chips, and few chocolate chip cookies.

     As soon as she got home, she would change into something more comfortable, pour herself a glass of wine, have one of the salmon sandwiches, turn on the laptop, and dive into work.

     At some point she had to talk to Jordan. She had thought about calling every day this week; Jordan was a good listener. But she didn't want to burden him. Besides what would she say?

     Sunday she'd go for a long run. Or better yet, she'd curl up with half a pint of Haagen Daz, her chocolate chip cookies, and some movie on Lifetime.

She parked her car in front of her townhouse and stepped out. The day was warm. Maybe she'd change into shorts and go jog now.

"Gabrielle?" A voice behind her startled her. She froze, hoping the voice was a figment of her imagination. But it called out to her again. "Gabrielle." She refused to turn around until it called her a third time. "Gabrielle."

She had been too swallowed in her thoughts to notice Brad's car parked on the street. Had she seen it, she would've kept driving, avoiding him and the resurgence of raw emotion she was struggling to keep submerged deep beneath the surface. But now he was standing almost within reach of her, arms extended in a gesture that was half helpless and half come-to-me. His dirty blond hair was tousled as if he had been running his hands through it, he was wearing his white physician's coat.

How many cards, emails, and voicemails had she gotten from him this week?

How many peers had she lied to about the reason she kept receiving flowers at work?

How many times had one of her coworkers said, "He must really love you," and she had agreed?

He took a step closer, she took a step back.

"Gabrielle," his shoulders sagged. "I am so sorry." She suppressed a desire to clamp her hands over her ears. Instead, she put out a hand to stop him from coming closer. When she did, a work file slipped out her hands and the papers scattered to the ground. "What can I say?" Brad asked as he bent down to help pick up the papers. "Anything?" He took another step forward as he handed them back.

She took the file without touching him.

"I was cruel ... I know," he continued. "I was an ass. I deserve you never speaking to me again. But believe me, I am so sorry. I was so … I guess I felt betrayed and I overreacted. But there is no excuse. None."

He took a step closer. Gabby willed the tears back.

"Can I come in? Can we talk?"

Afraid her voice would crack, Gabby said nothing.

"You are right, I'm going to therapy." He pulled out the card of the therapist she had called. "I went on Monday. That's one of the reasons I've been trying to call you. I wanted to let you know. I've got to learn to get control of my ... my moods. For you ..."

Gabby shivered, although the sun shone brightly.

"Another chance, please. I'm begging you. Gabrielle, I'm sorry. I love you. It's ... it's my family. There are things I've never told you. But ... you know the problems families can have."

Family was the one thing Gabby had held withheld from Brad. But she knew all too well the stress family could cause.

"Neither one of us is close to our family. We need each other. I need you. A second chance. That's all I'm asking." His eyes welled with tears and he reached out to her.

Everybody deserved a second chance. Everybody did. He was going to therapy now. So Gabby walked past him, up the stairs, through the front door, and let him in.

Brad followed her inside, humbly shut the door behind them, and begged forgiveness until she finally said, "It's alright."

She couldn't sleep that night, though. And she couldn't make love. Every moan and every orgasm had been faked for Brad's benefit. Hours later, as she stared at the ceiling and he slept peacefully beside her, she wondered if she should have been so forgiving. Once granted, Brad had moved around her place like they had never had an argument. She, though, had had a knot in the pit of her stomach all evening.

Quietly she slid out the bed. "Where ya going, babe?" Brad murmured. He touched her and his skin was hot on hers.

"To get a drink of water," she replied before she kissed him on the forehead. She padded down the steps, poured herself a glass of wine, and laid across the couch.

Brad came downstairs around three am and woke her up. He asked her to come back to bed. She did. But she couldn't get back to sleep once she got there.

Chapter 18

March 31st (Monday)

Stan's sits on Greenville Avenue, a dive bar with a strange juxtaposition of people coming through its door. Levis and Wranglers shoot pool with True Religion and Addicktion. Sorority girls and their fraternity boyfriends dance the Texas two-step to a jukebox loaded with Kenny Chesney and Alan Jackson, but sprinkled with the observations of Fabolous and Biggie Smalls. A large Bud Light neon sign adorns the wall behind the bar, the centerpiece for a hodgepodge of pictures, trinkets, lights, and other incongruous items.

The scenery was lost on Gabby. All she could do is think about Brad. She had been on the verge of sharing her angst with Jordan. But Chris had walked over. Jordan would be a level-headed voice of reason. Chris, on the other hand, would say something sarcastic and she didn't have the energy for it. Not today. So she stopped talking and hoped Chris hadn't noticed. She also cut the evening early with claims that work had her exhausted. But work wasn't wearing her out. Work was her solace. Not knowing if she should have let Brad back in was wearing her out. Not confiding in Jordan was wearing her out. Wearing a happy face when she wasn't happy was wearing her out.

Her cell phone vibrated with Brad's text tone as she

turned her car on.

I need you to come by. Now.

Her stomach churned. If Brad didn't know she always checked her messages, she would have ignored it. She counted to ten and then hit the call button. He didn't answer. **On my way,** she typed back and headed in his direction.

In spite of having a key, she knocked on Brad's door. She braced herself as she heard him descend down the stairs of his University Park home.

"Babe," he exclaimed when he opened the door. "Why the long face? And why the knock? That's why I gave you keys." He grabbed Gabby by the hand and pulled her into the foyer.

"Brad, I thought something was wrong."

"Oh there is." His tone changed and Gabby stiffened. He turned away, picked up a piece of paper and handed it to her. "Read this."

"What is it?"

"Just read it," he said sternly.

She read. It was a receipt for two tickets to Sydney, Australia. Gabby's eyes widened when she saw her name on the itinerary. "Brad," she gasped.

Brad beamed. "I love it when you smile."

"But Brad, I can't. I can't accept these …"

"Of course, you can."

"And I don't know if I can even get the days off."

"Of course, you will."

"Brad, I …"

Brad pulled her close. "You know I would do anything for you. I know sometimes I get a little moody. But I love you. And I appreciate that you accept me for who I am."

As incensed burned and Sarah Vaughan sang *Lover Man*, they made love on the living room floor.

Chapter 19

March 31 (Monday)

Chris left happy hour right after Gabby left. He could tell Jordan wasn't pleased and Chris felt a twinge of guilt over it. That twinge kept him from ringing David's doorbell.

I shouldn't be here, he thought. I shouldn't be here.

The guilt that suppressed his movement was only equaled by his concern over what Gabby and Jordan had been saying. Gabby had clearly stopped talking when Chris got back to the table. Had they been talking about him?

He put his hand down and turned back to the street. Who was David anyway? And why did Chris feel compelled to keep coming back to his house? And what was Juliana's story? All Chris knew was that she was hot and totally cool with the threesome. She didn't blink an eye when David went down on him; she encouraged it. Memories tumbled through Chris's head and he wasn't sure whether to lock them away or let them flow freely.

Getting head from a guy during a threesome was one thing, he could justify that. Didn't gay dudes claim they gave the best head? Justifying last Saturday was a different matter - if he could remember last Saturday. He recalled kissing David. But he couldn't remember anything after that except waking up naked.

It must've been the ecstasy.

He cupped his hands together and blew into them, finally sensing the coolness of the night, and turned to go home. The outside light flickered on just as Chris reached his car. David opened his front door and stepped outside. "Are you coming in?" He asked. Chris turned around to find David standing in boxer briefs even though it had to be 40 degrees.

Chris tried to avoid looking at David's muscular chest, his flat stomach, his hip cuts. "Uh …" Chris started. "It's getting kinda late."

"It is getting kinda late," David agreed. "But you might as well come in for a few minutes. You're here. Besides, it's cold outside."

As Chris passed through the threshold, David patted him on the back. "Glad you came over," he said with a devilish grin. "I've got something to keep us warm." His hand lingered on Chris's back.

As the door swung shut behind them, Chris felt an odd sense of horniness and a prickly sting of guilt. And he wondered again if Jordan and Gabby had been talking about him.

Chapter 20

April 4th (Friday)

The spreadsheet on my Dell stared at me with blurred lines of useless reporting. The clock on my work PC said one-thirty, reminding me that I had three more hours in this hellhole called work, and a half cup of lukewarm coffee sat on my desk.

I was eager to get in my car, head down the tollway, and go home. Not that I had any weekend plans. My forecast was monotony with a chance of depression.

In the past, I could've counted on hanging with Gabby and Chris. We didn't even have to make plans to have them - weekend plans went without saying. Now I could barely get thirty minutes out them, much less a weekend.

Plus, I was neglecting Alicia. I knew that.

My lack of friends was fucking up my love-life. And my lack of love-life was fucking up my sex life.

I had called Alicia a couple times and sent several texts. She always responded enthusiastically but my attention wasn't there. We hadn't hung out since our trip to the mall. My fault. Even with her rotating schedule, she was more than willing to try to connect. I, on the other hand, required space, lots of space when I was sifting. For the past few weeks, I felt like I had been doing nothing but sifting.

But Alicia and I did not have a title. So didn't that give me some grace?

I hate these fuckin' moods.

I was sitting at my cube, somewhere between a trance and sleep – still staring at the spreadsheet - when Mike, a coworker of mine, invited me to lunch.

Mike has got me by about a decade and a half. But the guy parties every weekend like it's 1999. I'm guessing this is partly due to his double life as a swinger.

Who would've thought that a Republican state full of mega-churches (think Joel Olsteen – 43K members and counting – TD Jakes – 25K members and counting) and conservative Christians would also be chock full of swingers? But yes, the state is. About a year ago, the police busted up a swinger crowd in Dallas suburbia. I'm not sure why the police would care about who-is-doing-who in the privacy of their own home. Mike claimed it had something to do with some obscure Texas laws on sexuality. Go figure.

Conservative folks putting conservative legislation into action usually results in conservatism.

And lots of people acting on the down low.

Somewhere in the Mid-cities of the Dallas metroplex – and several other areas – suburban housewives and their white-collar hubbies are meeting other couples for lascivious orgies.

Mike lives in the suburbs. He lived there with his wife until she left him for some guy they swung with.

The clock said two. Not only was my bellybutton hitting my backbone but Mike would take my mind off my present self-loathing. I locked up my desk and followed him.

We wandered downstairs to the new building restaurant that claimed to be a NY deli. Mike promptly ordered us pastrami on rye. I've never been a fan of pastrami. But he swore by it.

Ten minutes later we were chowing down on sandwiches that were from anyplace but NY and washing them down with flat Cokes. Mike began to tell a story about a girl he met at a

Kanye West concert and how they had fucked all night. He was telling me how they were swinging from chandeliers, rolling around on the bathroom floor, doing it in the sink. He was going into graphic details, sharing techniques straight from the Kama Sutra. Finally I said, "How old was this chick?" And he said, "I dunno … twenty-two, twenty-three." And then I was staring at the dude. Because, as I said, he's like fifty-two and I'm wondering how the hell he had the stamina. Not that a guy stops having sex at fifty, think Hugh Hefner. But he is talking about busting a nut five times that night. I mean, if he hadn't had the cell phone pictures to prove it, I wouldn't have believed it.

Trust me, no one should see those pics.

So I asked him, "What's your secret?"

He looked at me as if I might be wearing a wire tap, then checked left and right as if an undercover agent might be sitting close. "These," he said leaning over the table.

He had some little yellow pills in a bag.

I went, "Geritol?" I didn't even know they still made Geritol. And I didn't know it was an aphrodisiac.

"No, you idiot." He stuffed the pills back in his pocket in obvious offense. *What I say?*

"What are they?" I asked.

He looked around again. "Cialis, dipshit. They're Cialis."

"Really?" My eyes opened wide. "Where did you get them?"

Mike was acting covert, like the situation was black market. Maybe it was. He kept looking around.

"My doctor gave me some to try," he said. "Not that I needed them," he quickly added.

Who cared if he needed them? I was friggin' amazed at the reaction his body had to them. I must've had that lean and hungry look in my eyes because he said, "You want some?"

I almost said no. I almost denied wanting them. But then I thought, *if he has the courage to take pics of his naked body and under-*

endowed totem pole slamming some blonde with double D tits, I can admit I'd like a little yellow pill.

"Sure," I said not trying to hide my eagerness.

"Here," he handed me the bag.

"Wait ..." I started to say. "Don't you need ...?"

"Naw, my ex-brother-in-law is a pharmaceutical rep. I get them from him." *Ex-brother-in law? Doctor? Who knew with Mike.* He gave me a congratulatory handshake, as if he was welcoming me into his fraternity.

"Thanks man," was all I could say.

"Anything for a friend." He did a ridiculous thumb up. I wasn't sure if he was going to want a full report or pictures after I had tried the pills. He wasn't going to get either. My only plan was to pop a few as soon as I got home.

I made one mistake. I failed to ask him how they worked, how many to take, should I take them with milk - the usual instructions for taking medication.

Fast forward to seven pm and I was standing in the bathroom, gazing into my mirror, with a glass of water in my left hand and a couple yellow pills in my right.

Should I take these on an empty stomach? Or am I supposed to eat first?

Shit! Maybe I should call a pharmacist.

Once I got that out the way, I'd call Nicole.

Chapter 21

Me So Horny

April 5th (Saturday)

There are girls that you wife, and there are girls that you fuck.

Alicia – wife, Kelly – fuck, Nicole – fuck.

But I couldn't call Kelly, she only called me. And Nicole wasn't answering her phone - which made Cialis a very *very* bad idea.

Me so horny and nobody to fuck. Every time the wind blew I got a hard on. Screw the wind. Every time my briefs rubbed against my dick I got a hard on. So I was free-balling in the house, doing it commando.

It didn't help. My dick was saluting everything in my loft and I had no way to bring it down to half mast. No way outside the internet, JO, and lube. Not nearly as fun as it might sound. Mix my need for a plot in my porn with the fact that lotions dries up before I can get the necessary rhythm meant release wasn't easy to get. Nevertheless, desperate times call for desperate measures. A two hour search was rewarded with the discovery of an almost empty bottle of KY Jelly. Combined with a viewing of *Debbie Does Dallas* and I was able to coax my dick down – three times. Most importantly, the erection hadn't lasted more than four hours, so an emergency room visit wasn't necessary. Thank God.

Chapter 22

April 7 (Monday)

I was sitting solo at Jim's when Raheem Cole walked in the door. His shoulder length locs fell loosely on his shoulders, tatts covered almost every inch of his unexposed body, and his pecs must have made shirts difficult to find. Any casual gesture made a muscle stand at attention.

"Where have you been?" I gave him some dap before he sat down beside me.

"Working on the merger," he said. Raheem was a sales leader at Wachovia Bank and Wachovia had been acquired. Raheem was none too pleased about the acquisition. "Been in Florida for the past three months."

"Sorry about that."

He shrugged. "Eh. Whatev. But ..." he smiled devilishly. "Miami does have some fine senoritas and mamacitas."

"Lemme guess. You pretended to be Cuban."

"Perhaps," he said slyly. Raheem had a reputation as a player and more than a few people found him intimidating. While he relished both facts, in actuality, he was one of the coolest guys I knew.

I had met him about five years ago when he had first relocated from Atlanta to Dallas and had introduced him to Chris and Gabby. Raheem had been working as a part time trainer at 24 Hour Fitness on Royal. He had claimed it was for extra cash; we both knew it was a way to meet ladies. While we weren't nearly as close as Chris and I, he was a good friend.

And I was always amused by the fact that he was the only guy I had ever seen make Gabby blush.

I was about to ask him about one of the many exploits I assumed he had had when Chris walked in. He strolled over, gave Raheem a head nod, and spoke directly to me.

"So what were you guys talking about last week?" Chris asked me.

"Who?" I said.

"You and Gabby. Last week you two were talking about something but you stopped when I came over. What were you talking about?"

Raheem leaned back in his chair.

"We weren't talking about anything," I said.

"So why did you guys stop talking when I walked over?"

"Um," Raheem interrupted. "You guys need some alone time?" He stood.

"No," we both said in unison. Raheem sat back down.

"Chris, I promise. We weren't talking about anything. Gabby was upset about something and I was trying to find out what. But she never told me."

"Oh," was Chris's only reply.

I looked at Raheem for support and he nodded as if my statement sounded reasonable and truthful. Chris, though, didn't look like he was buying it.

"So where did you go?" I asked. The question sounded tit-for-tat. But it wasn't. I really wanted to know.

"Huh?"

"Why did you leave so early?" I asked. "It wasn't even seven and you exited."

"I had business," was all he said.

"Oh," was my only response. I turned to Raheem and this

time he raised one eyebrow.

"Are you guys alright?" He asked.

"We're fine," Chris said.

"Great," I added.

But we weren't fine. Chris knew it, I knew it, and Raheem knew.

Chris must have had more business that night. Because he left at six-thirty.

"What was that about?" Raheem asked after Chris left.

"Hell if I know."

"By the way, who is Chris's new friend?"

"What?"

"I was working out downtown and saw him and some guy working out together. They seemed pretty chummy."

"Hell if I know," I repeated and I took another sip of my drink.

Chapter 23

April 14th (Monday)

"Gabby," Brad called from the bottom of the steps. The irritation in his voice was crystal clear. They were running late. Her last meeting had gone overtime and there had been an accident on the way home. Work-life balance, she thought to herself.

"Almost ready," she called back to him. She went to put in her earring but the back slipped out her hand and rolled under the dresser.

This night was important to Brad; the hospital was giving him an award. Not to mention, he hadn't had an ugly mood since the episode three weeks ago, much less raised his voice. She didn't want to ruin the streak. "I'm sorry," she called back. "There was an accident on the road," she explained for the fifth time.

He didn't respond.

Please, not tonight, she thought. She needed this night to be a good one, especially if she was going to broach dinner with Jordan. She planned on suggesting it, right after the ceremony.

She was glad she had opted not to tell Jordan about her brief break up. He was overprotective and wouldn't understand. She had to figure out how to get all the men she loved in a place where they would like each other.

"Gabby, are you ready?" Brad called from the first floor landing. He was losing patience.

"Be right down," she said.

She felt guilty about missing happy hour. But Brad's therapy sessions were on Monday and she wanted to be there to support him. The first two sessions had gone well and she would do whatever it took to help.

"Gabby, we are late."

She heard him ascend the first step.

"Ready," she said as she stepped to the top of the stairs. Her hair was swept-up elegantly, with two small wisps of hair carefully dangling on both sides of her face. Brad had given her a beautiful string of pearls to wear. Her red dress gathered at her tiny waist and fell right below her knees.

"Beautiful," Brad said. The tension in his face faded and, as she walked down the steps toward him, his face morphed into a wondrous smile.

Chapter 24

April 15th (Tuesday)

The sweet and spicy smell of Cajun pasta wafted through the loft. The dish was one that I had learned from my mother and perfected in her honor. Making it always reminded me how much I missed her.

Tonight, I made the dish for Alicia.

"This is delicious," Alicia said after she took her first bite. A small piece of tomato sat on the side of her mouth; I brushed it off.

"Did you have any doubt?" I teased.

"Absolutely," she teased back. "But obviously, I shouldn't have."

I liked Alicia, far more than the randomness of my attention implied. Beautiful eyes, deeply compassionate, and a wonderful listener. Plus, she had no expectations. She didn't complain when I didn't call and she was always willing to get together. I knew I needed to do more. So today I was playing catch up. It's a game that some of us guys play. We don't do things right the first time – even when we know what right is – then go into overdrive to fix what we should've done in the first place.

"Hey," I said, grinding some fresh black pepper onto her plate. "Gabby texted me about a triple date. You, me, Gabby, her boyfriend, Chris, and whoever he invites. Are you down?"

"Absolutely," she said. She picked up a piece of garlic bread and munched down. *How could anyone eat so much bread and have such a fantastic body?* "When?"

"Saturday. Is that cool?"

"I work seven to three. So Saturday evening is totally cool."

Jackpot!

"I got a movie," I said. "And dessert." Valentine's Day had been a disaster; I need to infuse romance into the evenings. I relit a candle.

"What did you get?"

"Something with ... Jennifer Aniston and cheesecake."

"Really? Sounds fun."

I cut the cheesecake, slid in the DVD, and cuddled with a blanket beside her on the couch.

The movie ended around midnight with Alicia cradled in my arms. She looked at her watch. "Wow ... it's gotten late ..."

"Yes, it has." I paused for a moment or two. "Would you like to stay?"

"I ..." she began.

"It's cold outside," I said. Although it wasn't.

She tilted her head to one side and smiled at me. "Yes, I think I'd like that."

I wanted her badly. But I also wanted to prove I was interested in more than just sex. So despite the fact that I slept in only my boxer briefs and despite the fact that she slept in a tank top of mine, all we did was cuddle. With my groin pulled far enough away so she couldn't feel my hard on.

Between my horniness and the residual effect of the Cialis, I worried about vascocongestion, better known as blue balls. I hoped I was too old to get them. Because if I wasn't, I'd have them in the morning.

Somewhere around three am, Alicia rolled over and

kissed me. She scooted into me so that our bodies were close and I couldn't help but kiss her back.

I kissed her again and again. Until we were making love. And it was good. Damn good. The best all year. Which kinda scared me.

Chapter 25

April 19 (Saturday)

Brad stood at the door wearing a pair of blue basketball shorts and a white wife beater. His gym bag was slung over his shoulder.

"Brad," Gabby said with more than a bit of dismay, "we are supposed to meet Jordan and Alicia for dinner at seven."

Brad stepped inside. "I'm sorry. It completely slipped my mind."

"Well," Gabby began. "You have an extra pair of slacks over here. I'll go ..." She walked back toward the laundry room for the clothes. Brad called out to her.

"Gabrielle, I don't really feel like going." He set his bag down and leaned against the wall.

"What?" Gabby's heart sank.

"I'm tired, I don't really feel like going."

Gabby turned around slowly. "Brad ... we talked about this. We talked about this yesterday. You promised. And I really want you to meet Jordan."

Brad walked over to her, slapped her lightly on the ass, and then sat down on the couch. "I know, I know. I'm sorry. But ... I'm tired. It's been a long day." He put his feet on the coffee table and turned on the television.

To argue or not to argue. That was the question that

always caused discord growing up. When to speak when not to speak. Her mousy mother had rarely spoken but when she did, it was always at inopportune times. Gabby wouldn't do the same. She took in a deep breath. "I know you've had a long day, honey," she said delicately. "But can't you go? Just for an hour?"

He didn't respond for a moment, as if he was completely caught up in the news, and then he looked at her and smiled. "Why don't you go, Gabrielle? Go and enjoy your friends. I'll just sit here by myself. I can run to Blockbuster or to Redbox and pick up a video." Gabby hesitated and Brad read her reticence. "Or you could just call him and and reschedule. He's your friend. Sounded like a great guy when I talked to him. I'm sure he'll understand." He continued, "I sure would love to have you here with me tonight. It's been a long day and it would be nice to relax in your arms. I can make some popcorn. Order us some sushi. We still have that bottle of wine in the fridge ..."

She stayed. Although, she didn't know if she was staying because Brad needed her to stay or if she didn't want to invent a reason for Brad not showing.

"You know I love you, right," Brad asked. "I really cherish the time we can spend together." He gave her a broad smile.

Gabby sighed deeply. "I know you do." Slowly she walked over and slid into his arms.

Brad was happy: Jordan wouldn't be. Gabby was between that rock and that hard place. At least Chris will be there, she thought.

Chapter 26

April 19th (Saturday)

Chris was eating. But it wasn't at a restaurant. He was between the brunette's legs – nibbling, licking, flicking his tongue back and forth. She trembled.

She grabbed the back of his head and shoved his face in deeper. He was happy to please; he took pride in every quiver of her body. As her breath quickened, he crawled from beneath her legs, his face wet from her juices, and slowly began to lick his way up her body, to her navel, to her nipples, to her neck.

Slowly he sank inside her - slowly - and then he pulled out. Damn she was wet; his dick was rock hard. He slid in again and again, pulling out then diving in, making love at times, and fucking at other. She whispered how good he felt inside her until whispers gave way to uneven moans. Right as she climaxed in a volcanic explosion, her nails dug into the skin of his back and she screamed his name.

He winked at her as he pulled on his jeans, blew her a kiss as he buttoned his shirt, and promised to call as he walked out the door. But he didn't know her name, he didn't have her number, and he didn't like the club well enough to go back and look for her again. Yeah, he thought as walked to his car, I'm straight.

****

Alicia and I were having a blast at dinner, waiting for Gabby and Brad to show. Then I got Gabby's text. *She wasn't coming.* The text killed the evening for me. And my disappointment killed the evening for Alicia. She suggested we end the evening early. I didn't want to do that. So we continued. But we should have; I know I wasn't one ounce of fun.

Chapter 27

April 23rd (Wednesday)

Gabby's brother Luis rarely called during the work day.

"Mom's sick," he said. Anxiety filled his voice.

Gabby waved her admin out of her office.

Luis was her only sibling and she loved him dearly. Handling situations with their Mom was his gift, not hers. Her hand tightened around the phone. "Does she need money?" Poorly chosen words tumbled out her mouth.

Luis let out a low sigh. "Gabby," he said earnestly, "she needs you."

Gabby's trips home were random and infrequent. "I would but I am so busy with work and you're so much better at this than I." Silence ensued. She spoke again. "Let me know when you know what's wrong. I'll come ..."

"Gabby, they think she has cancer."

Gabby inhaled sharply.

"You need to come home." Another beat of silence ensued.

"I will."

"And, Sis," he said gently, "you need to let some things go. She did the best she could."

Although his tone was tender, Gabby bristled. "Please, no speeches ..."

He laughed lightly. "Gabrielle, I would never give you a speech. You are too hard-headed to listen. What I'm doing is asking you to come home for a weekend. Because I need you and Mom needs you. Will you?"

"Yes, I said I would."

"Soon." His voice a gentle plea.

"Yes."

"This weekend." He bartered.

"I can't ...," she began.

"You can." He cut her off. Luis, two years older than she - her support, her listening ear, her protector when they were young.

"Yes," she agreed.

"Great! It will be fantastic having you here for a few days. Amy and I have missed you. Your nieces have missed you. And Mom has, too."

While she didn't admit it, Gabby missed them too.

She got off the phone, logged into American Airlines's website, and booked a flight to Dulles International using her frequent flier points.

Chapter 28

April 24th (Thursday)

"So when will you be back?" Brad asked.

Gabby folded a pair of jeans and put them in her overnight bag. She stood with her back to him, methodically preparing for a three day trip. "Sunday, Brad. I told you I'll be back on Sunday."

"I don't understand why you're going."

"My mother is sick, Brad."

"I understand sick, Gabby. I'm a doctor. All they're doing is running a few tests. For all you know, she has the flu."

"Brad, she *is* my mother and Luis said it's cancer."

"Yes, I know what he said. But they are running tests. You know how you overreact to things. He is probably doing the same thing."

"Brad ..." she began.

"How is it, that I'm your boyfriend but I have no say over what you do? How is that a relationship?"

"Brad, can we not do this right now?"

"This," Brad said caustically, hearing her unintended emphasis on the word. "What is *this*? *This* conversation?"

She ignored him. "What I want, what I need, is your support ..."

"That's what I want, Gabby. Your support."

She didn't respond. Instead she tucked another pair of jeans in the bag.

"All I know is," he continued, "that when we get married you aren't going to be running to see your family at every whim."

When they got married? Family at every whim?

"Unless you don't want to get married."

"Brad, I didn't say I didn't want to get married."

"I know, you didn't say anything," he spat at her. "Fuck it." He slammed the door and stormed out the bedroom.

Ten minutes later Gabby stood beside him in the living room.

"Are you going to take me to the airport?" She asked tentatively. "Or should I take a cab?""

He took her but she would've preferred a cab. They drove the thirty minutes together in utter silence.

Chapter 29

Chris had agreed to go with David under three conditions. First, they would sit in the back of the club where as few people as possible could see them. Second, they would go to a club that was out of town. Third, they wouldn't get there before one am.

David had agreed to all three stipulations and now they sat watching a show in the smoky corner of a gay club about twenty miles upstate. Chris downed his third margarita in two large gulps. What had he been thinking? A gay club? Drag queens? While he shifted uncomfortably, the men around him clapped with the fervor reserved for shows like *The Lion King*. They held an admiration for the vamping and the lip-syncing of men dressed like Lady Gaga, Cher, and Madonna - an admiration Chris didn't understand.

The effeminate emcee sported heavy blue eye shadow, ruby red lips, and a taffeta dress. He oversaw the theatrics with amazing gusto and punctuated most statement with the words "bitches." The crowd roared.

Chris was not a bitch. This was not his crowd. He never should have agreed to come.

"You okay?" David leaned over and asked. The music made it hard to speak and harder to hear.

Chris swallowed in response and David pushed the glass of water over to him.

"You look like you are about to pass out," he said. "Relax." He reached over and gingerly covered Chris's hand with his own. Chris yanked his hand back and put it under the table.

"What?" David said. He shook his head, scooted his chair away from Chris, and turned back to the show.

Chris didn't care. The exit door light beamed about fifty feet away. Maybe, Chris thought, he should make a run for it.

"And now, bitches," the emcee's announcement pulled Chris's attention back to the stage, "our headliner."

The lights dimmed momentarily and the crowd was swathed in the glow of disco lights. Smoke rose from the floor and Chris wondered if Madonna herself was about to take the stage. The beat of the song followed.

"All the single ladies, all the single ladies ..."

Something was familiar about the song, Chris thought. He racked his brain for why it struck a chord but couldn't figure it out. At least not until Gary took the stage – dress, heels, wigs, make-up, and microphone.

What had Gary said when he first met him? *"I have a show every other Friday through April."*

As the whole club erupted with cheer, Chris bolted for the exit door. Had he thought about it, he would've moved quietly. But it was a knee-jerk reaction. As such, it was noticeable, even to Gary.

Gary turned toward him. Their eyes met. Gary winked at him and then went back to "Uh oh uh oh uh oh ..."

"What the hell is wrong with you?" Chris looked up to find David standing outside beside him.

"Look man, I told you I didn't want to come here. I ... I don't like it. And I'm not gay ..."

David let out an exaggerated sigh. "Nobody said you

were." His nonchalance grated on Chris.

"I'm just not down with the experience, okay?" Chris walked toward the car.

David smiled smugly. "You were down for the experience last night."

"Fuck you, bro," Chris turned around. "I don't need ..."

David held his hands up. "Hey, forget it. I was tired anyway. It's getting late. Let's go back to my house and chill for a little."

"I just wanna go home, man."

"Man, you are all wound up." David walked over to Chris and reached out to massage one of Chris's shoulders. But Chris shrank away. "You know I have something that will relax us both. We can take the edge off the night and forget about it."

"I dunno."

"Com'on," David said. "We'll have fun." When they reached the car, David tossed Chris the keys. "Here, you drive."

Chris caught them in the air. "Hey, I don't ..." he began. He didn't want to drive. He wanted to sit in the car, put the seat back, and forget it all. Instead he hopped into the driver's seat, turned the ignition, and blasted David's Kings of Leon CD.

He ignored David when he put his hand on Chris's thigh. But fifteen minutes later, as David gave him head while he drove, he found David pretty hard to ignore.

Chapter 30

April 27th (Sunday)

I was parked outside baggage claim, hoping the police wouldn't shoo me around the airport again. Maneuvering through the maze was irritating and I wanted to get Gabby and go.

When she called last night and asked me to pick her up, I had wondered two things: why Brad wasn't picking her up and if I should call Chris and invite him along for the ride. I had asked neither.

Gabby emerged from the airport after my second shooing. Her hair was pulled back and her face bore a grimace.

I hopped out the car to give her a quick hug, she held onto me for a couple beats.

"You okay, beautiful?" I asked as I unlocked the trunk.

She stepped back, gave me a half smile, and nodded. We both got into the car.

"Tough trip, huh?" I asked.

She stared out the window.

"How's your Mom?"

"They are still running tests."

"I'm sure they were glad to see you ..."

"Yes," she said quietly.

"When was the last time you were ..." I began.

"Almost two years ago."

We drove the next ten minutes without saying a word.

"How's Brad?" I asked.

"He's okay."

"Everything good between you two?"

"Yes ... usually ..." Her voice got lower. "Sometimes."

I stared straight at the road. The light rain that had been falling had begun to morph into sleet. Bad. If someone spits on the road in Texas, people have accidents. Sleet and ice would have people all over the highway, in the ditches, in the median, and probably a couple people in trees. An overly-nervous driver pumped his breaks. I turned on my windshield wipers and moved from behind him.

"What's wrong?" I asked.

"It just ..." she still looked out the window. "He's so moody. Difficult. Sometimes he treats me like a queen. Sometimes he treats me like ... shit."

I have to admit, part of me felt good - Brad was a dipshit. But part of me felt angry - Brad had a beautiful woman inside and out but didn't appreciate her. Mostly I felt sad. In spite of my jealousy, I wanted Gabby to be totally and completely happy. Now I find out she isn't.

On second thought, mostly I was angry. I took a deep breath. "Gabby, you know I love you, right? And you know I want what's best for you.

"You deserve a guy who loves and cherishes you. I don't know if that person is Brad or not. But whatever you decide, I'll do my best to support you."

She reached over and squeezed my hand.

"You need anything before we get to your house?"

"No ... nothing. Thank you."

We drove the rest of the way in silence because silence felt like the best choice.

By the time I reached her house, the sleet was falling freely and loosely, splattering on the ground and genuinely impairing driving conditions. I pulled the car to a stop directly in front of her house.

"Brad is here," she said in a whisper.

"What?"

"Brad is here." She pointed. "That's his car."

"Aah," I turned off the car and got out with her. "Do you want me to come in?"

"No," she said. She gave me another hug. "Thanks for the talk and for the sweet words. I love you, too."

I watched her as she walked inside.

Brad was home but the lights were off. That couldn't be a good sign.

I waited for the lights to flicker on and then I started my car and drove to Alicia's house.

Chapter 31

April 27th (Monday)

Why had she given Brad a key, Gabby thought as she walked toward her townhouse. The question stopped her at the door, and though the cold rain pelted her, she felt none of it.

What she wanted, no needed, was some time by herself. She didn't have the energy to deal with Brad tonight.

Her visit home had been a lit keg of unresolved resentment and anger that felt inappropriate and selfish.

Her mother might be dying. The idea could not be wrestled in a day or a weekend. And it was muddled by all the other emotions she felt – and didn't feel – for her mother.

She slid the key in and pushed the door open.

"Brad?" Why were all the lights off? Four months of dating and she hadn't learned him. She turned on the living room light, "Brad?" and walked upstairs.

"Brad?" She repeated at the top of the steps.

The house was silent; the master bedroom door was closed. Was he napping?

"Brad?" She whispered as she gently pushed open the door.

"Surprise!" Brad yelled as he threw on the lights. Gabby jumped. A gift sat wrapped in his hand and his eyes danced with glee. He plunged in before she could speak, "I got you something," he said. "I wasn't very thoughtful the day you left. And I wanted to make it up to you." He handed her the small box.

"What is it?" Her heart raced from the scare.

"Open it," he said. "You'll love it."

Anything, she thought, but a ring.

"Open it," Brad repeated. "Just tear it," he said as she turned the box over and over.

"You know me," Gabby said. "I'm sentimental. I want to keep the wrapping." Please don't be a ring, she prayed.

"I'll get you more wrapping. Open it," he insisted.

She tore the wrapping slowly and let out her breath when she took off the lid. A pair of circle drop diamond earrings sat inside. "Brad, these are beautiful."

"And," he said, "I have these." He pulled two tickets out of his pocket for the play *Dreamgirls* at the Dallas Music Hall.

"Oh my god," a smile spread across Gabby's face. "Are you serious?" She had wanted to see the play in NYC last summer but hadn't been able to find the time. Now Brad had gotten tickets for the traveling show. "When is this?" She took the tickets and looked at the date. Her smile faded. "Brad, these are for tonight ..."

"I know." He still smiled.

"But Brad, I just got home and I'm exhausted," she said. "My mother is ..."

"Com'on, Gabrielle. Do it for us. I want make things up to you. And I'm dying to see you in the earrings."

"Brad, I am so tired and it's ..." She started to say and it's sleeting. But something flashed across his face that she couldn't read. So she didn't. Instead she said, "And it's going to be fantastic."

Brad pumped his fist. "Yes," he said. "Now get dressed. We only have about two hours before the show starts."

"Okay," She went into the bathroom, turned on the shower, stripped down, and stepped inside. She was exhausted. All she wanted to do was sleep. But it was nice to have Brad in a good move. So maybe the compromise was worth it.

Chapter 32

April 28th (Monday)

Perhaps the moon was in the seventh house and Jupiter had aligned with mars. For somehow we had all managed to do something we hadn't done in weeks - get together for happy hour.

Jim had made some renovations since our last visit and the results were pretty impressive. Biker friendly had become upscale chic. The bar stools were gone, replaced by plush couches and love seats. The 60's rock had morphed into Pop 100 and the back-splash for the bar was silver metallic.

I wasn't sure if Jim had sacrificed his authenticity or if he was a savvy business man. In any case, the anti-establishment 60-something revolutionist were now ultra chic hipsters.

The evening was feeling pretty good.

"Unbuttoned your shirt," I said to Chris. "Sit a while."

He smiled and obediently unbuttoned a couple buttons on his shirt.

"Did I tell you," Gabby said, "that Ryan Seacrest is buying a condo in Turtle Creek?" She sipped her vodka and cranberry.

"He is not buying a condo in Turtle Creek." I scoffed.

"That's what I heard."

"You did not hear that."

"I *swear* I heard it."

"Dallas would like to believe someone is buying here. Like this is the heartland of diversity and culture. Give me a break."

"George Michael has a condo in Turtle Creek."

"Oh please," I began. I nudged Chris.

"He does. Gary told me that he saw him one day on Cedar Springs."

"Gary?" Chris repeated. He shook his head with distaste. Gabby ignored him.

"Gary told you he saw George Michael dancing in the gay district of Dallas," I almost guffawed with laughter. "Seriously? And you believed him?"

She gave us the middle finger. "Both of you are pessimistic bastards."

"Not pessimists, cynics. There's a difference."

"Agreed," Chris said.

"Yes," Gabby said. "The heart of a Grinch."

I waved a waitress over. "Another round."

"So," Gabby paused dramatically, "let's play Mysteries of the Genders."

Mysteries of the Genders is a game one of us made up. I don't know who. It was no more than an excuse for sharing bizarre stories with each other, asking intimate details of our sex lives, and generally bonding over relationship trivia – sometimes useful, sometimes not.

"Who's going to go first?" She asked.

"I will," I volunteered, happy to have us sharing a moment. "So my friend La'Shonda told me about six months ago that foreplay is for guys with little dicks."

"What?" Chris scowled.

"No, I've got it wrong. She said that prolonged pussy-eating is for guy with little dicks. She said getting eaten out is cool, but if a dude know how to work the dick, he doesn't have to be good with eating pussy. True?"

A grin sat on Gabby's face. "I can only speak for myself. For me, undoubtedly."

"What?" Chris repeated.

"I can't speak for all woman. But think about it, it was meant to have something in it that's thicker and longer than a tongue. Although, a talented tongue is never a bad thing."

"And how is Brad at it?" Chris asked.

"Good with his tongue." She laughed.

"Well I am a pussy eating specialist," Chris bragged.

I poked Gabby's side. "Little dick," I said. She giggled. Chris punched me in the arm. "I do box," I said to him. "I will hit you back one day."

"Yea, right, Mr. Pacifist."

Someone who looked familiar sauntered to the back of the bar.

"Hey, isn't that Gary?" I asked Gabby.

"I think it is." She called his name. He didn't stop.

"Maybe we can lay this Ryan-Seacrest-George-Michael rumor to rest." I called him too.

"Excuse me for a sec," Chris said abruptly. He lumbered in Gary's direction.

"How are things with you and Brad?" I asked Gabby.

"Good, I guess. I came home and he apologized for how he had been acting. He even bought me some earrings and didn't give me any grief when I said I wanted to hang with you guys tonight. We are working, trying to make things right. That's what's important."

"You know we still haven't met him," I said demurely.

"I know. And we are going to change that very soon."

"Good. I need to know who's stealing my best friend." We exchanged smiles.

Gary hustled by without speaking, even as Gabby called

his name. A few seconds later Chris reappeared at the table.

"Were you just talking to Gary?" Gabby asked.

"Yea ... uh," Chris responded. "My mom wants a bag from Nordstroms and I thought he might be able to get it at a discount."

Chris was lying.

"Why didn't you ask me?" Gabby pressed. "I could've helped you with that. I shop there all the time. I probably have a couple brand new ones in my closet. You wouldn't have to even spend the money."

Chris hesitated, opened his mouth, and kinda shrugged. "I wasn't thinking I guess."

"Okay," Gabby said slowly. She looked suspicious.

"Hey, I got another drink coming for you ..." I changed the subject.

Gabby, though, is not easily distracted. She turned back to Chris to continue her interrogation but he was standing. "Sorry. But I've gotta run." He gave Gabby a quick hug and me a fist bump. "Next Monday."

Just as I opened my mouth, Gabby's phone beeped with a text message. She read it and looked at me.

"Brad?" I said.

"Yes," she replied.

"If he needs you, you gotta go," I said.

"Thanks for not making me feel guilty," she said. She gave me a big hug and a quick peck on the cheek. "Next Monday."

Then she was out the door like Chris.

All in all it was a good happy hour. Almost as good as the past.

Chapter 33

April 28th (Monday)

What Chris had told Gary was that if he said a word to Gabby about seeing him at the club, he'd make certain Gary didn't get one more drop of business from Gabby. She was a pipeline of referrals for Gary. Whenever female clients, friends, business partners from the east coast came to town, she referred them to Gary. He might have been a big mouth drag queen but he was also a savvy businessman. He wasn't going to say shit.

Chris was pissed as fuck. Pissed that he kept bumping into Gary and pissed at the stream of guys - tall, short, fat, thin, good-looking, butt-ass ugly - that marched steadily in and out David's house.

David knew Chris was coming by tonight. What the fuck was David doing? Having a party? Or was this what he meant by pharmacist? Fuck it! He didn't need David. This was a phase. Once he worked through it, these visits would come to an end anyway. Who cared who or what David did?

Chris mulled returning to the bar. But that would be awkward if Gabby and Jordan were still there. So he hauled ass home. He was halfway through chugging a Coors when he decided to workout. He poured the Coors down the sink and changed into sweats and a tank top. A few reps would relieve the tension.

Ninety minutes later he was drenched in sweat. Too tired to even put the weights back, he stood up, stripped down, and hopped in the shower. When the phone rang at twelve-fifteen, he was sound asleep.

"Hello," Chris mumbled.

"What happened? I thought you were coming over." David was on the line.

"I did come by," Chris explained. "But you had company."

"And?"

"And?" Chris sat up in bed. "I don't want to meet anybody, dude."

"You need to get over this."

"Get over what?" Sleep fled and Chris snapped.

"Your crazy paranoia. It's getting kinda old."

"What the fuck?"

"I'm saying. Live your life. It's yours."

"Look, if you don't care who knows about you, that's on you. But for me, this is just a phase."

"Here we go. Here we go with the phase thing. Let me tell you, you are too old for a phase."

Chris slammed his phone shut and ignored David's call back. He turned off the phone and tried to go back to sleep. But sleep escaped him. At three am, he found himself staring at the ceiling.

He rolled out of bed, turned on his PC, and tried to play a few video games. Within minutes he was bored. So he went to Craigslist to see if anyone was selling any new games.

He was sure he had seen the personal ads before. He shopped Craigslist pretty often. Clearly, they hadn't registered. Today they did. *Men for Women, Women for Men, Men for Men. Men for Men.* The words glowed like a neon light. An all too familiar guilt stung him, he hesitated, and then he clicked on the link.

About forty listings down he came across an ad that read GOODLOOKING GUY VISITING, NEW TO THE SCENE. The guy sounded like Chris and his picture was great – 6'1, 175, six pack – he looked like a runway model. Chris glanced at the clock. Three-forty five am. What the heck? No harm could come from responding. He quickly typed an email and hit send. Seven minutes later new mail sat in his box. His heartbeat quickened.

WHAT ARE YOU INTO?

I'M NOT SURE. Chris typed back.

Ten minutes passed before the guy responded. DO YOU HAVE A PIC?

NO. Chris typed. He waited five minutes, ten minutes, fifteen minutes. At the twenty minute mark, he moved to turn off his PC. He sighed with a mixture of relief and disappointment. Suddenly an email appeared.

YOU WANNA COME BY MY HOTEL?

Chris glanced at the clock. 4:30. There was no way he was going to this guy's hotel – no matter how good-looking the guy was.

Chris typed "no" onto the screen. Before he hit the send key, another email arrived.

DO YOU PARTY?

Party? What was the hell was this guy talking about? Chris typed back question marks. Two minutes later Chris had another email. PARTY. YOU KNOW – X. That's what partying was, Chris thought. Using X? Hell yeah, he was cool with that. He would go over and party with the dude. Nothing more. They'd chill for a minute and Chris would alleviate his boredom.

YES, Chris typed back. I PARTY.

Twenty minutes later Chris pulled into the DFW Hilton. Hands shaking apprehensively, he took another gander at the note he had written - room 713 - and stuffed it into his pocket.

He quickly scanned the lobby for the elevator as he

breezed past the front desk as casually as he could.

What was he doing? He didn't even know the guy's name.

He stopped outside the room, listened to the sounds of *Family Guy* floating into the hallway and tried to steady his breathing. A light knock on the door got no response; he waited, took a deep breath, and then knocked louder.

"Unlocked," a voice called from within.

Chris pushed open the door timidly. "Hello?"

"Hey guy," the voice called back. He stepped into the foyer to meet Chris.

Chris mouth fell open. This guy stood 5'8 and looked like a candidate for liposuction. "What?" Chris stammered. "The pic ..."

"I know, I know, man. I'm sorry. But I'm discreet. I have a family. I can't have my real picture floating out there. You know how it goes." He took a step toward Chris. "But you are hot, dude. And since you're here, you might as well let me give you head." He reached out and grabbed Chris's crotch.

Chris shoved his hand away hard. "I'm outta here." Their bodies banged as Chris turned to leave and the shorter guy stumbled back.

"Asshole," the guy spat at him.

"Fat fuck," Chris mumbled.

An hour later Chris was back in bed – more pissed, still horny, and wide awake. He stared at his ceiling until seventy-thirty and then he called the office to say he wasn't coming in.

Chapter 34

May 1st (Thursday)

Alicia once said that I needed to share. I wasn't ready.

I've dated women who interpreted my lack of sharing, and the entire male species lack of sharing, as being a detached and unemotional creature.

What is this bullshit that men are a stoic species from another world, adhering to the edicts of ESPN, our sole mission being to practice procreating?

The Church of ESPN is powerful and good. And I don't know a guy who doesn't enjoy practicing the procreation process. But stoic? That's a behavior learned from social programming. Dad teaches it, brothers teach it, the guys on the football field teach it, the Church condones it. Truth is, men are some of the most emotional people I know. Raw emotion rages right beneath the surface – tears, angers, confusion, frustration, sadness. But we are always told to control it. Men don't share and they don't the cry. The poor slob who is introspective enough to be a communicator and in touch with his feelings get labeled as gay.

A five year old girl breaks her Barbie. She runs to Mommy who sweeps her up and says, "It's okay." Okay to be sad and okay to cry. A five year old boy breaks his model train and just as Mommy sweeps him in her arms, Dad says, "Put him down, stop babying him." And then he says to his son, "Stop crying. You'll get you another one. Big boys don't cry."

And so the cycle has begun. Only to be repeated again.

And again.

And again.

Is it any wonder we struggle for words when a women says, "Tell me how you feel. Talk to me." Are you serious? Here is what we are really hearing: Speak Latin.

Find the words of a language that is dead to us and articulate it fluently.

And that's why I wasn't ready to share. I was searching for words.

Besides, is not talking necessarily a bad thing?

I picked up the phone to call Alicia. Not to have *the discussion* but to hear her warm voice.

No answer. I left her a message, picked up the clicker, and caught the second quarter of the Mavs game. They were up 42-24.

Chapter 35

May 1st (Thursday)

Brad moved around the kitchen as if he was channeling Bobby Flay. Spinach sautéed in olive oil, potatoes lay sprinkled with rosemary, and steak was deftly grilled over an open flame. He uncorked another bottle of Merlot and topped off Gabby's three-quarters full glass.

Gabby liked red wine but it always gave her a headache. Since there was already a dull throbbing at her temple, she wanted to push the glass away. She didn't.

She cleared her throat. "The doctor called today," she began as Brad placed her plate on the table.

"Uh huh," he said. He sat in the chair beside her and began to cut her steak.

Gabby continued. "He wanted to know when you were coming back."

"Uh huh," Brad answered as he continued to cut.

Gabby reached out and stopped him. "Brad," she repeated, exasperation slipping into her tone, "The doctor called and wanted to know when you plan on coming back." Brad stared at her blankly.

"Brad, when did you stop? I thought you were going

every Monday. You promised."

He sat back in his chair. "I promised to go. I didn't promise to go indefinitely."

"But ..."

"Com'on Gabby, haven't things been fine? We haven't had one disagreement."

"But ..."

"And when I am irritable, it's just because I'm stressed. That's all. I haven't lost my temper. Right? Right?"

"Right ..."

"So why am I going? I'm managing. I'm fixed."

"Brad, nobody is trying to fix you. The doctor ... I ... we just want to understand where the anger comes from."

"Where it comes from? Give me a break. People get angry. I'm only human.

"Look, if you want me to continue, I'll go back." He cupped her face in his hands. "I'll go back to four more sessions. Okay?" He moved her head up and down. "I'll go for you." He paused. "Because I love you.

"Now," he said. "Eat your steak. This promises to be the best meal outside Ruth Chris. Mangia!"

She picked up a piece of steak he had sliced for her. He was right. They hadn't had an argument, at least nothing along the lines of their first one. But not arguing didn't mean things were as they should be.

If she and Brad were in the good place he claimed, why did she always feel like she was walking on eggshells around him?

She wished she had the energy to sort, but she didn't have the strength to determine who was right. So she decided to enjoy her meal and think about it later.

Chapter 36

May 3rd (Saturday)

"Turn left," Chris slurred his words.

"What?" I said. "You don't live this way."

"Just do it," he insisted.

I knew where we were: The Gayborhood. Homo Heights. The Gay District. Boy's Town. I wasn't sure why we were there. We had just left a club – a fine club with hot chicks. I hadn't left it to go to a sausage party.

I clenched my teeth and turned left.

This is what I get for calling him.

May 3rd – 102 degree outside, the humidity was oppressive, and I was restless. More so than anything, I was used to hanging out with Chris on these hot summer nights. We hadn't done it in a while. So I called, even though I was a little leery about it. I mean, things had been touch and go between us. Plus, May tends to be a pretty busy month for him.

Chris was a sales consultant at Mediotronics. The company sold electronic software and prided itself on charitable donations and giving back to the community. For the last five years, Chris had helmed an annual fundraiser for children with disabilities. Gabby had met him and I at one of the May fundraisers.

When I called him he said he wasn't helming it this year and that he would be happy to go out. I'm not sure which surprised me more.

Around eleven, I drove fifteen minutes down the tollway to his house and we took off for this spot called The Limelight.

NYC once had a club called The Limelight. Their Limelight and this were not to be confused. The one thing they did share in common was discretionary admission - admission that had a throng of two or three hundred twenty and thirty-somethings trying desperately to get in.

Waiting in a line in NYC, yeah. Waiting in a line in LA, maybe. Waiting in a line in Dallas, absolutely not.

Fortunately, I knew the bouncer manning the door, the one that looked like Ving Rhames. We used to bartend together and occasionally I saw him at the gym.

Chris and I meandered to the front of the line, where we were greeted by a head nod, and a removal of the velvet rope.

It's not what you know but who you know.

"Fuck you," someone called from the middle of the line.

Fuck me? Fuck you. You're the one standing 2000 people deep in a line waiting to get judged like an American Idol contestant. I flipped him off.

Removal of the velvet rope didn't mean removal of the cover charge. We paid the pretty cashier thirty dollars, had our hands stamped, and then walked into the main foyer. What was immediately clear was the fact that the people outside the club were having it much easier than the people inside the club. The people inside were packed like sardines. The Limelight wasn't letting anymore people in because no more could fit.

Chris and I pushed our way through the swarm of sweaty bodies, navigated to the bar, ordered a couple drinks and learned the lay of the land from a server.

Level 1 of the Limelight: Top 40 and Pop: The Blackeyed

Peas segued into Coldplay who segued into Rhianna. Pretty blondes and brunettes danced and pranced around seductively on the floor.

Level 2: Hip-hop: Jay-Z, Kanye, Lil Wayne, Daddy Yankee -. Black and Latino women with bodies ranging from Halle Berry to Serena Williams to Monique grinded on the dance floor, surrounded by the many men who loved them. It was Springtime. People had been waiting to get out their clothes. Here they could - titties, ass, and legs abounded on every floor.

Level three was my favorite. House and electronica prevailed. Lisa Shaw, David Guetta, Kaskade, Colette. The floor was least crowded of the three but had the most diverse crowd. Everything and everybody dancing with anything and anyone.

I danced to a couple songs but Chris refused to move from his perch. He didn't scan the club for potentials. He didn't make a move on anyone. The only thing he did with any enthusiasm was drink.

"You okay?" I asked for the umpteenth time.

"I'm fine, man. This is great." He kept answering. But he looked uncomfortable.

The crowd was still jumping at two in the morning. But Chris was drunk and he had told me, "I love you, man," about twenty-two times.

"I love you, too," I said.

"No really, I love you," he slurred for the twenty-third time. He flicked my nipple through my shirt when he said it.

I called it a night.

Ten minutes later, the valet pulled my car around. A ten dollar tip – it was all I had – brought my spend count to $125 for the lousy evening.

We were navigating through downtown when Chris said, "Turn here."

"What? You don't live this way."

"Just turn here," he insisted.

"Chris, where are we going? Do you know?"

"Ssshhh," he said. "I know."

Yeah, he was definitely drunk. We zigzagged down a couple streets and landed on Cedar Springs.

"Turn right here," he said. "On Throckmorton. Okay, okay … slow down. Yea, stop."

Chris unbuckled his seat belt and hopped out the car. He smiled, "I'm good." Chris is either very happy or very confused when he's drunk. At the moment, he was both.

He stumbled to the door and rang the bell. I sat in my car and waited. Ten minutes later, he was still ringing. I was about to call him back to the car when the outside light came on and the door swung open.

Chris waved at me and stumbled into the house.

I started my car and drove off. But I didn't wave back.

Chapter 37

May 4th (Sunday)

David opened the door and led Chris inside. "You're drunk."

Chris laughed. "I'm fine, dude." He tripped and lurched forward. David steadied him.

"Chris, I really don't appreciate your coming to my house drunk." Chris pushed him aside and toppled on the couch.

"What?" Chris asked too loudly.

"You're drunk, I don't appreciate ..."

"Aw shutup." He waved David's words away with his hand, turned on his side and pulled himself into a semi-fetal position. "Turn the TV on dammit."

David walked over to him. "Chris, I'm talking." Chris closed his eyes in response, so David knelt down to face him. "I'm talking to you." David's warm breath made Chris open his eyes again.

"You want to kiss me, don't you?" Chris teased. David didn't respond. "You know you do. Go ahead, do it. Kiss me." Chris closed his eyes again and David complied with a kiss.

They made out, touching and groping for the next few minutes.

"Hey, I gotta take a leak," David said. He got up to go to the bathroom but had trouble pissing because he was hard. He stripped as he walked back to the living room only to find Chris snoring on the couch when he returned.

Chapter 38

May 4th (Sunday)

"Has anyone ever told you," Alicia began, "that you look like The Rock?"

"I don't look like The Rock."

"You do ... kinda sort. Maybe it's the eyes or the grimace." She laughed.

"Lo que sea. That's Espanol for 'whateva' ." I laughed and put more half and half in my coffee.

"What's wrong with The Rock? He's a good-looking guy."

"I didn't say he wasn't. But I don't look like him."

She shook her head. "You do," she insisted with an adorable grin. "So ... how was last night?"

"Let's not talk about it," I said. Today was cheat day, which meant I could eat anything I friggin' wanted. What I was eating was blueberry pancakes. I reached across the table and doused them with some good old fashion maple syrup. No story about Chris was going to ruin my meal.

"It couldn't have been that bad."

"Trust me. It was." I stuffed my mouth with pancake. *O my God, these things are delicious.*

We were having Sunday brunch at the Grand Lux and, at

eleven-thirty, were just ahead of the church crowd. You know the type, good people but terribly hungry after Sunday service. They are out the door as soon as the reverend says, "Amen", and they have been known to increase the brunch wait time tri-fold.

My Sunday mission: Get to brunch before the last "amen".

"Ever noticed," I said, "the uncanny resemblance the Grand Lux bears to the Taj Mahal? And look, there are like three hundred and twenty-five items on the menu. How does a chef get good at three hundred and twenty-five items? Answer: he doesn't. He gets good at twenty-five. All the other items he is about average on. Fortunately, these pancakes are on the list of twenty-five." I took another piece of pancake, rolled it in syrup, and gulped it down. Pancakes made me happy. They were also what my mom used to make every Saturday growing up as a kid.

"No, I haven't noticed and you are avoiding the topic."

"Am I?" I hadn't come prepared to talk about Chris; I hadn't found my words yet. "Okay, okay. Um … the night was … not what I expected."

She tilted her head to one side and her hair fell into her eye. I suppressed a desire to reach over and move the lock. "What do you mean?" She asked.

"Let's just say Chris wasn't himself last night."

She raised one eyebrow. "Care to share?"

I hadn't wanted to tell this story. "Well … we leave the club early because he is drunk off his ass. I get him in the car and I'm about to take him home, when he starts giving me directions. Turn here. Go straight. Take a left. Next thing I know, we are parked in front of someone's house in uptown. Chris gets out the car just as happy as he pleases. And goes in."

"So you dropped him off at some girl's house," Alicia said. "You said yourself he is a lady's man. Why would that bother you?"

"Say it wasn't a lady's house."

Her eyebrows furrowed.

"Say it wasn't a lady's house," I repeated.

"What do you mean?"

"I mean …. Never mind."

Alicia looked at me thoughtfully. "Say it wasn't a lady." She cut her omelet and took a bite before continuing. "Say," she said, "say it was a man. What difference would it make?"

I opened my mouth to answers but words weren't forthcoming.

"Chris was drunk and he had you drop him off at some guy's house. That may mean nothing at all."

"Oh it means something," I mumbled.

"What, Jordan?"

I hesitated. "Let's just say he hasn't been acting himself."

"What has he been doing?"

I didn't respond.

"Where did you drop him off?" She asked.

"Cedar Springs."

"Oh," she said. "Huh, so … you think the guy was gay?"

"I have no idea."

"And you think Chris ..."

I put my fork down and looked at her. "Please don't ..."

"And what if he was, what difference would it make?" She persisted.

I didn't answer.

"Here's what I say, he got dropped off a guy's house. That's all you know. But if there's more to it, if he's gay or if he is at some sexual crossroads, remember that it's his sexuality. It's not about you, it's about him. He has to come to peace with who he is."

"It's just that," I tried to explain, "we used to chase women together."

"Who said that will change?"

"I ..." Another question I didn't have an answer for.

"Be a friend, support him. I mean ...," she smiled, "if it wasn't a lady." On that note, she reached across the table and dug into one of my pancakes. "Are you going to eat all of these?" She tasted one. "Oh my God, these are good."

I moved my plate out her reach. "Get your own." I teased.

"Greedy." She stuck out her tongue. "By the way, I've been meaning to ask you. You said Gabby's boyfriend's name is Brad, right?"

"Yeah."

"And he's at doctor?"

"Yea, he is."

"Which hospital?"

"I don't know. Why?"

"I … there is a doctor at our hospital named Brad. I was wondering if he was the same guy. "

"What's he like?" I asked.

"He's an egotistical asshole," she said without missing a beat.

Alicia never cursed.

"Can't be him," I said. "I know that Gabby has had some ups and downs with the new guy. But she'd never go for the egotistical type."

"Good," she said. "I haven't met Gabby but from what you've said, she sounds very special."

"She is."

Ninety minutes later we were sitting in a the last row of the AMC 16 Valleyview – our feet plastered to the sticky floor, the smell of stale popcorn floating through the air, couched in uncomfortable chairs. Not that we cared. We positioned ourselves in the back row and made out like teenagers.

The tongue action was pretty hot. Hot enough for me to get wood and to forget all about Chris, the club, and his ten rounds with Jose Cuervo.

Chapter 39

May 5th (Monday)

We went to Sangria's on Monday. I'm not sure why. Sangria's serves tapas, which meant that the eight small plates sitting on the table between us three had come nowhere close to filling us. I'm not sure if Sangria is technically part of uptown, nevertheless it's a great place to be seen. People sit outside so they can watch folks traipsing by and the folks traipsing by can see who's eating. Or in the case of tapas, who's not eating much.

Chris, Gabby, and I were watching the people go by, which was a good thing as Chris and I weren't making eye contact.

"How was the Limelight?" Gabby asked.

"It was great." Chris replied.

Gabby looked at me. "No review?"

"Nothing to report," I replied with a shrug.

She looked back and forth between us before changing the topic. "Memorial Day is almost here. Whose turn is it to bbq?"

She was right. Memorial Day was almost here. The three of us rotated throwing some type of party during the summer. One of us took Memorial Day, one of us took July 4th, and the other took Labor Day. We'd been doing it for three years now. "It's Chris's turn, I think," she said.

I looked in Chris's direction but not at him. "You got it covered?" I asked.

"I got it," he said without enthusiasm.

Gabby continued to look at us quizzically.

"You need us to bring anything?" I asked.

"I got it," he repeated.

"But we always chip in, Chris," Gabby started.

"I said, I got it."

Gabby's eyes met mine and I gave her the wide-eye look. *Ignore him,* I thought. "Are you bringing Brad?" I asked.

"If Chris doesn't mind," she said.

He must have sensed he had been sharp because his toned softened tremendously. "Anything for you, Gabby." He shot her a smile and a wink. *Flirting? Seriously?*

Gabby blew him a kiss. "And who are you two bringing?"

"I'm bringing Alicia," I said.

"Really?" She said. "Alicia sounds like she is morphing into a full-fledged relationship."

I made a face. "I wouldn't say that. But ..."

"What would you say?" She asked.

"I dunno. We are just enjoying each other's company."

"Hmmm," Gabby said, "I wonder what she would say." She turned to Chris. "And what lovely damsel will you bless us with?"

"I think I'm gonna go it alone this year," he responded.

"What? Jordan, do you hear this? Chris, you never go alone ..."

Chris waved her off. "I'm a turning into a brand new man," he said.

Yeah, more than she knew, I thought. Hastily I changed topics. "Gabby, how's your Mom?'

Emotion ran freely through her face. "It's cancer."

"Gabby, I'm so sorry." A flashback of losing my own family caused a wave of emotion to flood through me.

"Your mom is sick, Gabby?" Chris leaned forward and put his hand over hers. "I didn't know. I'm so sorry."

Well buddy, you should have known. You aren't being much of a friend, you aren't keeping up with Gabby, and you abandoned me for some gay dude on Saturday. There! I had processed!

Gabby's response was far more generous. "Don't worry about it. We've all been a little busy. How could you know?"

"Is there anything I can do?" Chris asked.

She looked down into her empty glass. "You know we aren't close. But I think I'd be devastated if something happened to her." Gabby rarely talked about her family.

"She will be fine," Chris said. "And anything you need, *anything*, we are here for you. Because that's what friends do. We are here for each other when we need to be."

Chris was holding Gabby's hand when he said it, but when I looked up I saw he was staring at me.

Chapter 40

May 10th (Saturday)

"So are you coming over?" David asked.

Chris sat on his couch playing *Left for Dead* on his Xbox. He didn't want go out the house. He didn't want to see anybody. He wanted to be left alone. He cradled his cell phone between his shoulder and his ear. "Naw, man. I think I'm just gonna chill tonight."

"What the fuck? You said you were coming over when we talked earlier this week." David didn't attempt to hide his frustration.

"I know, man." Chris took a series of shots at the zombies on his screen. "But I think I'm gonna relax. It's been a long week. I should just chill at home tonight."

"And why is that?" David snapped.

"Uh ..." Chris hesitated. "I dunno. Just think I should."

"You know what? This is crazy. You come over last week sloppy drunk. You puke all over my floor. You don't do shit. You didn't come over Monday. And now you just don't feel like coming over."

Chris paused the game. "Look, I'm sorry. I didn't mean

..."

"It's funny how you can manage find your way over here when your horny."

Chris winced.

"Or when you want to get your dick sucked ..." David continued.

"Okay, okay." Chris wanted to clasp his hands over his ears. "I got it. I get it. So what do you want me to do?" He restarted the game.

"I want you to come over."

Chris stopped the game again.

"Besides," David said. "I've got X."

Chris didn't respond.

"So are you coming?"

Chris knew he should stay at home. But he didn't do loneliness well. Right now, he was feeling a bit lonely. The X always made for a good time and made the memory a bit hazy.

"Yes," Chris said with more than a trace of embarrassment. "Let me throw on some jeans and I'll be right over."

****

Old habits die hard. Chris and I had stopped having regularly weekend plans a long time ago. Yet, in spite of last Saturday's fiasco, I hoped we still might get together. *Another Saturday night and I ain't got nobody.*

I ordered a pizza from Zini's, I made myself a couple martinis, and fell asleep while watching *Let The Right One In.* My TV was far too loud for my neighbor, I'm sure. But we have an agreement, she doesn't complain about the sounds of my stereo and I don't complain about the sounds of her screeching five year old twins.

Unfortunately, the TV was also too loud to hear the

phone ring when Alicia called.

Chapter 41

May 12th (Monday)

The time to pay the piper comes around for everyone.

Mike had been on a couple business trips over the last few weeks. I hadn't seen him since our Cialis exchange. Now he leaned over my cube. "Hey, buddy," he said. I hate being called buddy and I particularly disliked how Mike said it. He would draw out the uh sound and add a slight accent to the e. It sounded like, *buuuhDE.*

"How ya doing?" He asked.

"I'm good," I said slowly.

He didn't move. He smiled and waited with control exuberance. "Had any fun lately?" Gently he attempted to mine precious details of my non-existent sexual escapades out of me.

Did we have to do this now, Mike? I stood and pretended to stretch. What could I tell him? I had had some fun with Alicia. That, though, didn't have anything to do with his Cialis. All that resulted from his prescription was two empty bottles of KY jelly and calluses on my palms. He had, though, tried to improve my sexual satisfaction. That alone earned him some kind of story.

"Com'on," I said. "Do you have to ask?" I walked past him and headed toward the elevator like I had someplace to go.

"I knew it! I knew it." He clapped his hands together as his exuberance broke forth. "Do you need more? I can talk to my neighbor. What was she like?Did you blow her back out? What were her tits like?"

"Three girls," I said. I shouldn't have said it but I did.

Dumbfounded is what Mike was. "What?"

"Three. There were three girls. One of them was a little older, but still ..."

"No way, no way. You are shitting me." Mike was beside himself.

"I shit you not, my friend."

"You gotta tell me more," he begged.

I was going to pay for this. No doubt. But I couldn't help myself. So I continued. "One was like a movie star, oh my god she was beautiful." I pushed the button for the elevator.

"And ..."

"The other," I said, "was much more the girl next door type. But she was equally as pretty."

A little bit of drool leaked out his mouth. "And?" he said.

The elevator dinged and the door opened. "The other was a little older but very refined, I could tell she had a lot of money." I stepped into the elevator.

"No way, man. This is crazy! I gotta hear it all. Where did you meet them? Can I meet them? We should get something going. I'm all about the foursome. What were their names?"

"Names, names," I said. "O yeah, one was named Ginger. The other was Mary Ann, and the older chick was Mrs. Howell. You wouldn't believe the snatch on Mrs. Howell. Moist like Duncan Hines."

It took a moment for Mike to digest it. Then he said, "You sonofabitch, you better tell me ..." The elevator doors closed and I didn't hear the rest. I'm sure I would though. We all have to pay the piper sometimes. Me and Mike included.

Chapter 42

May 14th (Wednesday)

At least, Gabby thought, as she kicked off her pumps and pulled her feet into the chair, her work life was good.

Was the work load heavy? Always. Was succession planning tedious? Certainly. But did it provide her a necessary distraction? Without a doubt.

If she took some time, she could almost connect every major promotion to an unsuccessful relationship. Maybe she owed a debt to some of her exes. Her break up with Augustine had gotten her the vice-president title four years. Two years ago, her break up with Greg had resulted in her being one of two HR members who had been invited on the company's annual sales trip to Bali.

She picked up a confidential file that held the names of potentials successors for several of her company's executive leaders. There were more ass-kissers on the list than real candidates but she saw a few names she would endorse.

Her admin knocked. "Your brother is in on the line, Gabby."

She lifted the receiver. "Hello?"

"Sorry to call you at work, Gabby. But I couldn't reach you on your cell."

"It's no problem. I had it turned on mute. What's going on?"

"I wanted to give you and update. Mom's not responding as quickly as we had hoped to the oral chemo."

Gabby didn't move.

"Although the good news is that she is in good spirits. That always helps."

"Do you need me to come home?"

"That would be great, Gabby. We would love to see you again. But let's plan it a little better. I know this isn't your favorite place."

"I want to come."

"And we want you to be here. Maybe longer than a weekend this time. Tell you what, take a look at your calendar. If you have time, maybe you can come for a week in June."

"I'll do it."

"Okay sis, I'm gonna let you get back to work. I just wanted to give you a call. Love ya."

"Love you, too." Gabby said. "And tell mom ... I love her too."

Her brother hung up the phone. Gabby buzzed her admin and told him she was leaving for the day.

She would go to the gym, run six miles, and clear her head. The succession plans could wait.

She answered the phone one more time before she walked out the office. The call was from Brad's therapist's office.

Chapter 43

May 16th (Friday)

    "Why are you nagging me about this?" Brad scowled.

    "I'm not nagging you," Gabby said with forced patience. "You said you were going to four more visits and you didn't."

    "So you're checking up on me now?"

    Gabby rested her head in her hand and took a deep breath. "I'm not checking up on you. You said you were going to go. I called the doctor to tell him so. When you didn't show, they called back."

    "Why are they talking to you anyway?"

    "We were going together ..."

    "Well I don't need it and I'm not going. And I'm going to call that doctor and give him ..."

    "Brad, that's the point. You're supposed to be working on your ..."

    "Give it a rest, Gabrielle. Damn! Can't I be human? What? I'm not allowed to ever get angry? To ever have any emotion besides happiness? Fuck."

    "No .. that's not what I'm saying ..." She stood, walked

over to his sink, and poured herself a glass of tap water.

"Then what are you saying? I did that stupid shit to make you happy. But clearly it didn't work. Because all you do is nag me about it."

"What? This is only the second time I've brought it up. And if you had kept your word ..." the words slipped out her mouth.

"So are you calling me a liar? Is that what you are saying?"

"Brad, you promised to ..."

"You know what Gabrielle. This is really pissing me off."

She put the glass down. "What's that supposed to mean?"

"You've got Mom and Dad issues and you take them out on me."

"What? Brad, I have never talked to you about my family."

"First of all, you don't have to talk about them. It's clear from the way you are all clingy and needy. Second, you didn't deny that you have issues. Third, you are so busy trying to fix other people. Why don't you try fixing Gabrielle?"

"Don't you dare make this about me or my parents! This is not about me. It's about your temper."

"No, it's about the fact that every time I'm anything but happy you starting whining. You not perfect either, Gabrielle. Big shock, huh? You aren't perfect either."

Gabby picked her keys off the kitchen counter.

"Where are you going?" Brad asked. "Oh now you don't want to talk. When the spotlight is on you, you run. Where the fuck are you going?" He caught her wrist as she reached for the knob of the front door. "Where are you going?"

"Anywhere," she said through gritted teeth, "but here." She jerked her wrist out his grasp and stormed out the door.

"Gabrielle, wait. Don't go," escaped just before the door slammed shut. Pride kept her from running to her car. She turned off her phone, drove back to the office, and completed the succession plans.

Chapter 44

May 17th (Saturday)

Do you want to come over? Alicia's text stared at me and I could only imagine the fun we could have. I hadn't answered it, though. Because when I went to reply Nicole's message came through. **Do you want to come over?**

Chris – the *old Chris* - would have interpreted the moment as a stamp on his player's card, he would've typed "Abso-fuckin-lutely" and figured out a way to make both meetings in one night. But I wasn't Chris. I'm a processor.

Nicole's appeal was unencumbered emotional detachment. She offered fuck-n-go, instant gratification. Medicine for the dick, she was.

Alicia had as much sexual appeal but it was wrapped in emotional attachment.

Nicole was medicine for the symptoms; Alicia was medicine for the illness. I knew which I needed but I didn't know which I wanted.

I put the phone down.

They say that doing mundane tasks allows the brain to

process information more easily. So I cleaned out the shower, washed a load of clothes, and answered email.

At eleven, I went to the boxing gym for a couple hours.

At two that afternoon, I was at Northpark Mall returning a shirt.

At a quarter after three I texted back: **I'd love to. What time?**

Chapter 45

May 17th (Satuday)

David turned off Lemon Ave and onto Oaklawn.

"Where we going?" Chris asked.

"I want to stop by a friend's for a moment. You don't mind?" David answered casually.

Chris shrugged. Four margarita swirls – top shelf - from Mi Cocinas had him pretty relaxed. Sixty seconds later they turned right onto Cedar Springs and Chris found himself in in a place he had not too affectionately called Homo Heights in the past. He suppressed the desire to slide down in his seat – liquid courage pulsing through his veins – and sat stoically as they drove slowly down the four-block strip.

The courage lasted no longer than the five minute ride. For as soon as they reached David's friend's condo, Chris regretted coming. Bass poured out the front door; a multitude of shadows moved to and fro within the condo. He and David hadn't just stopped at a friend's house, they had come to party.

As far as Chris could tell, the ratio of men to women in the house was ten to one - which translated into about 70 or so men of varying degrees of masculinity and the six or seven women who loved them.

David grasped his hand as they moved through the crowd. Chris held on limply, not wanting to hold hands but not wanting to let go.

"You're new."

Chris turned to find a guy with piercing blue eyes and the whitest teeth he had ever seen talking to him. The guy's tank stretched across his chest and abs revealing a body that was gym-centric.

"Excuse me," Chris said. He looked for David but he had vanished into the crowd.

"I've never seen you before." The guy flashed his million dollar smile. "You must be new to town. Or David's been hiding you someplace. I'm Peter."

"You know David?"

Peter's eyes were like pools of deep ocean water. He laughed. "Do I know him? Who doesn't know him?" He leaned into Chris. "We used to be lovers. But then ..." he cast his gaze around the room. "Who here hasn't been lovers?" Peter winked and Chris couldn't tell if he was joking. "You're a good-looking man. David's done well for himself. How long have you two been together?"

"Together?" Chris repeated. He started to say, "We aren't ..." but the conversation was interrupted by the antithesis of Blue Eyes. The intruder was short with a doughy Pillsbury face and sported a too-small button down. "Who's this?" He asked Peter.

"This is David's boyfriend ..."

Chris opened his mouth to protest.

"Damn you are fine," Pillsbury said. He placed his pudgy hand on Chris's chest. "Mmm, whatta man," he growled.

Chris pushed his hand away. "I need to use the bathroom." Hurriedly he walked away.

One of the six women at the party led the way to a third floor bathroom. She walked away with a giggle as Chris pushed open the bathroom door. He took one step in the room and stopped in his tracks. Two guys seemed to be playing *"60 Seconds in Heaven"*, except this version required one to be on his knees in front of the other guy.

The dark-haired guy didn't bother to zip when the door swung open. He leaned his head back and let out a low moan, and then he motioned Chris to join.

Chris scurried back downstairs. He'd pee when he got back home.

By midnight, Chris had made up so many aliases he couldn't remember them all.

At one he found David. "I can't find my wallet. Can I have the keys? I think I left it in the car."

The temperature was about 72 degrees. Chris opened the door, sat down in the seat, leaned it back as far as it would go, and closed his eyes. He woke up at three startled by the sounds of David banging on the door.

Chapter 46

May 18th (Sunday)

Sirens screamed in the distance portending winds of impending disaster. When Gabby had first moved to Dallas, the sounds had made her nervous. Now the sirens registered as no more than part of the fabric of Dallas's temperamental weather. Although, today, their prophecies seemed to portend more of Gabby's future than anything else.

"Are you listening to me?" Brad asked.

She turned her gaze from the darkened sky, the rain they had begun to fall, and the people hurrying to their cars, and gave Brad an empty look.

"Do you need anything?" Their strawberry-haired waitress stood beside them, a carafe of coffee in her head, smiling broadly.

"Nothing for me." Gabby covered the top of her coffee mug with her hand.

"And for you, sir?" The chipper young lady asked. Brad ignored her. Her friendliness was not deterred. "I'll be back to check on you in a minute," she promised and moved to another table.

Brad repeated his question. "Are you listening, Gabby?"

She hadn't been listening. Not when he called to apologize again last night. Not when he had invited her to brunch. And not now, as they sat at Ziziki's having brunch.

She picked up a piece of bacon, took a small bite, and placed it back on her plate

"Gabby, there are ups and downs in every relationship. You … we … we can't just bail every time there is a disagreement or an argument." He scooted his chair closer to hers and took one of her hands in his.

Gabby gently pulled her hand away and picked up her coffee. "Brad," she said quietly. "You know and I know, this isn't working."

The sky was darker now. Clouds huddled as if they knew that the light rain was only the beginning of the devastation that was about to be unleashed.

"Gabby it is working. It's working like it's supposed to work. We've hit some bumps in the road. That's all. You'll see. You know I love you."

But Gabby had stopped listening. All she heard was the sound of the rain pelting against the restaurant windowpane.

Brad repeated his words. "I love you. And I will never let you go."

Gabby still wasn't listening.

Chapter 47

May 19th (Monday)

"I don't like him," Chris folded his arms and sat back in his chair.

"You haven't even met him," Gabby responded.

"Well … I don't like how he treats you. How about that? Based on what you've told us today."

Gabby looked to me for support. I didn't like him either.

"I knew I shouldn't have told you two," Gabby said.

"This has nothing to do with telling us, Gabby," I said. "The guy doesn't seem right for …" I paused. "What does he say when you talk to him about it? You do talk to him, don't you?" Gabby didn't respond. So I continued. "Gabby, you're a communicator. When did you start changing who you are to be with him?"

"Aren't we supposed to compromise in relationships?"

"I … yes .. yes, we are. But that doesn't mean we change who we are. That we walk around like half people. The beauty of a relationship is that we've found someone who will allow us to be one hundred percent ourselves. You're a special woman,

Gabby. You deserve to be treated like the queen. From what you've told us, he doesn't do that."

"What Jordan is trying to say," Chris chimed in, "is that Brad is a grade A asshole and you need to kick him to the curb." He picked up his glass and chugged down the remainder of his beer.

"Appreciate the subtlety there," I said.

"Subtlety, fubtley." He slammed his glass down. "If the guy is an ass, he's an ass. No need to sugarcoat it." Chris was buzzing and punchy. "Besides, if he was that great of a guy, Gabby would be standing up for him."

He had a point. Gabby had offered no defense of Brad.

"Besides Gabby," I said, "you have other things to worry about. You don't need the stress. How is your Mother?"

"She has started on some oral chemo. My brother says it makes her so sick. I … I really need to get back. I'm planning on going in a couple weeks."

"I'm sure she will appreciate that," I said. "That's the real drama of life. You don't need somebody creating drama because of their own insecurities."

"Is he coming to the picnic?" Chris asked.

"What?" I turned to Chris.

"Is Brad coming to the Memorial Day picnic?"

"He said he was," Gabby answered, sounding as if she preferred he didn't.

"He doesn't have to come, Gabby," I said.

"I just feel like I should try," she explained. "I should give this one more chance."

"Let him come," Chris said. "I want to meet this guy."

"Chris," Gabby started, "please don't do or say anything …"

"I won't, I won't. I …" Chris slowed and said the next words deliberately, "want to meet him."

"Okay," she said cautiously. "And who are you

Sometimes Ya Gotta Laugh   143

bringing?"

"No one," Chris said.

"No blonde?" She asked. "No brunette?"

"Nope."

"No redhead?"

"Nobody."

Disbelief riddled Gabby's face. "I'll believe it when I see it." She turned to me. "Alicia?"

"Yes, I am bringing Alicia."

"This should be an exciting night," Chris deadpanned as he waved the hostess over for another round. He was hard to read lately.

Gabby's phone rang. "It's Brad."

"Don't answer it," Chris said.

"What?"

"Don't answer it," he repeated.

"Brad gets so irritated when I don't ..."

"Let him get irritated," Chris responded. "Does he need to know where you are every second of the day?"

"He's a man. He likes ..." Gabby began.

"We are all men," I said. "I don't need to know where my girlfriend is every moment of the day."

"I don't either," Chris concurred.

"That's because you have space issues," Gabby said. "And you," she turned to Chris, "have too many girls to keep up with."

"The fact remains," I pointed out, "only insecure men need to monitor their girlfriends."

The phone stopped ringing.

"Or men with small dicks," I added.

Gabby's mouth fell open.

"Got'cha," I said. I gave her a wink.

She kicked me under the table and said, "Whatever."

Aah. Good times.

Chapter 48

May 20th (Tuesday)

"Don't you think it's odd that Chris isn't bringing anyone to the picnic?" Gabby asked into the phone.

"Huh?" I said.

"Long ago, in a distant land ..." blared from my TV. I was watching another episode of *Samurai Jack. This guy really knows how to overcome adversity.*

"Don't you think it's odd that Chris isn't bringing anyone to the picnic?"

"Um ...," I watched Jack pull out his sword and devastate evil Aku's robot army. "What do you mean?"

"You know what I mean. And could you turn the TV down? I can barely hear you." I complied. "Chris brings a date to every picnic. One year, he even brought two women. Remember that girl last year?"

How could I forget? The girl looked like a Vogue model but she was a dumb as a box of rocks. When asked if she preferred sweet or dry wine, she said she preferred wet.

"Yeah, I remember."

"And remember that time he brought twins?"

"But they were fraternal."

"What does that have to do with anything?"

"I'm just saying that … you could tell them apart."

"So what? That means it doesn't count? How does a man convince two able-bodied women to be his date at the same time? And two sisters at that?"

"Beats me."

"But this year he isn't bringing anybody," she said.

"That's what he says."

"Jordan, that doesn't make any sense. I've known Chris for over four years. I've never seen him go someplace without some girl on his arm. And you've known him three times as long as I have. Have you ever seen it?"

"No," I admitted reluctantly as I sat up on the couch.

"He's acting differently, isn't he?"

I wanted to say "you just noticed?" But with everything going on in her own life and considering how much we had drifted apart, I wasn't surprised she hadn't.

I wanted to share. But what? The conversation Chris and I had had months ago? The fact that I had dropped him off at some guy's house? "Maybe he is. Maybe he isn't. He probably has things on his mind like the rest of us."

"Maybe," she conceded. "But this is very out of character for Chris."

"People are strange sometimes."

"Yes, I guess you're right," she answered. "Oh shit, I hear Brad at the door. Gotta go. I'll call you later."

She hung up the phone; I turned the volume back up on *Samurai Jack*.

Chapter 49

When David wanted attention, he demanded it. As evidenced by the twelve missed calls on Chris's phone.

He couldn't bring himself to delete David's number. So he did the next best thing: He avoided him. He hadn't answered any of David's calls since the party and he had gone to the gym on totally different days this week.

But a week of silence wouldn't deter … hadn't deterred David. At some point, David would find him and there would be a confrontation and a barrage of questions. Questions Chris had no answer for.

David's affections sometimes bordered on amorous – the kissing, the cuddling, the holding hands, the meeting friends, the weekends together sometimes felt more like dating. Sometimes it was all about getting high.

Chris could get high with a dude; he couldn't date one. He was an only son. He had to have children. What would his Mom say? Jordan? Gabby? He had been flirting with her for almost four years. What would she think? That he had been queer all along?

No. He loved pussy. He had proven that one thousand times over.

David's ring tone sang once again as his number flashed across Chris's phone. Chris picked up the phone and his thumb hovered over the "accept" button. But he was nowhere close to ready. So he let the call go to voicemail.

Chapter 50

May 25th (Sunday) Memorial Day

Raheem Cole was smoking a blunt and buzzing. I knew this because he called everyone *"my niggah"* when he was high. And *my niggah* was exactly what he had called me.

He strode in my direction, leaving his harem of three in frustrated impatience, and gave me some dap.

"How ya been?" He asked. Before I could answer he turned to Alicia. "And you are?" A West Indian accent escaped him, even though he was born and raised in Atlanta, Ga.

"This, my friend, is Alicia and Alicia, this is Raheem."

He flashed his Colgate smile, nodded too approvingly, and grasped her hand with both of his. "Nice to meet you, A-li-ci-a."

"Likewise," Alicia responded with a shy smile. *Raheem's got swag for days.*

I shifted the ice from one hand to the next and tried to put my arm around Alicia's waist. "Have you seen Chris?" I asked.

"He was arguing with some dude." He pointed across the park.

"About?" I hoped he didn't know the answer.

He shrugged. "Who the fuck knows? Chris has been a little crazy lately." I wanted to know what that comment meant and thought about asking. I didn't have to. Raheem continued, "Maybe it's the heat, the heat will do things to you."

He was right. The heat would do things to you. And Texas is damn hot. As a matter-of-fact, we have two temperatures: preheat and bake. Today was bake. Ninety degrees in the shade and the humidity was playing a game of kick ass. It felt like 112.

You don't get used to it, you learn to endure it. Exall park was full of people blissfully enduring. Friends laughed with friends. Children ran giddily. The smell of steak and burgers filled the air.

Yeah, the heat will do things to you. But I don't think Raheem really believed it was the heat at all.

"Oh, okay," I responded. "This shit is getting heavy. We are going to go check on the host. We'll see you later."

Raheem nodded and walked back to his three concubines.

By the time Alicia and I reached Chris, his mystery guest was gone. I dropped the ice into the cooler with an exaggerated sigh.

"You all right, dude?" I asked.

"Why wouldn't I be?" He snapped.

Snap or not, I shook it off. Reconnecting, that's what this day was about. I stepped closer to Alicia, took her hand, and said, "Chris meet Alicia. Alicia meet Chris."

Chris gave Alicia the same approving look that Raheem had given her. "Have we met before?" He asked.

"New Year's," Alicia said with a grin.

"Are you sure? I don't remember. And I'm positive I'd remember meeting a girl like you." Chris was flirting. I appreciated his attempt to be the old Chris.

I pulled Alicia even closer. "Oh you met alright. I have a Kenneth Cole shirt stained royal pink to prove it." We all laughed.

"Have you seen Gabby?" I started to ask. But before I could get the words out I heard Gabby call our names. I whirled around to find Gabby and Brad walking toward us.

"How long have you guys been here?" I embraced her.

"Maybe thirty minutes or so," Gabby said. She stepped back with a smile. "We … um … were mingling." She paused. "Well …this is Brad. And Brad, this is Chris, Jordan, and … Alicia, right?" Alicia gave Gabby a broad smile; she gave Brad an empty one.

Brad was muscular with dirty blonde hair and a strong handshake. Within twenty minutes, he was on his second beer, chatting me up about boxing and offering Chris needless pointers on how to grill.

His charm was disarming and by the end of the night, I had almost forgiven him for stealing Gabby away from me. I was thinking that maybe he and Gabby could find a groove. Maybe tonight was a watershed moment for our friendship.

I held onto that belief as the day beat on – as Chris reverted back into carefree Chris, as Brad interacted so easily with all of us, as Raheem was careful not to flirt with Gabby. *We were connecting.*

Fueled by turkey hotdogs, Texas-sized steaks, Alicia's special potato salad, a lazy game of flag football, and too many beers to count, the day quickly bled into night. Before I knew it, we were all saying goodbyes and walking back to our cars.

I closed my trunk and turned to find Alicia frowning. I opened her car door. "Are you okay?"

"That was the Brad I was talking about," she said as she sat down.

"The Brad?"

"When we were at the Grand Lux, remember?"

"Yes, you said you knew a guy at the hospital. That was him?"

"Yes."

"Hmm," I closed her car door, walked to the other side, and got in. "I remember. You said he was an asshole. I know he and Gabby have had some ups and downs. He's kinda moody, I guess. But I think she is trying to give it a little more time. You know, see if they hit a groove."

"Jordan, it's more than being moody ..."

"He seemed nice enough tonight."

Her frown refused to go away. "You trust me, right?" How could I not? "It's more than moody," she continued. "He is condescending, manipulative, and has a horrible temper. There's something about him that sometimes scares me a bit ..."

I'm a processor. "I don't understand. Did you say anything to Gabby?"

"No, I didn't. I'm not sure if it's my place."

"But if he's all that, why wouldn't she have told me? She's like my sister. Maybe he isn't that way with her."

"Maybe," Alicia said quietly. "But I doubt it."

"Gabby is smart, she's strong, she's beautiful. How could she get caught up with ..."

"Honey, sometimes we meet the wrong people. And unfortunately we don't realize they are the wrong person until we're emotionally involved, until we're in love, or we think we're in love." She gazed out the window. "It's so easy to say, someone should be strong when you aren't connected to the situation emotionally. But that's an unfair statement. Some of the smartest and most beautiful women in the world have found themselves in love or involved with the stupidest of men. And vice verse."

Chapter 51

May 25th (Sunday)

Gabby sighed with relief as she sat back and buckled her seat belt. She had been so worried. But everyone had connected. She really liked Alicia. She was easy to talk to and looked a little like Kerry Washington. No wonder why Jordan was crushing on her.

Brad pulled out of Exall Park, turned onto Live Oak, and chuckled to himself.

"What are you laughing at?" Gabby asked with a relaxed smile.

"So those are the happy hour guys?"

An all too familiar sarcasm filled his voice. Her relaxed feeling dissipated.

"And I was worried." He chuckled more. "One is a flamer."

"A what?" Gabby sat up.

"A flamer. A queer. A faggot." He laughed loudly. "Well,

maybe he isn't a flamer. But the dude he was arguing with was a little light in his loafers. No wonder you wanted us to hang back and let them finish their 'discussion'. Know what," he continued. "I'll give Chris credit. He is very masculine. But the other dude … total queen."

"How dare you say that about my friends."

"Oh … little Ms. Intuitive didn't know her best friend is gay. Imagine that. And the other dude … what was his name? Jordan? What is he anyway? Black? Hispanic? Italian? A mutt?He must have something going for him. He's dating Alicia. She's an average nurse but she's almost as hot at you are."

"Brad, you won't talk about my friends like that," Gabby snapped.

"Calm down and give it a rest. You wanted me to come. I came. You wanted me to meet your friends, I met them. I don't have to like them." He laughed again. "And I don't."

"You're being an ass."

Brad shrugged. "And you are a bitch."

They were sitting at the light of Washington Street and Lemon Ave. Gabby unbuckled her seat belt.

"What are you doing?"

"Getting out." Her relationship with Brad could not and would not work. It was a fact she had been denying for far too long. Most important, she thought as she opened the door, was the fact that she no longer wanted it to work. "'I'll call a cab," she said calmly. "Go home. We can talk later. I need to clear my head." She was in control.

"Bullshit." Brad yanked her back inside the car and the door swung open as the handle slipped out Gabby's hand. "You aren't going a goddamn place."

A scream that had been bottled up for months came pouring out. "I'm leaving, Brad! I've had enough. You're possessive, you're insecure, you're an asshole! I won't continue to allow you to alienate me from my friends any longer."

Brad released the steering wheel and shook her hard. The car slowly drifted into the middle of the intersection. "Who the hell do you think you're talking to, you stupid bitch?"

"Get … off … me!" Gabby pushed him away. "I said I'm getting out. I don't want to fight."

But they were fighting, Brad pulling, Gabby pushing, until he slapped her. When he did, a thousand painful memories tumbled through her head. "See what you've made me do!"

The car door was open; her seat belt was not latched. Gabby rolled out the car and felt her lip split open as she hit the pavement. Brad stopped the car immediately and jumped out. By that time Gabby was up and sprinting.

"Gabrielle!" Brad cried. But Gabby had no intention of stopping. He ran after her but she lost him in the Target parking lot, still two miles from home.

If he was at her house, she would wait somewhere until he left.

She was sure he didn't realize she had changed her locks on Tuesday.

One more chance. She had given him one more chance and he had blown it forever.

Chapter 52

May 26th (Monday)

Gabby took the ice pack and put it to her cheek again. Five months with Brad and his final gift had been a busted lip, a bruised cheek, and battered self-worth. How could she have been so stupid? She rummaged through her bathroom for some blush that would cover the bruise.

Her phone rang. She hesitated when she saw Jordan's number flash, found her happy voice, and answered. "Hello."

"Hey Gabby, it's me."

"Hey."

"Are you okay?" Jordan had heard through her happy voice.

She sighed deeply. She had to tell him. "It's me and Brad."

"What happened?" The concern in his voice almost brought her to tears.

"We broke up."

"When? When did you guys break up? You looked like you were having a great time last night."

"I know, I know … afterward. We had … some words." Her throat grew hoarse at the strain of not crying.

"I'm sorry," Jordan said, although he was really relieved. "How are you feeling?"

"Stupid."

"What? Why?"

"There were so many signs, Jordan. I knew in my heart this wasn't working but I kept on working at it."

"Gabby, don't be so hard on yourself. Sometimes we get caught up with the wrong person and when we think we love them," he said, quoting Alicia. "Feelings can be confusing. We make mistakes. Look, why don't I come by and pick you up? We will go get some Mexican at Taco Diner."

"No, no," she said a little too quickly. "I … I'm kinda tired. I think the heat took it outta me yesterday. And then the argument with Brad."

"Are you sure? We don't even have to talk."

"Thanks, Jordan. But yes, I need some alone time."

"Okay, okay. I understand. But call me if you need me."

"I will."

After they got off the phone, Gabby put her head down and sobbed. She wondered if she should have told Jordan about the fight, about Brad hitting her, about running home. But she thought the situation, at least, was over.

Chapter 53

May 27th (Tuesday)

"What happened?" Alicia asked into the phone.

"I don't know. Gabby didn't go into a lot of details. She said they had an argument. I guess she was fed up."

"How is she doing?"

"I invited her out but she said no. She said she needed time alone, which is totally not Gabby. I think she's blaming herself. I told her not to worry about it. I told her it could happen to anyone."

"Did she feel better?"

"I'm not sure ... I don't know. I don't think so."

"You're sweet, Jordan. My guess is that there probably wasn't much you could say. But I know she appreciates your support. Give her some time to work through how she feels. I get the feeling that she really really liked him. Love can be hell sometimes. Take it from a woman who knows. You're a wonderful friend to her, Jordan."

Finally Gabby's words clicked. Gabby says fuck buddies don't spend the night, NOT because it implies some level of emotional intimacy but because if you do it enough, you do become emotionally intimate. I was feeling pretty emotionally intimate with Alicia. *I'm not ready, Alicia. I'm not ready.*

"Jordan, I need to get back to work," she said into the phone. "I'll call you later."

Chapter 54

Epiphany

May 30th (Friday)

Gabby could see the slip of white paper waving gingerly out her door as she unlocked her gate. The sight of it made her stomach churn. She stopped at the top of her steps. Every day she had come home that week a note waved from her front door - begging, pleading, demanding that she come back. The emotion of the notes changed like Texas weather – sometimes warm gentle pleas, sometimes harsh cold accusations. Which Brad would she get with this note?

She needed to confide in Jordan and Chris. But what could they do? Brad was just leaving notes. Still, there was something disconcerting about coming home to find emotional diatribes in her door every day. She had run away from Brad but somehow she still rode his emotional roller coaster.

She pulled out the fifth note she had received that week and read it.

Her new neighbor passed by and honked. Gabby glanced up from the note and waved.

As her neighbor's car faded into the distance, she took one last look at Brad's proclamation of forever love and then ripped the note into pieces. She tossed them into the air as she stepped into her home, and the warm breeze caught them and scattered into the street.

Chapter 55

May 31st (Saturday)

Gabby came out, carry-on in hand, and slipped into the front seat of my car. Her hair was pulled back from her face in a ponytail, she had on 7 For All Mankind, sandals, and a light blue top.

"Don't you look lovely," I said as I pulled the car into the street. We were headed to DFW airport. Gabby had a ten am flight home.

"Thanks," she said with a slight smile.

"And how are you feeling?"

She mustered an "Okay."

"Heard from Brad?"

The word search was lengthy. "I ... I've gotten a few notes from him."

"A few notes?"

"Yes, a few notes. Sometimes ... when I get home from

work … there's a note stuck in the door."

"Really? What have they said?"

"In one of them he said he was sorry for everything he did and that he loved me and that we should be together forever. In the next one he said I was to blame and who did I think I was treating him like I did."

"Seriously, Gabby?" My eyebrows furrowed. "That is weird." I looked in my rear view mirror and changed lanes on I-183. Behind me was a black Mercedes E-class. I was going to get one of those cars one day. Or a BMW.

"I know."

"So what are you going to do?"

"What can I do? They're just notes."

Should I problem-solve? She hadn't asked me what she should do. "Maybe you should go to the police." I couldn't help it; it's a guy thing.

"And tell them what? That my ex-boyfriend is leaving me notes?"

"I guess you're right." I checked my mirror again. Brad had evolved from asshole to creepy asshole.

"So how's Alicia?" Gabby asked, then she changed my radio station.

"Alicia?" I repeated.

"Yes, Alicia. The girl you're dating. You remember her? How is she?"

I think I blushed a little. "She's fine. And you know better than to touch a brutha's radio." I turned it back.

"A brutha." She laughed and switched it again. "How long have you two been seeing each other now?"

"We've been friends …. I don't know … maybe five months now."

"Friends? Is that what you call it?"

"Yeah, sure. Friends. What else would I call it?" I didn't want to talk about this.

"How often do you two get together?"

"Once a week ... sometimes twice ..." I guessed.

"And you call that friends?" I could see her sly smirk out the corner of my eye.

"Com'on Gabby, you know I have a hard time opening up. It takes me a while."

Gabby sighed. "You take too long and I move too fast," she mumbled under her breath.

"What?" I said, although I had heard her clearly.

"Nothing," she responded, although she knew I had. She was right. She moved too quickly, I moved too slowly.

Five minutes later I pulled up to Terminal A. We sat in the car for a moment before she got out. "So how is your Mom?" I asked.

"Good days and bad days," she said. "She may have to take steroids ..."

"I'm glad you're going home."

"I am, too," she admitted. "It will be good for me to get away and I really need to spend more time home."

"Do you need me to pick you up?"

"Please?" She leaned over and gave me a quick peck and slid out the car.

I put the car back in drive and worked my way back home. At the MacArthur exit, I looked in my rear view again. Was it me or was that the same Mercedes I saw on the way to the airport? I slowed down from 75 to 60 but the car didn't pass. So I exited Mockingbird. It wasn't my exit but I took it. The E-class continued to hum down I-183. I drove down Mockingbird to Harry Hines Blvd and took the long route downtown.

Chapter 56

June 1st (Sunday)

"Time to get up, sleepyhead." I opened my eyes to find Alicia leaning over me, her lips inches away from mine. I puckered to kiss them but she pulled back playfully.

"What time is it?"

"Almost one." She rewarded my waking by blowing me a kiss and fully displaying her naked body. My morning wood got harder.

"Don't you wanna come back to bed?" I reached toward her. But she stepped beyond my grasp, tied a robe around her, and opened a window shade. "Don't," I said. I threw my hands over my eyes in defense mode. She giggled.

"I'm going to hop in the shower," she said. "There is coffee brewing. What would you like for breakfast?"

"You," I said.

She laughed.

"I'm serious." I was serious. Last night our bodies had been in total sync. I wanted to experience that sensation again. "We can do a quickie. Or take our time. You know I'm easy-like-Sunday-mornng."

"I know you are easy, horny boy," she teased. "But I have to be at work at three, remember? I'll whip you up some breakfast, though. What would you like?"

"Scrambled eggs."

"You like my scrambled eggs." She grinned.

"I like you." I winked.

She blew a kiss and then padded her way to the shower.

What were we? Friends? Friends with benefits? Was this a relationship? Gabby was right. Alicia and I had been seeing each other for the better part of five months. That had to mean something. Or couldn't we just *be*?

I knew the answer. There has to be a destination or an end-game. Otherwise, what was the point?

Alicia was kind enough not to ask me about the next step. But she had to wonder.

Gabby wondered.

I wondered.

The bathroom door opened and Alicia stepped out. Her caramel tone seemed to glisten as she moved around the room. Her hair was wet and she had small hoops in her ears. She slipped on a pair of shorts and an American Apparel tank top and blew me another kiss.

Don't fuck this up, I thought. *Don't fuck this up.* But deep down I knew I would.

Chapter 57

June 2nd (Monday)

For Chris, happy hour had become more chore than pleasure. It was ninety minutes of making up stories about where he had been, changing the "him" in his story to "her", and hoping his friends couldn't see right through him.

He skipped it today. Gabby was outta town and he knew Jordan wouldn't expect him to show.

"I can't believe you didn't invite me to your party," David said.

Chris snapped back to the present and watched as David carefully poured coke onto the table. He divided it into four straight lines with amazing precision and then took the tip of his key and snorted. He lay back on the couch and grinned at Chris.

"I can't believe you came anyway," Chris said. "It was for my friends."

"Whatev. I'm your friend. By the way, there were a

couple hot guys there. You ever get with them? Who was the big black dude with the locs? I'm not into black guys but he was kinda hot.

"You know what they say, once you go black you don't go ..."

"Shut up," Chris said.

David laughed. "Aren't you the sulky boy today?" He shook his head. "You know, I didn't ask you to come over and kill my high. I asked you to get high." He laughed.

Chris stood. "I'm leaving."

"Sit your ass down," David said. Playfully he grabbed Chris's arm and tugged him. "Shit. You're too uptight. Worried about that someone is gonna see you. Worried what someone is gonna think. Fuck, man. It's your life. Live it. Gay. Straight. Pussy. Dick. Ass. Who cares? I don't give a fuck about what people think. You need to stop being a woose and do the same thing. Now let's have some fun. It's Monday night and I don't have to work tomorrow."

Chris hesitated. Why had he come? Because he felt some sort of connection with David that he no longer felt with his friends. And David had a point. This was Chris's life. He could do what he damn well pleased. So he sat down, picked up David's key, and did a line with him.

Chapter 58

June 4th (Wednesday)

I woke up this morning suspended somewhere between peaceful bliss and insidious self-pity.

When life lacks spice – when it's neither sweet nor sour, hot nor cold, you're probably sitting in some emotional purgatory. When nothing is horribly wrong in your life but it's still stale to the taste and everything feels the same, yup, that's emotional purgatory.

A couple years ago, I read the first fifty pages of a book on how to be happy. The book's strategy: Focus on happiness and let it overtake you. *Bullshit!* If I sit in a chair, my mind will mull, meditate, and probably meander. But it will not greet happiness at the doors. Happiness is far too elusive than just to saunter into one's life effortlessly. It requires real work. I know this. Nevertheless, I sit in a chair anyway. Anything is worth a second try. And I process:

I can't count on Chris anymore.

I'm only half connected with Gabby.

Alicia is the closest thing to real affection I've felt in years. But I'm frozen.

They are my family. My surrogate family. The one that have replaced the one I lost. Yet, I feel I'm on the cusp of losing them too. Lost 2; Jordan 0.

Self-pity is winning.

My mother used to say doing something for others makes you less selfish. I'm not sure how much I can do for Chris and Gabby but there are other people in the universe I can help.

I open the Viao and do a Google search. Maybe I could volunteer for the homeless, go work at a soup kitchen.

I surf the web until I find an organization that supports the homeless not too far from where I live. Yup, that's the ticket. I'll give them a call.

I reach for my phone and as I do, it rings. I pick up the phone and look at the ID. It's Kelly. What should I do?

On the fourth ring, the sound fades to voicemail.

The voicemail alert is followed by the beep of her text. **Can I come over?** Kelly asks.

The connection would be good.

Yes. I type back without hesitation.

I'll visit the homeless next week.

Chapter 59

June 8th (Sunday)

    I picked Gabby up at eleven-thirty am and we drove back
to Dallas in comfortable silence - saving our questions for brunch
at Breadwinners.
    Breadwinners routinely ranks as one of Dallas' best
brunch spots. It's not a ranking that I support but I'm in the
minority, as evidenced by the sixty some-odd people waiting to
get inside when she and I pulled up.
    We waited for almost an hour before we were seated by a
sexually ambiguous host sporting a tight black shirt and muffin-
top.
    Fifteen minutes later Gabby was raving about her egg
white omelet with feta and I was complaining about my
lukewarm pancakes. Typical.
    "So how was the trip?" I pushed the rest of the pancake

away and reached for a blueberry muffin. I do give them credit for providing a damn good bread basket.

Gabby sat back in her chair and chewed thoughtfully. "Good. Better than I expected."

"What were you expecting?"

She crinkled her nose. "Tension."

"But no tension?"

"None. I mean, there's rarely any tension between Luis and I. But Mom and me. That's another story."

"How is she?"

"No steroids. And the oral chemo does seem to be helping." She took a sip of coffee.

"Excellent. And your brother? Your nieces?"

"Wonderful. They are the absolute best. I almost cried when I had to leave. Playing with them was so much fun."

"I'm so happy. That's great." I hesitated before continuing. "What about Brad? Have you heard from him?"

"Absolutely nothing."

"Really?"

"Nothing at all."

"Wow." I didn't try to mask the surprise in my voice. "I'm impressed. Maybe he's growing up."

"Maybe," Gabby said with a shrug. She looked away. I dropped it, I didn't want to ask too many questions.

"Whatever happened with that wedding you were supposed to be going to?" I asked.

"They moved the date. Something crazy happened. Gary is coming over next week, though. He's got some new makeup to show me. You should stop by."

"Seriously? To watch you and Gary-the-drag-queen put makeup on each other?"

She laughed loudly.

"You ready to get outta here?" I asked.

"Yes, I've got some things I need to do. I've been gone for

over a week and didn't check email once while I was gone. I can only imagine the number of messages I have."

As we walked toward the car, I asked, "Can we do Shiela's Sky Diner next time?"

"It's Kathleen's. Kathleen's Sky Diner. Shiela is a waitress who works there."

"I know, I know. But she's my favorite waitress in Dallas. And their Eggs-From-Hell is quite the tasty dish."

"I thought Hibiscus had your favorite servers."

"Hibiscus has the best service staff. Bar none. But Shiela … well she just makes you feel at home. And the bartender, great bedside manner."

Gabby shook her head. "Whatever," she replied with a grin. Two minutes later we pulled up outside her home.

"You okay?" I asked when she didn't get out. "You want me to go and check the house?"

"No, no, I'm fine," she repeated. "Just thinking." She leaned over and planted a sisterly kiss on my forehead.

I hopped out the car and got her suitcase from the trunk.

"Will I see you at happy hour tomorrow?" I asked.

"I doubt it. I'm sure I'll be working late every night this week."

We exchanged a quick hug and then I watched her walk into her home.

I missed her but I was beginning to think it was time to close the book on a real happy hour. She waved to me before she closed her front door. I waved back and drove home.

Chapter 60

June 11th (Wednesday)

My boxing coach has a drill called the Super-Combo. It's a series of twenty-seven punches. You would never use the combo in the ring but he claims it's a great way to learn how to flow from one punching combo to the next. I don't know if he makes this shit up. But he's the coach, so I do the drill.

If nothing more, the drill is great exercise and a great stress reliever. The latter was why I was standing in the middle of my kitchen punching the wind when my phone rang.

"Have you talked to Chris?" It was Gabby.

"Nope. Haven't talked to him since the last time you and I saw him," I panted.

"What's up with him these days?"

"I don't know. What's up with us all?" I said nonchalantly.

She contemplated this. "Hmm ... I guess you're right. Things have been a little ... different this year."

"Asi es la vida," I said, still attempting to sound nonchalant.

"You know his birthday is next week. Are you going to do anything for it?"

"Gabby, I don't celebrate my own birthday. Why would I celebrate someone else's? He's a thirty-six year old man. Does he need a celebration?"

"Blah, blah, blah. You think birthdays are ego-driven and contribute to selfishness. I've heard the crap before. But I was thinking it would be nice for us to get together and do something. Maybe Cyclone's next Wednesday? You could bring Alicia. Wouldn't that be fun?"

"What would be fun is to not have to eat Tex-mex every time we went out together."

"Shut up. I'm being serious."

"I am, too." But only about the Tex-mex. Anybody ever wondered why TX is one of the fattest states in the union? Blame it on the Mexicans, goddamn them, and their fat-intensive diets. Plus, everything is bigger here. So you have a recipe for obesity waiting to happen. "Yeah, we could do that."

"Great," she said victoriously.

"The problem is getting in touch with Chris."

"I'm sure between you and I, we'll be able to find him. If not, we'll just go by his house."

"Sure, sure, sounds like a plan."

"Okay, I'm going to try to call him now. You call Alicia. This will be like old times."

"For old time's sake," I echoed.

But by Saturday, neither one of us had been able to reach Chris. He wasn't answering emails, his voicemail was full, and when I stopped by his office on Friday he was in a meeting.

Chapter 61

June 14th (Saturday)

Why was the elusive question. The search for the answer had Chris scouring the internet as the day darkened into night. He had turned off his phone, turned down the lights, and hid himself in his study.

The internet was a dumping ground of material and no shortage of it dealt with sexuality – heterosexuality, homosexuality, bisexuality, pan sexuality. Hours he had searched and yet he was at no greater peace than when he started. He pushed his computer away.

Straight guys never wonder why they're straight, he thought. They aren't confused about it. No straight guy ever sits back and asks why he likes women. But tons of gay guys sit back and ask themselves why they *don't.*

Was it environmental? Was it genetic? Was Dad weak and Mom overbearing? Did Uncle Bob touch you in your private parts? Was it that one time you played 'you-show-me-yours-and-I'll-show-you-mine' when you were eight?

He had jacked off with a couple guys in college while watching straight porn. Was it that? Or maybe just too much damn porn, period?

Maybe sex at too early an age made people bored with conventional sex when they got older.

And what about all the gays and straights who shitted on bisexuality, who claimed it was no more than waffling on true desire? Was he waffling?

He remembered having a wet dream about Keanu Reeves when he was eighteen. Yes, Keanu Reeves. Chris had gone to see the movie *Speed* with some friends. Six hours later he had woken up sticky and had to change his sheets. But he had always blamed that on some bad 'shrooms he and his friends had ingested between the two activities.

He looked at the clock on the wall. This was not a day he wanted to celebrate.

Chris walked over and stretched across his bed. He closed his eyes and tried to remember, who, what, when, why. But he couldn't think of anything, couldn't remember anybody, couldn't recall a date. And he began to wonder if the only person he had to blame for his life was himself.

Chapter 62

June 15th (Sunday)

I'm not a pessimist, I'm a cynic. Pessimists believe all is wrong with the world. Cynics believe all is wrong with the world but they desire to be proved wrong. The seeds of romance have actually been planted in us. We just need a helluva lot of watering to let the seeds blossom.

I'm a believer in miracles too. Odd, yes, coming from a cynic, but true. To be clear, not the call-up-to-our-Lord-and-Savior-Sweet-Baby-Jesus-you-are-clean-now-stand-up-and-walk kind of miracle. I'm talking about the nine month kind.

But I digress.

I'm bustling along at the Dallas Art Museum with a throng of people, on this journey solo. I love art. I'm moved by the aesthetics, the talent, the emotion poured into the work. It also makes me melancholy. Art is a reminder that we, and everything around us, eventually drifts into the past.

Is art a call to take the miracle of our short life and find a way to touch someone else?

Yes, I'm a believer in miracles.

What are the chances that any of us should be here? Had not Mom and Pops been in the mood at that right time, had Mom not been throwing it back at that particular moment (not a good visual, but stick with me here), had Dad eyes not rolled back at that wondrous second, had his trajectory not hit that certain egg and that certain egg been receptive, we would not be here.

That situation had to occur with Granddad and Grandma, Great-granddad and Great-grandma, Great-great-granddad, and great-great-grandma, and so forth and so on.

What is the mathematic possibility that we should be here?

Since we are here, shouldn't there be a reason? A purpose? At best, life is a bittersweet journey. A gift of love, life, friendship, and companionship but filled with the hopeful expectation that there is more, sometimes overshadowed by the fact that it eventually ends.

That's life at its best. For others: Life sucks, then you die. At least it did for my little sister.

Chapter 63

Something was wrong. Gabby could sense it. She walked back to her desk, picked up a report again and moved it back to its original stack.

No phone calls, no texts, no flowers from Brad. She should've felt at peace. Yet an ominous feeling gripped her.

She had studied psychology at Duke, had had three therapists in the last six years, and had read countless self-help books. In retrospect she thought it was all useless. All she did was run in circles – same patterns, same guys, same emotions.

She picked up another report. Work was her comfort zone, it was where she excelled. Three promotions in the last two years proved that. So she opened the file and forced herself to concentrate. Thirty minutes later she was lost in her work with thoughts of Brad floating in the recesses of her mind.

She worked until nine pm, long after everyone – including the cleaning crew - had left. But as she walked to her car in the dark empty parking garage, she couldn't help but think that something was not right, and she had the unsettling feeling that someone was watching her.

Chapter 64

June 22nd (Sunday)

Gary studied Gabby's face like DaVinci studied the Mona Lisa. He stepped back from his handy work and tried to suppress the grin that threatened to spread across his face. The attempt was to no avail. He caved as he stared at his own unabashed talent. "Take a look at you, girl. Tell me you don't look fabu."

Gabby took the mirror and gazed at herself. Gary was right. She looked stunning. "Oh my God, Gary. You are the greatest."

"You wouldn't believe how many times I hear that a day," Gary replied. They both giggled loudly, inspired as much by the drinks as by the comment.

Midnight had come quickly, slipping up on them between applications of shades of Mac, homemade Martinis, and several tirades against the male species. They shared many things in common, foremost among them were their love of makeup and their bad choices in men.

"You want another drink?" Gary asked.

"I do."

He stood up and placed his hand on the wall to steady himself. "I'll make it this time," he said. "You make them too weak." He was half way to the kitchen when someone knocked. He turned to Gabby. "Who could that be now? It's twenty minutes after."

Gabby got off her stool and walked to the door. She peeked through the peephole and then took two steps back.

"Who is it, honey?"

"It's Brad," she whispered.

"Brad? Your ex?"

"Yes."

"What the hell is he doing here?" He placed his hands on his hips.

"I … I don't know."

"Tell him to go. Do you want me to tell him?" Gary strolled toward the door.

"No, don't." She put her hand out to stop him. "Let's not antagonize him. He's got a temper. Maybe he saw you come in here and he's jealous."

"Saw me come in here? Honey, I've been here since seven-thirty. If he's been sitting outside your house for five hours, the motherfucker is crazy." Gabby waved his voice down with her hand.

They stood in silence; Brad's knock got louder. Finally he spoke, "I know you are in there Gabrielle. Open up."

"Brad," Gabby said trying to keep her voice steady, "go home."

"Who do you have in there with you?"

"You don't owe him any explanation," Gary said

scornfully.

But Gabby found herself explaining, "He's just a friend, Brad. Now go home."

"Gabby, I love you," Brad said with slightly slurred words. When she didn't respond he repeated himself. "Did you hear me? I said I love you.

"I saw you rip up my note," he continued.

"What?"

"The last note I left in your door. I saw you rip it up."

Gabby swallowed. "Brad, I ..."

"It's okay, I forgive you." He shook the doorknob. "Just let me in. We can talk about it."

"Brad, please go home. It's over. We never ..."

"No, it's not over. We were meant to be together. Gabrielle, you have to know this."

"Didn't you hear what she said, you dumbass?" Gary exploded and screeched through the door. "She doesn't want your stupid ass. Go home, bitch."

The words had barely escaped Gary's mouth before Brad threw his shoulder into the door. "Who the fuck are you?" Brad shouted.

"I'm the one telling you to take your ass home," Gary yelled back. Brad banged his shoulder against the door again. Gabby took another step back.

"Gary, don't ..."

"Gabrielle, you better let me the fuck in!" He kicked the door.

"Call 9-1-1," Gary said to Gabby. He turned back to the door. "Come through that door if you want to, bitch. And I will cut your motherfuckin' ass!"

Gabby fumbled with her phone. "No, no, let me call Jordan and Chris."

Jordan's voice was thick with sleep when he answered. "Hello?"

"Brad is here."

The fear in her voice struck Jordan like a ton of ice water. He sat up. "What?"

"He's here now. Please come."

Chapter 67

June 22nd (Sunday)

Free falling. Heart racing. Adrenalin surging. Body floating. An incredible fucking rush. That's how Chris would describe coke – a fucking incredible rush.

Tonight, though, wasn't about the coke. It was about the X. Same rush but followed but cool calm collection. The calm was a strange contrast to the increased sense of touch that made the sex so spectacular.

He never worried about what he was doing with David when they had the X. So calm. No worries. Just happy.

For a fleeting moment, he had thought he needed to let the coke go. He had had a problem in college. But this time was different.

That time he used the shit every day. This time he only

used it when he saw David.

That time he was buying it himself. This time he never bought it.

That time he was addicted. This time he was … no. Not now. Cool. Calm collection.

The Chicago house that came from David's speakers made Chris's skin tingle. Two of David's friends were over and they sat semi-naked making out as David slow danced with no one but himself. Occasionally he stopped to kiss the kissing boys. Each time he did, they peeled off some of his clothes. He laughed as they fumbled with his belt and they beckoned Chris with a grin. Cum.

Chris stripped down to his briefs and took one step toward them. He had almost joined them when Jordan appeared in the room, screaming and waving his hands. What the hell was Jordan doing here?

Chris fled to the bathroom. He locked the door and clasped his hands over his ears to block out the sounds of Jordan's screams.

"Go away!" Chris sat in the tub, eyes shut tightly, hands clenched over his ears, and begged Jordan to stop. He sat until the knocking ended, the noise subsided, his heartbeat dropped, and he fell asleep.

He awoke six hours later in the cold ceramic tub. The hallucinations were gone but the cramps had just begun.

Chapter 66

June 22nd (Sunday)

My car screeched to a halt in front of Gabby's house. *Where were the police? Why did the house look so quiet?*

I fell against the front door with a thud and followed that with several loud pounds. "Gabby! Gabby, it's me!"

Gary opened the door and I rushed to Gabby's side. "Are you okay?" I wrapped my arms around her.

"Where is Brad?" I looked at Gary.

"That motherfucker left." Contempt dripped from every word. He strode into the kitchen and fixed himself another drink.

"Where's Chris? Didn't you call him?"

"He never answered," she replied.

"And the police? Didn't you call?"

"Brad went away," Gabby responded, "as suddenly as he

had appeared. So we didn't call."

"You didn't want to call," Gary corrected from the kitchen. "But you need to. Somebody needs to do something about that sorry ass bitch motherfucker."

"Tell me what happened."

"The beginning," she smiled sadly. "I don't know ... He was so sweet in the beginning. So sweet. God, he made me feel like I was the most beautiful girl in the world. Always calling, always attentive, always giving.

"We saw each other every day. He's a doctor but somehow he managed to see me daily. He said he was making time for me and you know how I feel about time. It's my most precious possession. That he would share his time when he was so busy meant so much. And he said that making time was vital to any good relationship.

"We were spending so much time together that there was no room for happy hour or getting with you and Chris. I felt guilty bringing it up to him. I was his priority. Didn't I need to make him mine? When I finally broached the subject, he disapproved. He said that Chris was in love with me and you just didn't want to see me with anybody else, that you guys were satisfied with the three of us being single. I didn't believe him. But when the three of us would get together, everything seemed off-kilter. I thought you didn't like Brad and that maybe he was right. I ... I'm ... I'm so sorry ..."

I rubbed her back. "There is nothing to be sorry about ..."

"I guess after that, his control slowly increased. We'd have two great days and seven bad days. One day he loved everything I did, the next day he hated it. I didn't know what to think. Blissfully happy," she laughed bitterly, "every other day. When things were good, I felt like I should put more energy into it to keep it working. When things were bad, I felt like I should put more energy into it to fix it.

"That's why I left happy hours early. That's why I didn't

meet you and Alicia for dinner. That's why my communication was limited.

"I knew it wasn't right. But I wanted so much ..." she swallowed hard. "The night of the barbeque, we had a terrible argument. He was talking about you and Chris. He was being such an ass. And finally, finally, I had had enough. So I told him so. I said it was over. We were at a stoplight and I was going to walk or call a taxi. But when I tried to get out the car, we fought ..." Her voice faltered. "Physically."

I swallowed hard.

"He ... he slapped me."

A million shards of glass ripped through me and I hoped she didn't feel me tremble. My eyes met Gary's.

"That Goddamn ..." Gary started. But I shook my head. *Not now, Gary.* And so he changed his statement to a gentle, "Oh honey."

Why hadn't she told me? "I'm sorry, Gabby. I'm so sorry." I held her tightly.

"I'm dating my father," she whispered.

"What?"

"I'm dating my father," she repeated. "This is what he would do to my mother. He would come home angry or drunk and he would terrorize her ... he would slap her around. Then he would apologize. He would promise it would never happen again. But it always did. I don't know when it started. But it didn't end until I was fifteen. That's when Luis was physically strong enough to stop him. I swore I would never be in a relationship like that. I hated him and I hated my mother for staying. Why did she marry him? Why didn't she have the guts to leave? For seventeen years she lived with that man. Seventeen years."

"Did he ever hit you?" I asked.

"No, Mom would say she would call the police if he ever hit us. Not that he had to anyway. We were petrified of him."

"So she stood up for you but she wouldn't stand up for herself," I said.

"All those years, I hated her. And now I'm just like her ..." Her voice trailed off and she began to cry. The tears were silent streams at their onset. But soon they began to pour. They rolled down her face in inconsolable sobs and her entire body heaved, as if every tear she had ever locked away, every tear she ever refused to cry, was now free to fall.

Chapter 67

June 23rd (Sunday)

The knocking woke us. The sound was low, quiet, and insistent. The kind of sound that made you wonder how long it had been going on before you heard it.

We were sitting downstairs in Gabby's den. She had cried herself to sleep in my arms; I had dozed off with her. For how long, I wasn't sure. We woke with a start.

"What the hell is that?" I looked around for Gary but he must've left.

"It's Brad," Gabby whispered. She clenched my arm tightly.

"Where's the sound coming from?" I continued looking around. "The garage?"

She nodded almost imperceptibly.

"I'm going to go check it out."

"Please don't." She held me tightly. "Let's call the police."

"We will." Gently I pulled my arm from her grip. "Let's just make sure first."

I walked out the den, through the small foyer, and to the back door - the door that led to her garage. I stood there listening. But the knocking had stopped. *What the hell was it?* I waited. Nothing. But when I turned to walk back to Gabby, I heard the sound again. It was coming from the other side of the door. I whirled back around and reached for the knob. When I did, the entire knob and screws fell on the floor and the door swung open. Brad lunged from the shadows, and Gabby, who had been standing in the threshold of the den watching me, let out a scream. She ran back into the room. I stumbled back into the den and awkwardly lurched out his way. As I did my back clipped the den's door frame. Brad lunged at me again.

About a year ago, I started boxing. If you're not a fan of the sport, you probably believe boxers to be two idiots bloodying each other in a ring for the amusement of others. Dumb neanderthals. Truth be told, boxers are far smarter than most people give credit. They play a physical game of chess - calculating, predicting, and seeking the weakness in their opponent's strategy. The sport takes mental and physical prowess.

At the end of the day, though, boxing is a sport with rules and regulations. A real fight lacks both. No one stops someone from hitting you below the belt, or punching you in the back of the head, or shoving you down to the ground. While the speed, the power, the sight you learn in boxing are powerful weapons – especially versus someone who isn't a fighter at all – a real street fighter knows how to lock another man up. He knows how to take away spacing which makes the punches of a boxer weak or useless. People have died in the boxing ring. But never does a man enter the ring with such a horribly evil intent. On the other hand, many men have died in a street fight and death was often the intent.

Boxing is sport. Real fighting is brutal.

Brad punched the side of my face with a left jab as powerful as any man I had ever boxed. My head snatched to the left, as it did he leaned in to strike again. I saw that punch coming, blocked it, stepped toward him, and caught the bottom of his chin with an uppercut. My uppercut was followed by a quick left jab.

He stumbled back a couple steps – his eyes flashed surprise – and he smiled. He didn't forge back at me. Instead he scanned for a weapon. He spotted the poker to the den's fireplace – a fireplace Gabby never used – rushed for it and swung it at me. I jerked back, forced into defense mode as he pressed forward. My plan was to hop over Gabby's elongated leather couch and put space between us. But I banged my knee on top of her coffee table as I came down on the other side. Pain shot through my knee. As I rolled off the table, I barely avoided the poker that crashed down beside me. Gabby rushed out the corner and grabbed at his weapon but he shoved her aside as if she were Raggedy Ann and slammed the poker back at me. The thrust was long enough to rip the corner of my shirt, short enough to just graze my skin, and powerful enough to get lodged in the wood. He cursed as he jerked the poker but it refused to come out. Gabby ran at him again and this time he backhanded her; she seemed to hurtle across the room. I bounced to my feet intent on rushing him. But when I did, a sharp pain surged through my knee. It slowed my reaction by a millisecond - a millisecond too long. As I moved toward Brad, he turned on me with what looked like one of the martini glasses Gabby and Gary had been using. But the glass was broken. I halted less than an arm's length in front of him as he waved the jagged edge at me. He swung in broad strokes, as if he were painting a wall. I used my left and right forearms to defend myself, ignoring the blood that began to flow as he ripped through my shirt. He plunged at me with the glass. I pivoted to my right, grabbed his forearms, and attempted to roll. But my knee gave out mid-pivot and he came crashing on top of me. The glass slipped out his hand and shattered. But Brad was not to be denied. He snatched up a large piece and dragged it across the top of my forehead. Blood poured out. I took my knee and shoved it into his groin. He yelped and I pushed him off me. I stood wobbly, thrust my leg back and kicked him. Satisfied at the sound of his deep grunt, I swung my leg back to kick him again, but he grabbed my ankle and wrenched my knee. I fell down and instantly he was on top of me again.

I should have seen it before. Maybe I knew it all along. Perhaps it was inevitable. But it was at that moment that I realized it.

One of us was going to die tonight!

As Brad reared back to punch me, I reached to my side and came up with my own shard of glass. We swung simultaneously. He fist grazed my face. Right before the glass in my hand grazed his, he collapsed on top of me. I looked up. Gabby hovered over him. A cast iron skillet was in her hand.

Chapter 68

June 23rd (Monday)

The Metro diner is a hole-in-the-wall that caters to a motley crew of club-goers trying to coffee their way out a hangover, nurses and orderlies on break from Baylor Hospital, truck drivers passing through town, people changing shifts, and anybody else suffering from the case of the late night munchies.

The entire operation is run by a husband and wife and the place never closes. Well maybe on Christmas. It sits across from Baylor, which is appropriate as their food is designed to raise the blood pressure, clog the arteries, and make the cataracts fail.

That's not to say the food isn't good. It's delicious. Credentials verifying that tastiness of the cuisine decorated the walls – Best Diner in Dallas 1997, 2002-2004, 2007. I had a sneaking suspicion that few people stopped there for the health benefits anyway; Panera Bread it was not.

A jukebox played songs that were popular sometime in the mid-90s, circa Paula Abdul.

But then, people don't come into the diner for the music either. More than likely they come for the perfectly fried chicken fried steak that sat on the plate in front of Gary. Or the greasy cheeseburger that lay on Gabby's plate. Perhaps even the small pile of iceberg lettuce with ranch running off the side that sat in front of Alicia. I drank coffee.

The police had come and gone. They seemed to think the altercation was little more than a fistfight for which I had some culpability. Brad was drunk, I shouldn't have been there. *Change the lock. File a restraining order. Mind your business.* I don't recall all their sage counsel but that was the gist.

The four of us knew the incident was far more than a frat-boy fistfight. My right eyebrow had six stitches above it. My left knee was bandaged and bruised.

"I wish I had been there," Gary said. "I would've fucked his ass up."

The smile was painful but I gave him one. "I wish you had been too."

He turned to Gabby. "And I know you are gonna get a restraining order ..."

"Where's Chris?" Alicia asked before Gabby could answer.

We hadn't said much since sitting down at the restaurant. Actually, we hadn't said a whole lot since the police had left. Gary had done almost all of the talking, which was good. I don't think anyone else had the strength.

Gabby had called Gary for her benefit and Alicia for mine. They had gotten out their beds at four am and met us at the diner. That's what friends do. Chris was nowhere to be found.

"Fuck Chris," I responded.

Sometimes Ya Gotta Laugh   191

"Mmm hmmm," Gary mumbled. "Fuck 'em."

Gabby gave us both a disapproving look. "Jordan, don't say ..."

"I will say it. Com'on Gabby, how many times have we called him tonight? At least ten times? Are you telling me that none of those calls woke him up? He didn't think that after the first five calls there might've been an emergency?"

"Maybe his phone was off," Alicia offered.

"It wasn't off," I assured her. "I've known Chris a long time. He doesn't turn his phone off. He doesn't even like to put it on vibrate, afraid he'll miss a call. We needed him tonight," I said. "Where was he?"

Gabby rubbed my shoulder. "You were the hero tonight."

I shook my head. "No, you were the hero. I was the boy-in-jeopardy."

"The way I heard it," Alicia said, "Sounds like you two were a tag-team match."

We all laughed. Sometimes ya gotta laugh, if just to keep from crying.

"Seriously, though," Gabby said, "I'm not sure what I would've done tonight or if I would've made it through the night without you." Tears welled in her eyes. "Thank you, thank you." She hugged me tightly.

Alicia smiled at me. "And give Chris a break. I'm sure he'll come around," she said.

Gabby picked up a napkin and dabbed her eye. "He will," she concurred. "He always does."

When he does, I thought, I'm going to let him have it.

Chapter 69

June 30th – Monday

When words lack solace, when they can't convey the empathy, the concern, or the angst, friends come over and offer the solidarity of friendship.

They sit together.

Raheem, Alicia, and I called it having dinner at Sushi Zushi with Gabby. We had even made overtures at eating – a glass of Monchoff Estate sat in front of each of us, edamame adorned the table, and a limitless menu lay in each of our laps. But the wine was not drunk, the edamame not touched, and the menu not perused.

"What happened to you?" Chris asked. He appeared like an apparition. One minute he wasn't there, the next second he was. He looked oddly pale. "What happened, guys?" He asked again when no one answered.

I didn't look at him. "Who invited him?"

"I did," Gabby answered. "We all need to talk."

"I don't need to talk," I said. "I don't need to do shit."

"What's your problem?" Chris demanded. "Gabby said it was an emergency."

"My problem ... my problem?" I leaned forward in my chair as my voice rose. Raheem gently pushed me back with his arm. I dropped my voice. "What's *my* problem? My problem is that you are so goddamn selfish that you can't find your way around when your friends need you."

"What are you talking about? I am here."

"He doesn't know," Gabby said.

"I don't know what?"

"Just my point," I stated. "Maybe if Chris wasn't so wrapped in Chris, he'd know what was going on with his friends. Ten fucking calls didn't tell him something was wrong?"

"Fuck you," he said.

"I'm sure you'd like that," slipped out my mouth before I could stop it.

His face went ashen. Alicia's hand tightened on mine. "You think you are so much better than me, Mr. Perfect," Chris spat. "You've got your own fucking issues but all you ever see is everybody else's. Thanks for being around when I needed you." Then he turned to Alicia as he spoke to me. "And how's Nicole? You still hitting that?"

Alicia's hand went slack in mine.

"And what about Kelly? She get that divorce?"

Gabby called Chris's name as he marched out. She got up to follow but he was in his car and gone before she reached the door. Minutes after Chris left, Alicia excused herself and went home. Gabby immediately followed suit.

Raheem sat with me while we finished our wine. We

drank our glasses, we drank Gabby's and Alicia's, then we washed that down with one more glass. Afterward he paid and we went our separate ways without saying a word.

Chapter 70

The Month of July

Alicia never asked for an explanation. Perhaps she didn't think one was owed. Maybe she didn't want one. I didn't offer. But everything changed. I felt guilty so I called her less. She was friendly but less enthusiastic. Work seemed to be taking up more time. We didn't get together.

Gabby never asked for an apology. Perhaps she didn't think one was owed. But our conversations were a little less frequent, a lot less hearty, and never intimate.

Chris never called to apologize. Perhaps he figured we had said enough. *The sounds of silence.*

And so my Dallas summer began. My living space crowded with bright pink elephants that I squeezed around.

The only person I saw with any regularity was Kelly. I even bumped into her at the bar a couple times. Which was odd as I'd had never seen her outside of my apartment since the day we met at Kroger over a year. I had assumed she lived somewhere far north of Dallas. Plano. Frisco. Oklahoma.

Last time I saw her at Jim's she was sitting with a dude.

I had picked up my beer and strolled their way, deliberately slowing as I passed their table. A gold wedding band had adorned the dude's left hand. *The ring doesn't mean anything.*

But the next day, when she came over, I could barely keep a hard on - despite the Icy Hot condoms, handcuffs, and a can of whipped cream. Not with Alicia, Gabby, Chris, and wedding band guy running through my head. After an hour of faking it, I had clutched the sheets, whispered a guttural, "damn, baby," and pretended I had cum.

In July, I boxed at the gym more, I jogged more, I endured the sweltering heat, and I pretended like I enjoyed sex with Kelly. Thirty one days in July and for all thirty one I stewed in my own self-absorption. I should've gotten off my ass and did something for somebody else. My parents would have wanted me to.

Chapter 71

August 4th (Monday)

It's my fault, echoed through Gabby's head as she walked from the courthouse to her car. Had she paid attention to the signs, had she been more loyal to her friends, had she not been so needy, none of this would've happened.

And she wouldn't be living in fear.

She started her car and pulled into the street, relieved that Brad hadn't shown up today. Brad could charm most people easily; she had worried he would dazzle the judge. But despite knowing the date of the hearing, he had been a no-show. Wherever he was, he wasn't far.

It's my fault floated through her head again.

An angry horn blared behind her. The sound startled her and she looked up as the traffic light turned from green to red. The driver honked again.

She had gone out with coworkers on Friday and had bumped into Brad and his date. He never hung out in uptown. But there he sat smugly, and he lavished his date with a kiss as soon as he spotted Gabby.

Her first instinct had been to rush home. Her second had been to warn his date. She had followed her first, abruptly and awkwardly leaving her coworkers alone.

Two weeks ago she would've sworn she had seen Brad cruising down her street. Her response had been to dart into her house. Sitting in the house with the lights off and the shades pulled, she had tried to convince herself she was victim to an overactive imagination. Whatever it had been, it compelled her to finally get a restraining order.

The horn behind her blared again, angrier than before. As the driver stole around her, he flipped her off.

She looked at the restraining order that she had taken out against Brad. How far was he supposed to stay away? 500 feet? 1000? 10000? Did it matter? It didn't provide her with comfort; today she had received flowers at work. No name attached, no card, only a beautiful array of tiger lilies, her favorite flower.

She folded the papers and put them in the glove compartment. She needed to make copies, one for her car, one for her house, one for the office. The clear instructions were to call the police if Brad violated the order, yet she didn't feel safer. Her hands shook as she reached for her phone. Luis answered on the first ring.

"How are you?" She forced herself to sound happy as she pulled into the Exxon on the corner of Lemmon and 75 and parked.

"We're great. Just getting the kids ready for school." He paused. "How are you?"

"How's Mom?"

"Good," he said with a sigh of relief. "Improving. When will you be back? We always love seeing you."

"Soon. I was even thinking this weekend. If I can make it happen."

"That's great, Gab. Mom and the kids will be so happy. You know you can stay as long as you want. Take some time off work. Or work here. All you need is a laptop, right?"

"Right," she said through constricted vocal chords.

He paused for a moment and then lowered his voice as he stepped into another room. "So you didn't answer my question. How are you?"

The words came tumbling out so quickly Gabby barely realized she was saying them aloud. "I'm thinking about getting a gun."

"What?"

"A gun. I'm thinking about getting a gun."

"Gabby … are you serious? I mean, I know that asshole has you scared but ..."

Gabby burst into tears. "I'm beyond scared. I'm petrified. I see him everywhere … I don't know if it's me. If it's my imagination. I blame myself for what happened to Jordan. Had I not been so selfish, had I paid attention to the signs ..."

"Whoa Gabby, no one blames ..."

"I know, I know. No one blames me. At least that's what people say. But I blame me. A couple weeks ago I thought I saw Brad driving down my street. I ran back into the house and didn't come out for the rest of the day. What's going on with me?"

"Gabrielle, he broke into your home. He tried to hurt you and Jordan. He made you feel vulnerable. But … I mean a gun? Are you sure? Have you talked to Jordan? What does Jordan say?"

Gabby's answer was silence.

"You haven't talked to Jordan, have you? Gabby, you are a very intelligent woman and I am immensely proud of you. I trust you to make good decisions. Please think about this one before you do anything rash."

Gabby could hear the cries of "Daddy" in the background so she let Luis get off the phone quickly. He was right, getting a gun might be the wrong decision. At the moment, it was the only one she had.

Chapter 72

August 6th (Wednesday)

Chris grunted as he pushed the two hundred pound barbell upward.

Raheem smiled down at him. "Struggling?"

"A little," Chris answered as he lowered the bar. Actually, he was struggling a lot. His body felt like shit and he had been slack at the gym for a couple months now. He lifted the bar again and attempted another rep.

"What's the problem?" Raheem asked. "I've seen you do two twenty-five on this thing easily."

"I dunno, man. Think I'm tired." He sat up. "Guess I'm not into it today."

"Not into it?" Raheem mocked him with his pseudo West-Indian accent. "Not into it? Man, you're soft. You're getting fat."

"I am not," Chris shot back. "If anything, I'm losing."

"Same difference." Raheem shrugged. "You're becoming skinny fat." He added another forty pounds before he took his turn on the bench. "So when was the last time you spoke to Jordan?"

Chris gazed around the gym. He hated 24 Hour Fitness. Of all the gyms in Dallas, 24 Hour had to be the biggest social club. Seventy-five percent of the people wandered around in the latest sports gear doing nothing but talking. The rest stood in fanatical admiration of their bodies. He had a suspicion that he used to be one of the latter set. He was also uncomfortable because David worked out at 24 Hour downtown. He and Raheem were at the one on Royal but a membership at one place meant a membership at all. The last thing he wanted to do was bump into David while working out with Raheem.

"Son, where is your mind at today? You losing your hearing and your muscles too?"

"I'm sorry," Chris said. "What did you say?"

"When was the last time you spoke to Jordan?'"

Raheem didn't pry. When he sensed something was wrong, usually his concern was intoned in the words, "You okay, bro?" And Raheem rarely offered unsolicited advice. Today, though, he was prying.

"Huh?"

"Jordan, you know, your best friend."

Chris forced a laugh. "You're my best friend."

Raheem did one more set and then he sat up. The west-Indian accent was replaced with concern. "No, I am your substitute. Your best friend is Jordan.

"Listen Chris, Jordan came at your wrong in the restaurant. I'll give you that. But he was angry, he was upset, he was disappointed. He felt like they needed you. I don't know what was going on with you that night. But you know you should have been there. You should've been there for your friends." Chris looked down at the floor. "And what you said to Jordan. Shit. You broke the code, my dude. That was some real gay shit right there." He lay back on the bench and began another rep. "What you need to do is straighten it out."

He finished the rep quickly, flashed Chris his Colgate smile, and popped him with his towel.

"I gotta hit the showers, dawg," he said. "My new baby mama wants to see me tonight."

"You don't have any kids," Chris responded.

"Not yet," Raheem replied. "But we gonna work on one tonight."

Chris removed fifty pounds of the barbell and sat back down on the bench. Working out always helped him clear his head. But this time, he couldn't get Raheem's words out of his head. He couldn't stop thinking about what happened to Gabby or how he let Jordan down. He also couldn't get the images of a naked David out his head.

Chapter 73

Aug 9th (Saturday)

Four days later Raheem's words were still resonating with Chris. Chris knew he had messed up. He had probably broken Jordan and Alicia up. He and Jordan weren't even speaking. Almost twenty years of friendship. Over.

The duality of Chris's existence did not escape him. He had a life with his straight friends, at least he used to, and he had a life with David and David's friends.

Initially, the time with David was an easy escape, a way of exploring something he couldn't share with his friends. Now it seemed as convoluted as everything else in his life.

Last week they had gone to The Porch for dinner. How would Jordan describe it? *Style over substance.*

The Porch had been packed and the hostess had been very hot. So Chris had flirted. That's what men do. They flirt. What resulted was an argument with David that had lasted the rest of the evening.

His phone rang and Gabby's number appeared. He snatched it up. "Hello." He hoped she hadn't dialed his number in error.

"Chris, it's Gabby."

He shook his head. Had he made himself such a stranger his best friends needed to identify themselves? "Yes, I know."

"Can I ask you something?"

"Of course, anything." His chest constricted.

"Can you help me get a gun?"

"What?"

"I need … I want … a gun."

How frightened was she? Had he really not comprehended what she was going through? The pain in her voice made him pull into Albertson's parking lot and stop. "Gabby, are you sure? Have you talked to Jordan?" He took her silence to mean no. "Are you at home? I'll be there."

David was pretty pissy when Chris called to tell him that he wasn't coming over. But Chris knew he hadn't been there for Gabby last time and there was no way in hell he wouldn't be there this time.

As Chris pulled in front of Gabby's house, Raheem's other words floated through his head. "That was some gay shit." What did he mean by that, Chris wondered as he locked his car doors and walked up Gabby's steps.

Chapter 74

Ride of Your Life

August 10th (Sunday)

I couldn't do it. I got up and sat on the edge of the bed. Nicole sat up behind and rubbed my shoulders. "It's okay," she said. "It happens."

Shifting, mulling, pondering.

She was right, sometimes *it* does happen. She understood that fact well enough to have a modicum of sympathy in her voice. Although I knew, unless I turned it around, my lack of performance would hinder a future rendezvous.

Why am I here in the first place? What had Gabby asked

me before? Isn't there a time a man stops chasing ass and acts like ... a grown up?

Nicole pressed her hard nipples against my back. She kissed my neck. "You sure you don't want to come to bed?"

My dick stirred a little. *Is sex just easier? Easier than facing my demons? Is sex my escapism?*

Nicole reached down and stroked me. She was nibbling on my ear. "Com'on, baby. You know I'm about to give you the ride of your life." Blood left my head, funneled to my nether regions, and my thinking got hazy.

What about Alicia? Don't I owe her something?

Nicole moved from behind me to between my legs. She gazed up at me seductively as she moved in to take my dick in her mouth. Her lips touched the tip, I jumped up, and she fell back on her ass.

"I'm sorry ... I ... I gotta go ..." I pushed past her and hurriedly put my clothes on. "I'm sorry. I can't do this."

Nicole returned my apologies with the words, "Get out."

My shirt was unbuttoned, my pants barely zipped, and my sneakers unlaced as I hit the door to leave. The last words I heard her say were, "And why don't you lose my number?"

Chapter 75

August 16th (Saturday)

"Guns don't kill people. People kill people." At least, that's what Annie Oakley believed. She repeated the words like a mantra, occasionally punctuating the statement with the words, "That's why we teach gun safety. And for you ladies," Annie looked directly at Gabby, "this protection will help you sleep better at night."

Gabby prayed Annie was right. She needed some sleep. The Ambien wasn't helping anymore and the signs were showing in her concentration and her focus.

Gabby had expected her instructor to be a big burly

man with a cowboy hat and boots. He who would walk to the tune of an Alan Jackson song and he would be a proud Texan. If any of those things were true, they were ensconced inside a petite fifty-something blonde woman who looked better suited for dinner planning in Highland Park than instructing at the range. But instructing what was she was doing. She lectured on gun safety, had the class shoot at the range, and took them through the paces. Every now and then she'd say to Gabby, "Relax, it'll be okay." The class was a ten hour course that Gabby could remember little of. That fact was probably not the best thing when it came to safety. She stopped by Chris's and dropped off his gun on the way home.

"How did it go?" He asked.

"Okay."

He hugged her and kissed her forehead. "Everything will be okay, Gabby."

"Of course it will," she agreed. But her words rang hollow.

Chapter 76

August 18th (Monday)

Raheem was sharing the details of his latest workout diet: No carbs after six pm. A whey protein shake before bed. Plain oatmeal and five egg whites for breakfast. The diet sounded as tasty as a cup of gravel. But no one could deny Raheem's eight pack and v-shape.

I was drinking a Martini. No problem with carbs after six here.

He was in the middle of telling me how he held a plank for seven minutes last night when he abruptly stood and said he had to take a leak.

I'm sure I had a quizzical look on my face. But before I could even get a "huh" out my mouth, I felt a hand on my shoulder. I turned around and found Chris behind me.

"Gabby got a gun" were his first words.

"What?" I asked, shocked by his words and his presence.

"Gabby got a gun."

"And you let her?"

"Jordan, Gabby is a grown woman. She doesn't need my approval – or yours – to make a decision."

"I see," I said. "You know how Gabby feels about guns ..."

"Apparently that has changed. Look, under other circumstances, I'd be rubbing this in your face. But not this one. This isn't the type of thing I'd want to happen to anyone."

"Well thanks for telling me," I said dryly. I returned to my drink.

"Is that all you have to say?"

I didn't respond.

Chris took two steps away and stopped. "You know what, J? I'm sorry. I shouldn't have said what I said to you. I shouldn't have put you on front street like that. I'm sorry. And I wish I had been there for Gabby. You don't know how much I've beaten myself up over that." His voice broke. "I wasn't there for her. But you were. I thank God all the time for that. If you never speak to me again, I needed to say I'm sorry." Then he walked away.

Suddenly it hit me like a ton of bricks. It wasn't his fault that Alicia and I weren't speaking. It was mine. I was the one who had slept with Kelly. I was the one who slept with Nicole. I did owe Alicia something. I owed her an apology. I owed Gabby one, too.

And as for Gabby, I *had* been there. In the end, isn't that what mattered most?

I watched him as he walked toward the door. Until Raheem, who I'm not sure ever went to the bathroom said, "You gonna work that out?"

"Chris," I called. He stopped and I walked over to him. "I owe you an apology too. I was wrong. I shouldn't have said what I said. I miss you, my friend. Can I buy you a beer?"

So we drank. We drank so much that Raheem had to take us both home. But the hangover I felt in the morning was well worth the reconciliation.

Chapter 77

August 20th (Wednesday)

Knowing that you've done something wrong, admitting it, apologizing for it, none of those things make the pain go away.

It certainly doesn't excuse the fact that things weren't handled right the first time. Sometimes apologizing is too little, too late. Had I done things right the first time, I would not be hoping for forgiveness I wasn't sure I merited.

I called Alicia when I got home on Monday but got the answering machine. Thank God. I would've sounded like a drunk dialer.

I called again on Tuesday. Answering machine. Of course, my number had displayed on her caller ID. Unlike the Alicia of days gone by, she hadn't bothered to respond with a text or a call.

On Wednesday, I tried again. Again, I got no answer. I didn't want to leave a voicemail. I wanted to talk. But say she never answered, would she never hear my apology? Since I had hurt her, did I have the right to make demands on where and how I apologized?

So I called her once more on Wednesday. She didn't answer the second time either. But when the voicemail picked up, I left a message.

"Hey Alicia, it's Jordan. I just want to say, I'm sorry. I'm very sorry for what happened at the restaurant the last time I saw you, for embarrassing you, and for hurting you. It was immature, it was selfish, and it showed a gross lack of compassion. I want to say I hope I haven't hurt you. But I know I have. You are a beautiful girl. Inside and out. I learned a great deal from you, even if I didn't show it.

"I wanted to tell you this face to face, but I wasn't sure I'll get the chance. And like a friend said to me very recently, if I never speak to you again, I need you to know that I'm sorry." I hung up the phone. I didn't feel any better. But I knew I had done the right thing. I took a deep breath, picked up the phone, and called Gabby to apologize.

She picked up on the first ring.

Chapter 78

August 23rd (Saturday)

   Chris put down the second protein shake of the day and wiped his mouth. He was running almost an hour late for David's. Unless David was high when he got there, he would be angry. Which, honestly, would be par for the course of late. David had been bellyaching ever since they went to The Porch. He was mad about the girl Chris had flirted with, he was mad Chris had bailed on him to spend time with Gabby.

   Chris walked into the bathroom, skipped his usual manscaping and showered. Forty five minutes later, he pulled in front of David's house. No sooner did his car come to a halt than

David opened the front door. Chris turned off the car, inhaled deeply, and stepped out. He had been racking his brain for a good excuse for being late the entire drive and still hadn't come up with anything. Please, he thought, let's just not have this argument outside.

But as he got closer to David, he could see that David was smiling. "Glad you made it," David said. He handed Chris a gin martini as he stepped into the house and planted a kiss on his lips. The house smelled of weed.

"I have a surprise for you," David said. "We didn't do anything for your birthday and I feel like I've been giving you a hard time lately. So I wanted to make it up to you."

"What is it?" Chris asked tentatively.

"DP."

"Huh?"

"Let's just say it's a little something from the past ..." David grinned. "Tell you what. I'm going to go upstairs and get it ready. Make yourself a drink. I'll call you." David's eyes twinkled and Chris wasn't sure whether he should be excited or nervous. He poured himself a shot of tequila. He was on his third shot when David called him upstairs.

Chris ascended the steps slowly. "Where are you?" He called when he reached the top.

"The bedroom," David called back.

Chris gulped the last shot. Hesitantly, he pushed the bedroom door open.

"Turn on the light," David whispered. Chris obeyed. The light came on and Chris saw his surprise. David wasn't in bed alone. He was in bed with Juliana. She lay on top of the sheets completely naked. Her nipples were hard, one hand played with her clit, one finger was in her mouth. She oozed porn star.

DP. Double penetration.

"You getting in?" David said.

He didn't have to ask. Chris was already half naked.

Chapter 79

August 24th (Sunday)

Get to Kathleen's Sky Diner around one to one-thirty pm on Sunday. Any time before that and you're going to run into the after-church-brunch-crowd. (You know how I feel about the church brunch crowd). But around one pm, the crowd dies down and by two pm, there are just a handful of diners decorating the place.

My favorite waitress, Shiela, had left me with a cup of decaf, a mimosa, and a banana nut muffin. I was munching on all three when Gabby arrived.

I hadn't seen her since the sushi incident, probably

the longest I had gone without seeing her since we had met. She looked beautiful, a little darker because of the sun, her stride as purposeful as ever, her eyes as piercing. She also looked exhausted.

The bartender directed her to my table, where Gabby and I shared an extended hug.

"I'm sorry ..." she began. But I hushed her.

She ordered the Eggs Louise, I ordered the Eggs From Hell. We were halfway through our meal when I finally said, "Chris said you got a gun." She looked around uncomfortably and I leaned into her. "Is it on you now?"

"It's a concealed weapon. You know, concealed?" She mocked us both.

"Do you feel safer?"

Her shrug was undecided. "I think. I don't know. Sometimes ... maybe."

"Did you file the restraining order?"

"Yes."

"You have one in the car."

"Yes." She assured me.

"And I assume you haven't heard from him since."

"I have," she whispered.

"You have!" My mimosa remained suspended between the table and my mouth. Several guests turned and looked in our direction. "What do you mean, you have?"

Gabby scooted her chair over to mine. "I got a delivery of flowers recently. No note. No name. But my favorite flower."

"Tiger lilies," I mumbled.

"Yes, tiger lilies. It was the same arrangement that he sent when we broke up before. And last week there was a type-written note stuck in my door."

"What did it say?"

"*I'll never let you go.*" I covered her hand with mine.

"Well, that's why you have a gun. Right?"

She looked grateful for the support. "So you think it's a good idea?"

I thought it was a horrible idea. "If it gives you peace, babe, it's a wonderful idea."

Chapter 80

August 25th (Monday)

Chris was seeing red and I was still raging.

We were at Gabby's house. The plan had been to meet at Jim's. I had gotten there first and who should I see? Brad. I wanted to walk over and knock the stupid grin off his face. And I started to.

It goes like this. I walk into Jim's, sit at the bar, and order a drink. I'm looking around, taking in the sites, people-watching, as I wait for Gabby and Chris to show up. I turn to my left and who do I spy? Brad. The thing is, he had already seen me! He is sitting and grinning at me, arm around some girl.

When our eyes meet, he raises his glass and mouths the word "Cheers". What the fuck? I bolt from the bar and I'm in his face, "You goddamn sonofabitch, if you ever reach out to Gabby again ..."

Next thing I know, the bartender is yelling, the waitress is calling management, and Raheem is hauling my ass out the door.

He called Chris and told Gabby we would meet at her house.

"I should stop going out for a while," Gabby offered.

"You can't stop going out," Raheem said. "That's giving him all the power."

I nodded. "Gabby, you have to live life. He can't take that away from you."

"He already has," she said under her breath.

"I can't believe he had the audacity to show up at the bar," Chris added. "I thought you had a restraining order."

"I do. But it doesn't say he isn't permitted to go to bars. He was there. I wasn't. I can't wage a complaint about that.

"I'm really thinking I'm going to go and stay at my brother's for a while. I think it's the best thing to do. At least until all this passes."

"And what if it never does, Gabby," I asked.

She winced in pain. "Yeah, what if never does?"

Chapter 81

August 27th (Wednesday)

My iTunes blared so loudly, I almost missed her call.

"Jordan?" I turned down the music, shocked at the voice on the other end of my line.

"Alicia?"

"You sound surprised."

"I am surprised."

"I got your message. And I wanted to call."

"I'm glad you did."

"I wanted to say thank you. The message meant a lot."

"I meant every word of it."

"I believe you."

Silence drifted from the phone. It permeated the room and engulfed my entire loft. I wanted to ask, "Is that it? Is that all you have for me?" Instead I waited anxiously in the silence.

"Maybe I shouldn't have taken it so hard," she said. "We weren't in a relationship. We hadn't talked about exclusivity. But at some point you assume ... I assumed ... I don't know. Part of it was my fault for assuming ..."

"No," I said. "Not your fault. I ... I let you assume. I ... was wrong. But I want to make it up to you."

"Jordan, what's done is done. I'm not angry. I just ..."

"Please, please, let me make it up to you."

"I just wanted you to be honest with me."

"Can I see you?" I asked.

"I don't think that's such a good idea."

"Just as a friend. Your friendship means a lot to me. Just as a friend ..." my voice trailed off.

"Jordan, I forgive you. Don't feel you have to ..."

"Just as a friend," I repeated. "Please."

We sat on the phone without speaking. I even began to wonder if I was alone on the line. And then she said, "Just as a friend ..."

Chapter 82

August 30th (Saturday)

       Chris hadn't had a wet dream in forever. Yet something sticky was on the end of his dick. Last night's beers had woken him but now he was more concerned with why the front of his boxers clung to him.

       He walked into his bathroom, flicked on the light, and pulled his dick out. Something milky leaked out the head. His stomach knotted. He took a deep breath and relaxed so that he could pee. It was a decision he immediately regretted. The pain that ravaged his dick head was so sharp he yelped in pain. It felt like acid poured out the end of his dick.

He tried to control the flow of the pee. But it didn't help. Each drop – no matter the size – was as painful as the one before it.

When the pain finally subsided, he put on his jeans, grabbed his shirt, and drove to the emergency room.

Chapter 83

September 1st (Monday)

So we were sitting at Houlihan's in Addison, munching on corn tamales, calamari, and a petite filet.

I didn't like the idea of picking and choosing where we would go based on whether Brad would make an appearance. It gave him power he didn't deserve. But that was my hang up. The less chance of seeing him that existed, the better mood Gabby was in. I wouldn't deny her that. So when I got her text message, suggesting a spot twenty minutes from our normal rendezvous point, I accepted without hesitation. I'm glad I did. The conversation was one of the easiest we had had in months.

"Labor Day really snuck up on us this year," I said.

"I know. Usually we do something for Labor Day. BBQ. Martini party. Something." Chris agreed. "Oh well."

"I think we should still do something," Gabby stated.

"Really?" Chris asked.

"Absolutely … um … something small though. At my house, we could all invite one or two people. Just talk and relax, eat and drink. Wouldn't that be nice?"

"I don't see why not," I said. "Chris?"

"I guess ..."

"Who are you going to invite?" She asked me.

"Alicia." Her name stumbled out sounding more like a question than a statement.

Gabby had the look of "really?" on her face. But what she said was, "Nice." She turned to Chris. "Who are you going to invite?"

Chris opened his mouth as if he was about to respond. Instead he popped in a piece of calamari.

"Well, you can bring anybody," she said. *Did I imagine stress on the word anybody?*

"Thanks," Chris said. He looked awkward to change the subject. *Had he heard it too?*

"And who are you going to invite?" I asked Gabby.

"The usual crew. Raheem, a couple people from work. You know I have a new neighbor. Her name is Karen. She moved in about three months ago."

"How old is she?" Chris asked.

"Fifty-five," Gabby answered. "Why? You're interested in the cougar scene? When I think about it. You two *are* close to the same age," she teased.

"Whatever," Chris said.

"And Gary, of course. He'll probably bring a friend."

"Ugh," Chris said under his breath.

"You need to give him a chance, Chris," Gabby said.

"I don't know what your problem is with him."

"Aside from the fact that he's a man who prefers to act like a woman?"

"His life, bro," I said. "Beside, Gary's a cool guy."

"Oh, so you are Gary are best buds now?"

"What? Ugh. Geez. No we aren't best buds. But he's a good guy and he cares about Gabby."

"Sometimes, Chris Beauchamp, I think you are homophobe," Gabby said. "And you know what they say about homophobes."

"No," Chris said. "What do they say?"

I kicked Gabby under the table. "They say they're Republican," I said.

"I've got two words for you," Chris said to me. "And one word for you," he said to Gabby.

"And they are?" I asked.

"Fuck you," he said to me with a grin. And then he turned to Gabby. "Whatever."

Chapter 84

September 3rd (Wednesday)

I expected the call Monday night. It came on Wednesday.

I was propped on the couch catching some DVR'd repeat of Pinky and The Brain. Those two make me laugh. *Are you contemplating what I'm contemplating?*

My phone buzzed with a text. I leaned over casually and read the message. It was from Kelly. **Can you meet me for lunch tomorrow? 1 hour.**

I should've expected that text too. We had gotten together weekly for six weeks straight. But since my apology to

Chris and Alicia – nothing. I needed to be honest and let her know we had to stop. But I didn't feel like having that discussion I put the phone back down. Two minutes later the text tone went off again.

It was Gabby. **Can you talk?**

This was the call I had been expecting. **Waiting for your call.** No sooner had I hit send than the phone rang.

"Hola, Senorita."

"Is Chris gay?"

"Seriously, Gabby? The first question? How about, hey, Jordan, how are you?"

"Oh whatever! Just tell me, is he or isn't he?"

I sighed. "I don't know."

"You do know."

"No, I don't. I know he's been going through some things. He's been acting differently. But that doesn't mean ..."

"Brad said ..."

"You know I don't give a rat's ass about what Brad ..."

"I know. Just listen. He said that Chris was arguing with a gay guy on Memorial Day. That's all. Did you see him? Was he?"

"I didn't see him up close. And how would Brad know if he was gay anyway?"

"You didn't see him up close. But what do you think? I know that you're very intuitive."

I took a deeper sigh. "Yes, I think the guy was gay. Yes, Chris has done some things to make me wonder. Yes, I think I've seen the guy and Chris together before."

She chewed on this for a while. "And when he said fuck you at Sushi Zushi you said ..."

"I know what I said," I cut her off. "And I wish I hadn't said it. That's why I try not to speak out of anger. I say things I regret."

"We all do," she said. "But you apologized. Sticks and stones ..."

"Yeah, that adage applies when we are little. When we're grown we realize words hurt more than stones sometimes."

Again, she chewed. "Well, we need to get him to tell us."

"What?"

"He needs to be honest with us. We need him to tell us."

"No, no we don't need to get him to tell us."

"Why not?"

"Gabby, it's his business. It's his personal thing, what he's going through. When he decides to tell us, if he decides, then we'll listen. But we aren't going to make him talk about something he clearly isn't ready to discuss. Aren't you the one who said it doesn't matter?"

"I guess you are right." She sounded a bit deflated.

"You know I'm right."

"Look at you, all Mr. Mature and shit." She took on her home-girl Latina voice. That cracks me up every time.

"Get off my phone," I said.

"Okay, Papi. But I love you." She hung up the phone with a giggle.

And I love you, too, Gabrielle.

Chapter 85

September 5th (Friday)

"I have a question," I said.

"What's that?" Chris asked.

"Why is it that, on the rare occasion we get together at one of our places to eat, it's always mine?"

"Because you don't like my cooking," he answered.

"That's true."

Chris hadn't stopped by for dinner. He had called earlier to ask my help in downloading iTunes. iTunes isn't a complex science. The visit was an excuse to hang out, and I welcomed it. We fiddled for a couple hours searching for 80's hiphop before I offered to make us turkey burgers.

"Can I tell you something?"

My back was to Chris when he spoke, my arm outstretched, reaching into the cupboard for some sea salt and cayenne. "Anything." I formed the meat into quarter-pound burgers and placed them in a pan.

"I caught something," he said quietly.

"Caught something?"

"Yeah, caught something. An STD."

I kept my back to him. "Which one?"

"Gonorrhea and chlamydia."

"That's the one where you ..." I began.

"Burn when you piss."

"Ah," I replied. I flipped the burger and mulled chopping some onions and peppers. "So … do you know where you got it?"

"I had a threesome."

"Do you know their names?" Don't press the burgers down. That's the most common mistake people make when making burgers. It causes all the juices to run out the meat.

"David and Juliana."

"David and ..." I had sweet potato fries in the fridge.

"David and Juliana. The two I had the threesome with back in January."

"Oh … um … I thought you always wrapped it up." Had I seasoned the burgers enough? I probably needed to add some of the chili olive oil I had gotten at Whole Foods.

"You can get it orally."

"Really … wow … I didn't know that." Yeah, I was definitely gonna chop up some onions, and peppers, maybe even jalapenos.

"Yup," he said.

"So you got this from Julianna ..." I put fries in a

pyrex dish.

"I dunno."

"Have you talked to her?"

"I talked to David. He said he had no symptoms when I talked to him on Sunday. But yesterday he said he had it."

"And?"

"That fucker blamed me." I couldn't tell if he was angry or sad. "He said he had never had anything before he met me."

"What about Juliana?" I asked.

"He said he called her and she was fine."

"Chris, STDs don't spontaneously combust. Someone gave it to you."

"What does it matter? It's my fucking fault anyway."

"I don't understand. What do you mean, your fault?" I faced him.

"All this ... everything ... this ... this ...fucking around. This .. this ... shit."

"Chris, people get STDS for a lot of reasons. Usually, it's poor judgment. Poor decision. Unprotected sex. Sometimes people get them from people they trust and love. But anybody can get a disease. You shoulda used protection. But how many guys get head with a condom on? I didn't know that you could catch something orally. It could've happened to anybody. Talk to David again."

"For what?"

"To see if you can get to bottom of this. It does matter. Talk to him." I turned back to the burgers. "Shit. You are gonna make me burn these gourmet burgers."

"Yeah, I'll talk to him," Chris agreed reluctantly.

But as I served the burgers, I wondered if encouraging Chris to talk to David was the best thing.

Chapter 86

September 7th (Sunday)

About ten people converged on Gabby's house on Sunday including Gabby's new neighbor Karen. She was a mid-50's divorcee with an easy laugh and a perm that suggested she had once been a Def Leppard groupie. She fussed in a motherly sort of way, talked to everyone as if she knew them for years, and had a story for everything. She would make a good neighbor.

Gary brought a friend. She was cute, friendly, and

flirted shamelessly with Raheem, who returned the favor. She flirted with Chris a little too. Until she sensed that something was off between Gary and Chris or Gary said something. Everyone sensed it.

Alicia came. She was sexier than I remembered. I had offered to pick her up but she had opted to drive.

We played a game of Taboo, followed by WII tennis and bowling, and a curse-filled game of spades.

Karen told us about her divorce, how her husband had left her for a blonde twenty-something who only wanted his money, and how her two children – the apples of her eye – would be graduating from Rice and TSU. She concluded by stating that all men where dogs. She also cooked up a storm, practically catering for Gabby. Where Gabby had planned on serving hor d'eouvres, Karen made us dinner. Manicotti, stuffed shells, ravioli. If the dish was pasta-based, she served it. And it was all damn good.

At one point, while putting a heaping portion of shells on everyone's plate she turned to me and said, "has anyone ever told you you look like Roger Guenveur Smith? Oh … now that's one attractive man." *Roger who?*

For the most part, we avoided the discussion of Brad. Karen didn't know and she didn't need to know. Gabby, though, still blamed herself for everything. There was a brief moment, when Karen stepped out the room, that Gabby welled up a bit.

"I just keep asking myself why it took me so long to see it."

"Gabby," Raheem said, "sometimes we don't even know ourselves. Figuring out who we are, why we tick, peeling back those layers, can be a lifetime journey. If learning ourselves can take years, imagine how much harder it is to truly learn someone else. Be glad you learned when you did and you were wise enough to get out. Not everyone can say that."

I felt a twinge of jealousy at the smile of appreciation

Gabby gave Raheem.

During a round of Taboo, I playfully reached for Alicia's hand. But she withdrew it. She gave me a look that said, *Just friends, remember?*

By the end of the night, Gabby appeared to be in a good place. And, at midnight as we all said our goodbyes and I can remember thinking, the evening couldn't have been better.

Chapter 87

September 10th (Wednesday)

Alicia and I were *just friends.* Yet it still bothered me she had pulled her hand away. Yea, I had been an ass. I deserved it. But that didn't keep me from hoping for forgiveness and a fresh start.

Typical Jordan response: Sulk. I had tried that all of July. It hadn't really worked. I make poor choices when I spend too much time rolling around in self-pity. I've learned that much.

Better response: Be an adult. Go for a jog. Stop jacking off. Do something altruistic. Didn't I say I wanted to help the homeless?

I reached into my closet, pulled out shorts, tank, and sneakers and decided to jog over to Exall park. I'd circle it a half dozen times, and then decide what to do.

But what do they say about the plans of mice and men?

I opened my front door to find Kelly standing there wearing a raincoat, although it wasn't raining outside. My mouth fell open.

She smiled at me with cool satisfaction.

"Hey Vin Diesel," she said coyly. "I decided to take matters into my own hands." She placed her hand on my chest and gently pushed me back into my loft. As the door closed, the coat opened to reveal a t-shirt and panties. She let the coat fall and pressed against me. "Are you happy to see me?" She asked as she reached into my shorts. It was a rhetorical question. Any doubt about coming over had evaporated as my dick grew in her hand.

Emotional eating is what happens when food becomes the substitute for sorting out life, when food consoles us when we are troubled. If there is emotional eating, there must be such a thing has emotional sexing. Sex is our solace. Pussy or dick is comfort food – our mac and cheese, our potato salad – filling for the moment but unhealthy for the body, mind, or spirit.

So there I stood. Rejected by Alicia and on the verge of self-pity. Kelly had her hand down my pants; her lips were brushing my neck. I was about to indulge in some emotional sexing.

I guess emotional eating and emotional sexing are similar in that you have to know what's going on, why you're eating, why you're fucking, if you are ever gonna stop. If you are ever gonna get healthy. I needed to get healthy.

I grabbed her hand. "Kelly, no." My words were lost in the moment and she kept groping me and kissing my neck.

"Kelly," I said more firmly this time, "no." I pulled her hand from my briefs and pushed her away.

Her face was a series of emotions – confusion, shock, hurt, disbelief. The last one was anger. "Who do you think you are ..."

I didn't hear the rest. Did I need to? She was angry. Although I thought some of it was misplaced – *she* was cheating – I'm sure she found her own comfort in our unions. Maybe she suffered from emotional sexing. So Kelly yelled. She cursed. She called me an arrogant sonofabitch. She called me everything but a child of God. And I processed. After three straight minutes of insults, she stormed out the door.

I readjusted my dick in my shorts, put on my headphones, and went jogging. An hour later, when I got home, I called up an agency and offered to volunteer to help the homeless.

Chapter 88

September 11th (Thursday)

Washington DC was cold. Gabby stood outside baggage claim at Dulles, waiting for her brother Luis to pick her up. She wished she was wearing more than her work clothes. But she hadn't been thinking about the weather when she stopped at Macy's and bought travel clothes.

She hated to worry Luis. But what else could she do?

Where else could she go? She had already put Jordan and Gary in harm's way.

How could a day start so well and end so badly?

This morning she had been basking in the glow of her manager's compliments. The merger was going smoothly. The morning's strategic planning session had gone well. Quarterly earnings were ahead of pace. Yeah, she was definitely going on the corporate trip to the Dominican Republic. She had been thinking about asking Jordan to go with her. Until her phone rang.

"Honey," Karen had started. "I want to let you know there are some beautiful flowers sitting on your porch. They're lovely."

Gabby had swallowed.

"Honey, are you there?" Karen had asked.

"Yes, yes." Gabby had searched for composure. ""What kind are they?"

"Oh … well I didn't want to walk onto your porch and be the nosy neighbor." Karen had laughed. "But I believe they are lilies. What time will you be home? Do you want me to go over and get them?"

"Did you see who dropped them off?"

"No, I didn't. But I'll be happy to go over and get ..."

"No, just leave them."

"Are you sure? I don't mind."

Gabby's phone buzzed with a text from Luis. **Almost there.**

"You are so sweet, Karen," Gabby had replied. "I'm on my way out of town. But I'll send someone over to get them?"

"Oh really?" Karen had said excitedly. "Where?"

"Home." Although before that moment Gabby hadn't been going anyplace. Gabby had hung up the phone and booked a flight. She stopped at the Galleria, purchased an overnight bag at Macys, and filled it with clothes purchased there as well. She had called her brother on the way to the airport.

"I'm coming home," she had said to him.

"Great! When?"

"Tonight. Can you pick me up?"

Luis hadn't missed a beat, although anxiety filled his voice. "Of course, what time?"

"Nine thirty."

"I'll be there … Are you alright?" When Gabby hadn't responded, he had continued. "Come for as long as you need, Gab."

"Gabby?"

The voice startled her. She hadn't seen her brother pull up and get out the car. "Luis," she said. He wrapped his arms around her and held her.

"You okay?" He whispered in her ear.

She shook her head.

"You wanna talk about it?"

She shook it again.

"Okay, okay, well let's get in the car. I"ll take you home. I've told Amy, Mom, and the kids you are coming home. Everybody is excited."

He tossed her bag behind the seat and they rode in silence.

As they pulled up at Luis's house he said, "Why don't you turn off your cell phone? Get away from it all."

She sent a quick text to Jordan, Alicia, and Chris and then complied with his suggestion.

The beauty of running away is just that, you get away from it all. Going home was like running away and for parts of three days Gabby almost forgot about it all. She chased her nieces, gossiped with her sister-in-law, confided in her brother, and talked to her mother. Between the cobbler, the quiche lorraine, and the empanadas only her mother could make, Gabby swore she had put on five pounds. But the butterflies returned on the ride back to the airport on Monday. She sat anxiously as she waited to board and she didn't turn on her phone until she was sitting in the plane's cabin. One text from Alicia, one text from Gary, and a text and two voicemails from Jordan. She was about to breathe a sigh of relief when the phone rang.

"Hello," Gabby said.

It was Karen. "Honey, I'm so glad you answered. I've been trying to call you all weekend. Your friend never came by and picked up those flowers on Thursday, so I went over there and got them myself. And I'm glad I did. It rained so badly Thursday night. Not that I think it would've mattered anyway. You got another delivery on Friday, Saturday, and another one this morning. All lilies. Whoever's sending them must really be in love with you."

"Miss," the flight attendant said, "we need you to turn off your phone." Gabby did. But not before sending Chris a text and asking if they'd have time to go practice at the firing range in Plano this week.

Chapter 89

September 18th (Thursday)

"So what do you think?" I asked Alicia over the phone.

"About?"

About us, about starting over, about letting me back into your world. "About Gabby," I said.

"I'm worried about her, Jordan. She must be

terrified."

"She has a gun," I said.

"Yes, she told me."

"I don't think it's a good idea."

"I don't think so either."

"But what can I say?"

"Nothing," she answered. "All you can do is support. But I worry ..."

"About?"

"I worry that this is going to end badly"

"Please don't say that."

"You hear so many stories …"

I didn't want to go down that path. "I think Chris came out to me."

"He did?"

"Well … not really came out … but he did share that he had another threesome and implied something sexual happened between him and David."

"I guess that's kinda sorta coming out … although I'd be cautious not to put words in his mouth. Plenty of guys have had threesomes and *something* has gone down and they'd still consider themselves straight. Being gay is more than random sexual experiences."

"You're right."

"What did he say?"

"Guy talk. You know, we were just catching up." *He caught a STD.*

"Uh-huh." She didn't press and I appreciated that. "So what else is going on?" She asked.

I wanted to tell her that Kelly had come over half naked, tried to give me a hand and a blow job and I had kicked her out.

I wanted to get a smile of admiration like Raheem had gotten from Gabby.

I needed to earn some cool points.

But can you earn cool points when you do what you should have done in the first place?

"Nothing," I said. "Nothing." Then I changed the topic again.

Chapter 90

September 20th (Saturday)

Three days of excruciating pain, two weeks of arguing with David, and a guilty conscience - one of those things should have kept Chris home. Yet he sat in the parking lot of JR's – Dallas's largest gay club.

Fear kept him frozen in his car as he imagined the countless guys from the gym, his neighbors, and untold coworkers that must be roaming the club's halls. He sat for twenty minutes before he finally pulled his baseball cap over his face and he walked inside.

Men of all shapes, sizes, and colors filled the club. Chris weaved through the crowd, avoided eye contact, and occasionally got felt up as he searched for someplace to stand. He spotted a relatively empty corner, away from the deejay, and he took up residence.

Two minutes later a guy walked over and offered Chris a beer. "Hey, I got this for you," the guy said with a sly look.

Chris glanced at him peripherally. The guy had to be early twenties with sandy blond spiked hair with blue tips. He was shirtless, revealing a toned but slight frame. Something about the way the guy spoke, about the way he held the beer ever so delicately said "ladyboy."

Chris didn't respond.

"Hey, I got this for you." The guy spoke louder this time.

Chris ignored him.

Sixty seconds of awkwardness passed. Then the guy spat, "Bitch," and walked away.

Chris adjusted his baseball cap.

"Sorry about that." Another guy stood beside him. "She is in here all the time trying to buy drinks for the cute boys." The guy stuck out his hand and Chris looked at him – mid 40's, small belly paunch, salt-n-pepper hair, studs in both ears. "Look at her now," the guy said. "She's already on the tail of new meat." The guy laughed while his hand remained extended in midair between them. Chris spotted another corner and walked away without a word. As he left he heard the guy say, "You are a little bitch, aren't you?"

Chris changed his mind. He was going home.

"Well look who is here."

Chris looked up to find Gary standing in front of him. The color drained from Chris's face. He shoved past Gary toward the door but Gary grasped him lightly on the shoulder.

"Look, honey," Gary said. "I don't know what your problem is ..."

"My problem is I want to be left the fuck alone," Chris said in a harsh whisper as he knocked Gary's hand off his shoulder.

"Honey, you're the one who keeps showing up at my spots. Nobody here cares if you are gay ..."

"I'm not gay." He faced Gary. Several people moved in to listen. Chris heard someone mumble, "closet case."

"Whatever the fuck you are. Nobody cares. You got in my face at the bar. You didn't speak at Gabby's party. The only reason I didn't read you was because I respect Gabby too much. "

"And the money she throws your way."

"It ain't even about money. Gabby is my friend just like yours. And I know her well enough to know she wouldn't care if you told her you are gay."

"I'm not gay," Chris said through clenched teeth.

Suddenly Gary's voice softened. "Honey, all I'm saying is that if your friends really love you, they won't make judgments about you."

"Really," Chris spat as he pointed his finger at Gary's chest. "What about all the people who have lost friends and family because they came out the closet? Do they have any regrets? Do you think one of them might just think that it would've been better to keep their sexuality to themselves? Why does every faggot on earth think everybody should sing their sexuality to the rooftop? If you guys are so happy with your lives, why are you so busy telling others how to live theirs?"

Gary was undaunted. "Love is about acceptance. I ain't saying to tell the world. But you ain't happy, baby. And you need to figure out how to get there."

Chris whirled around, shoved through the small crowd of people that encircled them, and pushed to the door. As he yanked the door open, a hand touched his shoulder.

"Would you get the fuck away …" he yelled at Gary. But it wasn't Gary. "I'm sorry," Chris mumbled as he stepped outside. The guy followed.

"Are you okay?" The guy asked. "I saw what happened."

"Yeah, whatever. I need to go home."

"Listen," the guy held his hands up. "I … I don't know your business. But I did overhear. I think … I think the guy meant well. He was trying to help."

"Well he didn't," Chris snapped.

The guy chuckled. "Well don't let it ruin your night. There are plenty of places that are quiet enough to get a drink. What about Snookie's on Oaklawn? I don't like their drinks but they serve a mean basket of loaded fries."

Chris pulled his cap down as two guys walked past. "Uhh … I think I've seen enough for one night."

"Are you sure? I don't live far from here. Maybe three blocks. We could go to my house. I have stuff we can do, if that would help take the edge off and relax you some."

Stuff we can do, Chris thought. That's exactly what he needed. Stuff to do. To relax, take the edge off, and forget the evening.

"Where do you live?"

"Ilume. Maybe two blocks from here. Follow me."

Chris followed, uncomfortable in the slew of folks that wandered up and down Cedar Springs, but he wanted stuff to do.

"You sure picked a crazy night to come out."

"What do you mean?" Chris asked as they reached Ilume.

"It's Pride weekend."

Chris stared at him blankly.

"You are a straight boy, huh?" The guy joked. When Chris didn't laugh he apologized. "Sorry, sorry. It's a celebration of being gay, of being who you are."

"I'm not gay," Chris mumbled.

"You don't have to be gay to come to Pride," the guy said as he unlocked his door. "But I suppose it helps.

"I guess I should tell you my name. Make it official. I'm Shane." Shane stood six feet, slim, with shaggy brown hair, and brown eyes. His lack of facial hair made him look like he was in his early-twenties. Although, Chris would've guessed he was mid-thirties. Chris sensed that Shane was a genuine guy. It was at odds with the fact that they'd be doing X soon.

"Nice to meet you, Shane," Chris said. "I'm Mark."

"Nice to meet you, Mark." Shane ushered him into his living room and handed him the remote. "Make yourself comfortable. I'll be right back."

Chris sat on the couch tentatively and turned on the TV. To his surprise, ESPN appeared on the screen.

"I'm a big sports fan," Shane called from the distance. "Football, basketball, soccer, you name it, I'll watch it. But turn it to whatever you wanna watch."

Chris left it on ESPN.

"My DVD collection is minimal," Shane said, reemerging from the back. "So our choices are limited. I have *Gladiator* with Russell Crowe, a personal favorite and a classic. Ha! Let's see. *The Departed, Inside Man, and Madea Goes to Jail*. A guilty pleasure. Or we can just order something off HBO."

"It doesn't matter. *Inside Man* is a great movie."

"Great." Shane put the movie in and nestled beside Chris. His leg bumped into Chris's a couple times before finally coming to rest on it.

Chris shifted. Where was the X? He moved his leg

away from Shane's.

"You alright?" Shane asked. He casually put his hand on Chris's thigh. "Either your back hurts or you're restless. You keep moving around."

"I'm okay," Chris said. He turned to look Shane and found that Shane had leaned into him. Their eyes met, held the gaze, and then Shane moved to kiss him. As Shane's lips brushed against his own, Chris pulled back. "I'm sorry, I ... I can't."

Shane turned beet red. "No, don't apologize. I'm sorry, I guess I read you wrong. I've never been good at reading the signs. Totally my fault. I'm such an idiot."

"No, no, it's not that." Chris felt self-conscious himself. He hesitated. "Um ... what stuff do you have?"

"Huh?"

"Do you have any stuff? *Anything*," Chris repeated. Shane stared. Chris continued. "X or coke or ..."

"Oh ... that," Shane said. "Uh no ... dude, I don't. That's not my thing at all. I ..."

Chris felt like an idiot. The stuff wasn't X. The stuff was hanging out, the stuff was watching a movie. "I think I should go."

"You don't have to go. It's cool. I don't do it. But I'm not judging you. We can watch a movie. And I'll keep my hands to myself." Shane laughed.

"Really, I should go." Chris was halfway to the door.

"You sure you don't wanna stay and hang out? The company would be nice."

Shane was legit, which was all the more reason Chris felt like he couldn't stay. They shared an extended hug at the door. "Thanks for having me over."

"Anytime, Mark. And here's my number. Call me if you ever want to hang out again. Next time I promise not to fuck it up."

But Chris knew that Shane hadn't fucked it up. He

had. So he tossed Shane's number out the car window long
before he got home.

Chapter 91

September 22nd (Monday)

Chris glanced over, saw David's number flash, and
returned his eyes to the road.

The ringing stopped and immediately started again.
David would call him all night.

"Yeah," Chris said.

"Where ya been?" David asked.

Chris was about fifteen minutes from the chore of happy hour. The faking was exhausting; he didn't need David sucking any energy out of him.

"Been busy."

"For weeks?"

"You may remember," Chris said evenly, "you accused me of giving you a STD."

"Yeah, well, that. No big deal."

"No big deal?" Chris shouted. "That is a big deal. Do you know what a STD can do to ..."

"Whoa ... whoa ... I said no big deal."

"And then you accused me of giving it ..." He swerved angrily to miss a car that had stopped short in front of him.

"Look," David interrupted. "I'm sorry. Okay? I shouldn't have done that. I was angry and I took it out on you. We probably got it from Juliana, the lying bitch." Chris said nothing. "Seriously, who else could it have been? I know you didn't do it. If it wasn't you and it wasn't me, who else could it have been?"

"I guess ..."

"Let's not fuck with her anymore. This kinda set us back and I hate that." When Chris didn't respond David continued, "Why don't you come over Friday? Let's talk about it face-to-face. We can work through this."

"I don't know if that's a good idea."

"Sure it is. We'll just relax. Have fun. Kinda like in the beginning."

The beginning was so vague in Chris's recollection he couldn't remember if it had been fun or if it had just been new.

"Maybe."

"Maybe nothing," David said. "If you can go to JR's, you can come to my house."

"What?"

"JR's."

"I wasn't at ..." Chris began.

"Don't lie, bud. I saw you there. No big," David said nonchalantly. Had he seen Chris leave with Shane? Arguing with Gary? "I was on my way over to speak but by the time I got there, you were gone. What happened to you? Look, I get it, man. I really do. You are exploring. You are working through this phase. Trying to get to the other side. I get it. It's a journey. And I know we've had some ups and downs. But in the end, don't I always take care of you?"

Chapter 92

September 24th (Wednesday)

Gabby had planned on stopping by Starbucks for a latte and a muffin for lunch. But when Karen called and invited her out, she couldn't resist. Karen was a sweet neighbor and reminded Gabby of the things she had missed with her own mother.

Karen had picked Nate's Seafood for lunch. The little pink building that sat off Midway Road would not have been Gabby's pick. Not because the lunchtime hot spot wasn't good, it was delicious. But Gabby couldn't recall anything on the menu that wasn't fried: catfish, hush puppies, chicken, french fries.

"Is that all you're eating?" Karen asked with mock disdain at Gabby's salad. "All of this good food and you want to eat a salad? Ugh!"

"I'm trying to pace myself," Gabby replied with a laugh. "The holidays will be here soon enough. I have to reserve some eating for those days or God forbid what I will look like next summer."

"I'll tell you what you'll look like," Karen said without hesitation. "You'll look like a size four instead of the size two you are now." She cut open a hush puppy and slathered it with butter. "I used to be a four ..." she paused, "teen" she added mockingly. "But that was too much work. Whew!" She wiped her brow dramatically then bit into the puppy. Gabby laughed heartily.

"So ...," Karen leaned forward in gossip fashion. "Did you ever find out who was sending you all those flowers?"

Gabby tried to keep her smile from faltering. "Can you believe I didn't?"

"Really,? You think a guy who sends flowers like that would reveal himself."

"It takes all kinds," Gabby said.

"Yes it does," Karen agreed. "By the way, where is our waitress? I am parched."

"I have to go to the ladies room." Gabby stood. "If I see her on the way, I'll point her over here."

"Thanks, Sweetie."

Should I tell Karen, Gabby wondered as she made her way to the restroom. She had already involved too many people.

The last thing she wanted to do was pull someone else into her drama. "Excuse me, " Gabby said as she bumped into a waiter. "I wasn't paying attention ..."

It wasn't a waiter, it was Brad. He grabbed her wrist. Heat rose in Gabby's face. She jerked her arm back but he held onto it tightly. "What are you doing here?" She said through clenched teeth. Terror and fury ran through her veins.

"Lunch," he replied as if she were stupid.

"You know you're supposed to stay a thousand yards ..."

"How was I to know you'd be here for lunch?"

Gabby cast her eyes over her shoulder. Her gun sat in her pocketbook and they both lay on the table beside Karen. Karen smiled and waved. Gabby forced a smile back.

"Brad, let go of my arm."

He let go with a laugh.

"If you ever come close to me again, I promise you, I'll call the police."

"Do as you wish," he said. "But know this, Gabrielle Garcia, I will always know where you are at. At work, at home, at Jordan's." He smiled broadly and added, "You look beautiful, by the way." Then he walked away. Gabby wandered back to her seat.

"Who was that?" Karen asked. "Oh my, he was good-looking. I'm not sure what he said. But he has you weak in the knees. You've lost all your color. I can't remember the last time a man made me feel like that," she chuckled.

"And I've gotta tell ya," she added before picking up another hush puppy. "He looks so familiar. I think I've seen him driving in the neighborhood a few times. Does he live close to us?"

Chapter 93

September 24th (Wednesday)

Gabby knocked on my door Wednesday night with a pillow and an overnight bag. I opened the door, gave her a hug, and escorted her inside.

She didn't offer an explanation of why she had dropped by and I didn't ask. Instead, I ordered a pepperoni pie and a side of wings from Zini's, I pulled a couple Deniro classics from the DVD collection and we hunkered down on the couch.

I saw a tear stream down her face and I slid the tissues in her direction.

Around ten-thirty pm she fell asleep on the couch. I had wanted her to take my bed but I didn't want to disturb her. So I tossed a blanket over her, turned on the space heater in case she got cold, and walked back up my stairs.

I ached with helplessness.

Around eleven-thirty, I made some tea and called Alicia but got no answer. I checked on Gabby once more to make sure she was still sleep, tossed what was left of the food into a small trash bag, crumpled up the pizza box, and walked it outside to the trash can.

I was three feet from my door when a black Mercedes rolled by. I couldn't see inside the car, the windows were tinted. But the car looked vaguely familiar. I stopped and stared as the car slowed down. I half expected the window to roll down and the driver to ask for directions. But when I stepped toward the car, the driver sped off. A tingle ran up my spine.

Suddenly my phone buzzed. I jumped. It was Alicia. "Sorry, I missed you," she said. "I was in the shower."

"You scared the shit outta me," I said.

"Huh? What are you talking about …."

"There was a car ..." I began. Then I thought better of it. "Gabby's here," I said instead.

"Is she okay?"

"I don't think so. She hasn't said. But I think something happened today. Something spooked her really bad."

Chapter 94

September 27th (Saturday)

      My phone rang just as I stepped into the boxing gym. I looked at the number, held up my index finger to my boxing coach, and answered it. He pointed at the clock. I was already five minutes late for a forty-five minute session that was costing me sixty dollars. But Alicia was on the phone. *I can take a L on the money.*

"Is Gabby still staying with you?" Alicia asked.

"No. I told her to stay as long as she liked. She spent one night and went home."

"Did she say what happened?"

"She saw Brad."

"Saw? Where? How?"

"At lunch with Karen. He threatened her."

"What did he say?"

"That he was watching her."

"Oh my God, Jordan. No wonder she's terrified."

"I know." I changed the topic abruptly and clumsily. "Do you think we'll ever go out again?"

"I don't know," she answered.

"I know I messed up. But ..."

"Jordan, we don't have to ..."

"I'm not asking for your hand in marriage, I just want ..." I sounded a bit desperate.

She laughed. "But maybe that's what I was looking for. Not for you to ask me to marry you. But something more. Something that you weren't ready for and I don't know if you're ready for now. I think you are scared of commitment, Jordan."

Is that what it is? Fear of commitment?

"And that's okay," she said. "*Llegaremos a tiempo.*"

"What does that mean?"

"Loosely translated, we will arrive on time. You'll eventually get there, when you're supposed to be there."

"You know I'm going to keep trying, right?"

"I know," she said.

My coach walked past me impatiently and pointed at the clock again. He made a hang-up-the-phone-gesture. I would've continued to ignore him, despite the fact that I knew he would make this workout hell. But Alicia had to go. So we said our goodbyes. As expected, my trainer put me through it. New punching combinations and new drills. But I was half-distracted, busy processing about my life with Alicia and all I had done wrong.

Chapter 95

September 28th (Sunday)

Chris envied Gabrielle. It was a stupid way to feel. But it was the truth. Yeah, Gabrielle had problems. Sure Brad was a lunatic. At least, though, Gabrielle had an infrastructure that supported her. She had Jordan and Alicia and himself. Not to mention, Raheem, and her family. Gabrielle was dealing with some crazy shit. But at the end of the day, she could unburden herself on any number of friends and they would support her.

His life was different. He couldn't gather his friends together and say, "Oh, I think I'm bi." Or "last night I fucked around with some dude. Does that make me gay?"

True, he had shared some things with Jordan. But Jordan's responses were always so measured; his methodical processing didn't help.

And that's why he was over David's. David offered infrastructure.

"You gonna join," David asked with glazed eyes. The all too familiar white powder sat on the tip of his nose.

When no one understands, who do you turn to? You turn to someone you think you can relate to, someone you think see things as you do, you turn to whoever or whatever will get you through.

"Dude," David said, "You've been uptight since you got here. Relax. All that stupid shit, all that stupid shit is behind us." He grinned at Chris and put his head back so each particle fucked a nerve ending. "Com'on, you know you want to."

Chris didn't have one friend who really could relate, one friend who could understand.

"Look." David sounded remarkably lucid. "I get where you're at. You're confused. This shit is tough. But you worry too much. Things will be okay. I know I've said and done some dumb shit. But this is a new day." He scooted over on the couch, patted the seat beside him, and slid the coke closer to Chris.

Some people would rather be unhappy than be alone. Some people would rather have bad support than no support. Maybe Chris was like that. As damaged as David's infrastructure was, Chris saw an authenticity to the connection. There was a part of Chris that only David saw, a part that David knew intimately.

Chris cast his eyes on David's ex, Peter "Blue Eyes", from the party earlier that year. Why was he here? He was stoned on the couch, eyes closed, not moving.

God, Chris envied Gabby. She had everyone. He had David. David smiled at him and patted the couch again.

Jordan flashed through Chris's mind, then Gabby. Even Shane.

"Atta boy." David beamed as Chris sat and snorted. "By the way," David added, "I've got this chick coming over later. Real freak. She'll do all three of us."

Chris wasn't sure he had heard him right. Not because the coke had overtaken him but because David had spiked his drink.

September 29th (Monday)

"He won't wake up!" David screamed. He sat on top of Chris, gripped his shirt, and shook him hysterically. "You gotta help me," he screeched, and saliva peppered Chris's face. "He won't wake up!"

Chris opened his eyes and stared at David. He wanted to ask "Who?" But he had exerted what energy he had in opening his eyes.

"Get up!" David screamed again. He hopped off Chris and Chris watched as he paced the floor mumbling to myself. "911. Should I call 911?"

Chris closed his eyes again. "Who?" He finally whispered.

"Peter," David yelled. He got on top of Chris again. "Com'on. You gotta help me. We gotta get him to the hospital. Get up! Get up!"

But Chris couldn't get up. He couldn't move. All he could do was lay there as the darkness came and overtook him.

Chapter 96

Oct 4th (Friday)

To say October fifth is Gabby's birthday would be a misstatement. More accurately, October is Gabby's birthday month. From start to finish she celebrates, planning events in advance, filling all our calendars with activities. Two years ago the three of us spent five days in Costa Rica to celebrate her birthday. Last year, she had a mini party every Friday in October and a huge party on Halloween. This year, though, she hadn't even brought up the subject. I got it - but there was no way I was going to let Gabby's favorite month pass by without notice.

So I, the guy who has never celebrated his birthday and who can't understand why anyone above the age of twenty-one feels compelled to do so, planned a surprise party. I ordered dessert trays from Two Sisters Catering off Gaston Avenue; Karen insisted on preparing the rest of the food.

Alicia coordinated; she sent out invites and went with me to reserve Kettle Art Gallery for the location.

And Raheem, the self-proclaimed deejay, loaded up his SUV, borrowed speakers from a friend, and offered to spin on the ones and twos.

Chris was out-of-pocket. But that was okay. Friends understand, right? He said he was coming and that's what was most important.

Gary couldn't make it, he had a show to do. But he had offered to contribute to the festivities and he dropped off a gift. We invited a couple of Gabby's coworkers, some mutual friends from past parties, and a couple guys from the gym who knew Gabby and thought she was hot eye candy. Mike – I still owed him one for the Cialis – came and he brought some twenty-one year old chick, who he promptly abandoned for conversations with Alicia and Gabby.

Chris got there a couple hours after the party had begun. He was distant. But the night belonged to Gabby and I figured I'd address it later. Gabby's face glowed and she swayed around the room. Alicia beamed at me; Karen showered me with motherly love.

Yeah, I was feeling all warm and tingly.

Until Gabby shrieked. The sound cut through the music and everyone in the room.

Brad was standing outside, face pressed to the

window. He held something in his hand.

I took my arm from around Alicia's waist and ran toward the door. Raheem left his turntables and followed. Chris didn't move. "Stay here, in case he circles back," I yelled.

By the time Raheem and I were outside, Brad was halfway up the block. He ran down Elm Street to Good Latimer and then he stole left, racing through the 7-11 parking lot. We lost him for a second in the crowd that milled on the street but saw him again as he crossed Commerce St. He was in arm's reach at Canton St., close enough for Raheem to take a large leap and knock him down. "Motherfucker!"

Brad fell and rolled. One hand went up to cover his face and he tried to crawl backwards. The bottle he had been holding crashed onto the ground.

But this wasn't Brad. We had chased down and accosted a homeless man.

The man spat curses at us, more angered by the lost of his alcohol than the shove to the ground.

"My bad, Dawg," Raheem said as he helped the guy to his feet. He reached into his pocket. "Here's a twenty for your troubles."

"Fuck you," the homeless man said. But he took the twenty.

"Here's another ten," I said, reaching into my wallet.

The man took the bill, studied it cautiously, then put it in his pocket. "Cheap bastard," he said as he dusted off his dirty black sports coat.

"Is she seeing things?" I asked Raheem as we jogged back.

"I don't know, man. Stress will play tricks with you."

"Did the guy even look like Brad?"

"I've only seen him twice," Raheem said. "But same height and build."

"Is it possible that Brad put the guy up to this? I

mean, why did the guy take off like that?" I asked.

"Anything is possible, my man." Raheem shook his head. "That's what makes this so fucking scary."

Chapter 97

Oct 8th (Monday)

"You look like shit," I said as Chris sat down. It wasn't the warmest greeting. But it was accurate. He looked ten pounds lighter than he had at the beginning of the year. He usually sported face-scruff but now it looked more like a raggedy beard, and his eyes were dark. *Why hadn't I noticed this?*

He ran his hand across his face and shifted in his seat. "Is it cold in here or is it me?"

We were at Chaucer's Steaks & Sushi in the Spectrum building in Addison. We hadn't returned to our usual haunts in uptown Dallas. "It's always cold in here," I replied. "I don't think they ever turn the temperature above sixty degrees. Must be for the fish."

He nodded vigorously and blew into his hands.

"I'm really worried about Gabby," I began. "Particularly after what happened at the party."

"I am, too," he said. "I'm worried." He licked his lips and then waved the waitress over for a glass of water. He drank the glass in two large gulps and then began to fidget with his napkin.

Shit, I was worried about Chris. "Chris?"

"Huh?" He was a million miles away.

"What's going on with you?"

"Nothing. Everything's okay."

I reached over and took the napkin out his hand. "No, everything isn't okay. What's going on?" I wasn't sure he was going to respond.

"I was at David's the other night." He scooted his chair to my side of the table and leaned into me. "I think someone may have overdosed."

Raheem walked through the door, at that moment. I put up my hand and raised one finger. He nodded and walked over to the bar. "What? What do you mean?"

"I don't know. I mean, Something bad went down. But I'm not sure what."

Process. "Who have you talked to?"

"Nobody," he replied.

"What about David? What did he say?"

"I can't get him to tell me."

"Chris, this is …" Whys and hows tumbled through

my head, questions I wanted to ask, and judgments I came close to making. "What are you going to do?"

"I don't know."

"Maybe you should leave David alone ..."

He bristled. "It's not David."

"It's not David?" I tried to keep the incredulity out my voice.

"I mean ... you just gotta know the guy. Besides ... he understands me."

"I ..." I started to say, understand? *He understands? I understand.* But did I? I wasn't sorting through my sexuality. I had never taken his journey. *Process.*

"Maybe he does understand," I said. "Maybe he understands better than I do. If he is a true friend, though, he's going to support you. He's going to try to help you find peace. That's one of the things friends do. Is he doing that? I know you are working through some things, my friend. But if he's a true friend, he's gonna be honest with you. He's gonna let you know what really happened that night." I wanted to say more but when I looked up Gabrielle was half way to our table. So I waved Raheem over and reminded myself again that I needed to make Chris a priority.

Chapter 98

Oct 11th (Saturday)

David opened the door with a frown. His folded his arms and leaned on the frame to block Chris from entering.

Chris shoved past him. "What happened that night?"

"Nothing happened," David said with a shrug.

"No. Something happened. I remember you waking

me up screaming. What happened?"

"He took … he took too much shit."

"And what did you do? I woke up and you were asleep and he was gone."

"I didn't do anything. I mean, I overreacted. I'm sorry about it. He's fine. He was fine. Just strung out. That's why I broke up with him in the first place. He doesn't know when enough is enough. I couldn't wake him. I got worked up. We were all high."

"Did you take him to the hospital?"

"I said he was fine. I fell asleep too. When I woke up he was gone."

"Fell asleep?"

"Yeah, fell asleep. Eyes closed. Shit!"

"You can't get your ex-lover to regain consciousness. You think he could be dead and you fall asleep? You are one fucked up sonofabitch."

"What the hell? Don't you dare judge me. You were using the shit just like I was. I don't recall you doing anything."

"Maybe I would have if I hadn't been fucked up. What did you give me?"

"Something to help you relax, to help get the stick out your ass. You should be thanking me. I'm the only person who helps you chill out."

"Fuck you, David." Chris turned and opened the door. "And lose my number."

"Fuck me? Fuck you, motherfucker," David said with a laugh. "Who is gonna help you get off now? Who is gonna be your listening ear for when you whine nobody understands? You goin' back to your friends. Your friends that don't get you?"

"Yeah, I am."

"You'll be back," David said with surprising calm. "You can't live without this stuff. You aren't strong enough to give it up, baby."

Chapter 99

Oct 17th (Friday)

Around midnight, the friendly staff of Gloria's in Addison moves the dinner tables to the sides, clears spacious room on the floor, and allows the room to sway with the sounds of bachata, salsa, and meringue. It helps to have some rhythm, to be able to move the hips but keep the shoulders straight, and to feel the music.

Even if you weren't blessed with natural rhythm, their margaritas swimming in sangria will certainly convince you otherwise. I'm not sure if it was the sangria, the company, or the music, but we were having a good time.

I was celebrating two small victories. I had convinced my friends to get dressed and go party for Halloween. No small task as everyone was in a perpetual funk. And I had convinced them to come out and dance tonight at Gloria's. Had to pat myself on the back for this suggestion. We were having an unbelievably fantastic time.

I admit it. I was probably being a bit partial. But Alicia and Gabby were the two best looking girls there. Then again, maybe I wasn't being partial. Gabby couldn't get off the dance floor; her admirers were lined up. Alicia would have stayed on the dance floor too had I not been doing some major cock-blocking.

Chris isn't a dancer. He doesn't do much beyond the Texas two-step. But I saw him talking to a cute blonde.

As for Raheem, he doesn't need to dance. He stands, he flexes, he shows his pecs, and the girls wander over. We didn't leave until after two o'clock in the morning. When you are feeling that good, why go home early?

****

We pulled up outside Gabby's house around two-forty five am.

"Thank you," she said.

"For what?" I asked.

"For getting me out the house … for everything."

"That's what friends do. Besides … you would do the same for me."

She leaned over to give me a hug, reached for the door handle and stopped. "I don't recall leaving that light on."

The lights in her bedroom beamed brightly. "You sure?" I asked. It was a rhetorical question. I knew she was sure.

"Yes, I'm sure."

"I'll go check," I said.

"No don't, let's ..." she put her hand on my arm.

"Don't worry. I'll be careful. It's probably nothing." I got out the car and closed the door quietly. Quickly I ascended Gabby's steps. I reached out to grab the front door knob and the door swung open. My heart lurched. *Déjà vu*. I turned to Gabby and gestured for her to make a phone call. I hoped she understood, and I stepped quietly into the house.

What do you do when you think someone is in your home? Do you call out – hoping to alert them and scare them into running away? Or do you try to sneak up on them and surprise them? And what happens when they want you to know they're inside?

"Is somebody in here?" I called out. The darkness was my only response. I felt along the wall until I found a light. "I'm armed," I yelled. Although, I didn't have anything.

I turned the light on.

Shambles. Gabby's living room was in complete shambles, smashed as if with a sledgehammer. The coffee table was in two. The couch had been ripped open. Every piece of artwork, every picture, every vase lay in a million pieces on the floor. I felt like someone had kicked me in the stomach. I turned to go tell Gabby but she was standing behind me. Our eyes met and she sank into my arms.

Later on the police would say that this wasn't a robbery. It was an act of passion carried out by someone insanely jealous or with a grudge.

We knew that. What we didn't know was how to stop him or what he would do next.

Chapter 100

Oct 21st (Tuesday)

    Déjà vu.
    Alicia and I sat at Northpark mall, occupying the same seats that we had occupied so many months ago. A cup of Starbucks sat in front of us and throngs of people bustled by. This was the place where I first realized I liked her.

I could feel the memory.

"Earth to Jordan," Alicia said. "Are you there or am I that boring?"

"No, no, you know it's not you. It's me. I'm sorry. What did you say?"

She tilted her head to the side in the same way she had the very first time I had lay eyes on her. Her chocolate eyes met mine. This time I held the gaze. "Is Gabby staying with you?"

"She's staying with Karen tonight. But then she is going to stay with me for a while after that."

"Jordan, you have a one bedroom loft. I have a three bedroom townhouse. You know she's more than welcome to stay with me."

"I know. And I appreciate the offer. But considering how crazy Brad is, I don't think it's wise to get anyone more involved than they already are. The guy is obviously dangerous."

"Obviously," she echoed. "Did the police question ..."

"Oh they went by his house that night," I said. "They couldn't find him. They caught up with him two days later. But he had an alibi."

"Alibi?"

"His family ... they said he was in Austin all week."

"Bull," she said.

"You called it," I said. "Bullshit."

"So what does Gabby want to do?"

"She wants to sell her house. She's thinking about moving."

"I can't say I blame her. To have your home broken into is such a violation ... and to destroy your stuff ... Is she going to stay with Chris at all?"

"I don't know," I answered. "Chris has his own stuff going on at the moment." I paused. "I feel like I'm so supportive of Gabby, like I'm giving her all my energy and I'm not giving enough to Chris. Sometimes I feel like he and I have taken one step forward only to take two steps back."

She put one hand over mine and placed the other on my cheek. *I closed my eyes.* "Anybody can be a friend when times are good, Jordan. Anybody can. Remember when I told you that some friends are for a season and some are for a lifetime? I said you had to decide which your friends were. It's clear to me that Gabby and Chris are for a lifetime. So take a deep breath and reach out to them. You're stronger than you realize and more caring than most people realize. Let them lean on you as you've always done."

I opened my eyes. "Kinda like I'm leaning on you right now?"

She smiled with those eyes. "You're supporting them in a way that far surpasses how I've supported you. I'm a listening ear. You have been there for them in body, mind, and soul. Jordan Spencer, you are a wonderful friend to them. Make no mistake, it's a quality that Gabby loves, that Chris loves, and that I love about you."

I read once that crying is not hormone dependent. It's not about being male or female. It's in the soul. And so my soul let a single teardrop fall as I turned and looked away.
Chapter 101

Oct 25th (Saturday - morning)

Gabby had a restraining order that didn't seem to be doing a bit of good, her house had been demolished, and she had seen Brad in too many places. I wasn't sure how much more she could take. So I was surprised when she agreed to go with Karen and Alicia to the mall. Although, I doubt they would've let her refuse.

"Macys is having a sale," Karen had sung.

"When isn't Macys having a sale?" I asked.

"Oh you, hush," she replied with a wave of her hand."Thirty percent off," she said. "And fifteen percent off home furnishings." Regret flashed across her face as soon as she said the word *home* but she pushed on without missing a beat. "And Nordstroms, let's not forget Nordstroms. It's a girl's night out, right Alicia?"

Alicia happily agreed. "Absolutely, a girl's night it is."

"And then Bob's Chophouse for dinner," Karen proclaimed. "Best steakhouse in Dallas."

By the time they got Gabby to the door, Gabby was almost smiling. The time would be time well spent. It would also be a good time for me to reach out to Chris.

He answered on the first ring. "What's up, bud?" The same sing-song cadence Karen had was now in my voice.

"Nothing," he replied blandly.

"I'm surprised you're home."

"Nothing to do," he said. Silence flowed through the line and then he changed the subject. "How's Gabby? I've been meaning to come by."

"She's good. And we know you have."

"Been kinda busy. Things on my mind."

"Like ..." I prodded him.

"You know. Things."

I took a deep breath. "How are David and Juliana?"

"I dunno. Haven't talked to them."

Another moment or two passed before I continued. "Chris, what's wrong?"

"Nothing is wrong. I have a lot on my mind."

"Okay ... what's ... not right," I asked. "Because

something is definitely not right. I've known you for a long time. I know when something … isn't right."

He didn't answer.

"Can I ask you a question?"

"Yeah," he said quietly.

"Are you using anything … recreationally … outside the time you spend with David and Juliana?"

He waited a beat. "I'm not addicted, if that's what you mean."

"Good … good. That's great."

"And I'm not spending any more time with David or Juliana. That was a mistake. So I'm cutting it all loose."

"What can I do to help you?"

"Nothing … I have to do it on my own."

"No, you don't. That's what friends are for. So you don't have to do it alone."

"Thanks, Jordan. I appreciate it," was all he said.

We talked on the phone for a few more minutes. I even invited him out. He declined.

Oct 25th (Saturday - evening)

He hadn't lied, Chris thought later. The only time he got high was when he was with David. But right now, he wanted to get high. During the week, he sulked. On the weekends, he got high.

Was this addiction? He thought addictions were uncontrollable, sloppy, embarrassing, and painfully evident. But then again, he could barely control it, he was embarrassed whenever it came up, and he was beginning to believe it was evident.

David was right. He wasn't strong.

Why hadn't he accepted Jordan's invite?

He pulled on some jeans and a sweatshirt and snatched up his keys. He had to get out. His place was stifling.

He thought about going back to JRs. He could see if Shane was there, sit in the parking lot and see if the guy showed. Shane was a nice guy. Maybe he could help him sort. Or he could go over David's. David would give him a hard time but he would let him in. They would get high and do whatever David wanted. Chris pulled his door closed and walked outside. As he hit the remote to unlock his car, someone called his name.

"Chris." He turned at the familiar voice. Jordan was walking over to him. "Where are you going?"

Chris looked at the keys and then back at Jordan. "Uh … nowhere."

"Good," Jordan said. "I thought you might need some company. You … um .. you wanna go bowling?"

Chris stared at him. "Jordan, you hate bowling."

"Yeah, I know. Despise it, actually. But you love it."

Chris couldn't help but smile. Bowling would be nice, he thought. But the company would be nicer.

Chapter 102

War Of The Hearts

October 31st (Friday)

Gabby dropped her brother off at Love Field and headed back to her house. His visit had been exactly what she had needed. He had even offered a different perspective on selling her place: Keep the house, let go of the memories.

She had contemplated his words countless times and couldn't help but wonder how many times she had held onto memories far longer than she should.

She pulled in front of her house and pondered the "For Sale" sign that sat in her front lawn. Maybe she was moving too fast, although the weight of the gun in her purse said she wasn't.

She smiled at Karen's ghostly yard decorations and ignored her own overflowing mailbox. She'd grab the mail on the way out and sort it at Jordan's. Now she needed to get a couple things if she was going to stay with him longer. Besides she still needed to get dressed for the Halloween parade.

Her watch said eight forty-five pm. She had to hurry if she was going to meet Jordan and Chris in thirty minutes.

She took her steps by two and headed for her bedroom. A small suitcase sat the top of the closet. She dropped her purse on the bed, pulled the suitcase down, stuffed it with a few more clothes, and took the stairs two at a time back down. She stopped when she reached the last step.

Brad stood at her front door. The moonlight distorted his shadow and it stretched across the room. He stepped inside and locked the door behind him. "Did you really think that I wouldn't find you alone? That you could hide behind Jordan or anyone else?"

He took one step toward her, she took one step back. "I love you, Gabrielle. I did from the day we met. But you could never see that, could you? You didn't get it. But I told you. Did you think I was lying? I told you I loved you. And I do. I told you I would always know where you are, and I did. What I can't figure out is why you didn't believe me. Why didn't you believe me you beautiful stupid cunt?"

Gabby reached for her purse. But she had left it upstairs on her bed. Brad rushed at her; Gabby raced up the steps.

"Remember that girl?" Chris asked. He stood in my living room dressed like a Yankees team player. I was an astronaut.

"Don't you think you should've gone with the Texas Rangers?" I asked.

"You hate the Rangers."

"I do. But I don't want you to incite a riot. You know how Texas is about their teams. I mean, have the Rangers ever won a World ..."

"And you love the team that buys the series. Whatever," he responded. Then he repeated his question, "Remember that girl?"

That girl? Chris used to say it all the time. Now the words sounded foreign.

"The girl from Gloria's? The blonde?"

He grinned. "She's the one."

"I remember. She was pretty hot."

"Right?"

"You got her number?"

"What do you think?"

"Great," I said, although I didn't know if it really was. "You guys going out?"

"I haven't asked her. But I'm gonna." He looked at his watch. "Hey what time is Gabby getting here?

"Nine-thirty," I said. I looked at my watch. It was ten till 10pm. I turned to Chris, "I'm going over."

"Going where?" He asked bewildered.

"To Gabby's house."

"What? All I asked was what time is she getting here."

"And I said at nine-thirty. Which means she is twenty minutes late. Thirty minutes late by Gabby's standards."

"Why would she be at her house?"

"She had to drop her brother at the airport, and she's been saying all week she needed to get some stuff from her house."

"You're overreacting," he said.

But I was at the door. "Then you stay and wait for her. I'm going."

"Just call her," he said as the door slammed behind me.

I jogged to my car looking like Neil Armstrong bouncing on the moon, hopped inside, and started the engine. Maybe he was right, maybe I was overreacting. But before I could pull out the drive, Chris banged on my window.

"I called Gabby twice. I got no answer."

"Get in," I said, "Call Alicia and Raheem. Karen. Gary. Whoever."

"And tell them what?" He asked as we ran the stoplight at Hall and Elm Street.

"Find out if they've heard from Gabby. Tell them where we're going. Ask them to keep calling her."

"Jordan, what if we're overreacting? What if she just forgot her phone?"

"Then we overreacted." I really wanted to be overreacting. I wanted to be able to look back at this situation in thirty minutes and laugh. I wanted Gabby to call and say that her signal was bad or that she had forgotten her phone at work and had to go and get it.

I prayed that I was overreacting.

The black Mercedes, the one that had driven past my place, the one that had followed us at the airport, the one sitting outside her home, told me that my prayer hadn't been answered.

"Is that Brad's car?" Chris asked.

"You bet your muthafucking life it is." My car was barely in park, when we jumped out. Karen waved at us vigorously as she handed out candy to trick-or-treaters. We kept moving.

I hit Gabby's door expecting it to be open. It was locked. I had a key but the security bolt was on.

I banged on the front door. "Gabby, Gabby!" Every light in the house was off.

"What are we going to do?" Chris asked.

"You're going to call the police," I said. "And I'm gonna break a window."

"But what if we're wrong?"

"Wrong? Chris, Brad's fucking Mercedes is parked here. Gabby's car is here. The door is dead bolted from the inside." With those words I took my foot and kicked a hole through the front window. "Gabby!" I screamed.

I crawled through the window and called again. "Gabby, where are you?"

Chris was beside me. "Gabby!" Something *or someone* rustled.

"Brad, you asshole," I said. "I know you're in here."

I flipped a light switch but the house remained in darkness. The cracking under my feet told me why. Brad has broken out all the lights. I tugged Chris's arm. "Check downstairs," I said. "I'm gonna try to find my way upstairs."

I knew Gabby's house well enough. But still bumped into a love seat on my way to the staircase. I bounded up the stairs and ran down the short hall, shoving doors open one-by-one. As I approached Gabby's bedroom, I heard a muffled sound. I rushed to the door and flung it open. "Gabby!" I tried the bedroom lights and they flickered on.

Gabby was lying on the bed, her hands and feet were tied, and a scarf was stuck in her mouth.

"Oh my God." I raced over to her and took the

muzzle out her mouth. "Are you okay?" I reached behind her to untie her hands and she sank her face into my shoulder. "Where is Brad?" It flashed through my head that he might be downstairs with Chris; I was wrong. He was upstairs with me. He smashed a lamp into the back of my head. Gabby screamed and I rolled onto the floor.

"You need to learn to mind your own goddamn business." Brad's low voiced teemed with maniacal rage. "And I'm going to teach you." He dragged me across the floor to Gabby's bedroom bathroom, lifted up the toilet seat, and shoved my face into the bowl. He held it down for what seemed an eternity and then pulled it back up. He repeated it again and then a third time. Each time he would pull my head out, he would laugh. "Now what do you have to say?"

The third time he dunked me, I chuckled a response.

"What?"

I chuckled again.

He leaned in close to me, "What did you say?" He demanded.

I gasped out a breath. "Is that all you have asshole?" Then I bit his ear. I grabbed his ear with my teeth and I tried to rip the goddamn thing off.

He howled in pain and stumbled back. I slid on the floor and gasped for breath. "What have you done?" He screeched as blood rushed from his ear. He reared back and kicked me in the ribs with his boot.

"Get away from him!" Gabby screamed. She had finished untying herself and stood in the bathroom door, gun held high.

"Shoot him," I said.

"Get away from him!"

Brad guffawed, hand still held to his ear. Even I could see she was shaking. "You don't have what it takes," he said.

"Shoot him," I said.

"You don't have it in you, bitch."

"Shoot him!"

Gabby pulled the trigger. She missed.

The bullet whizzed by Brad and landed in the wall. "You bitch!" He rushed her.

Gabby squeezed off another shot but not before Brad reached her. The gun flew out her hand and the bullet landed someplace unknown.

"I'll kill you!" He fell on top of Gabby; his hands were wrapped around his throat. I jerked myself up and ran toward him. But Gabby isn't the only one who carries a gun.

Chris also stumbled into the room with a shiner that said Brad had clocked him downstairs. His first bullet caught Brad in his right thigh. When Brad fell back, Chris' second slammed into his shoulder.

There might have been a third bullet had the police not shown up at that moment.

Chapter 103

Nov 3rd (Monday)

Gary had met Alicia, Chris, Raheem, Karen and I at Terminal A to share in our goodbyes to Gabby.

"Honey, don't make me cry. You'll have my makeup

running," Gary said.

"Gary, it's four in the afternoon. Why are you wearing makeup?" I asked.

"Oh, it's just a little eyeliner. I had a long night last night and all I had this morning was this cheap eyeliner. Don't get your eyeliner at Walmart, honey."

"Um, thanks, Gary," I said. "I'll take that under consideration."

"Oh baby, I'm just playing. Mmm hmm." He turned to Chris as if seeing him for the first time. "Chris," he said.

"Gary," Chris responded.

Then Gary turned his attention back to Gabby. "I am going to miss you." He gave her a hug.

"You are coming back?" I asked.

"Of course," she said. "But my brother's demanding that I come home. And I think I need to. It'll do me some good."

"Of course it will, honey," Karen said, crocodile tears rolling down her face. "Come here and give me a big hug."

"Will you be back for Thanksgiving?" Chris asked.

"Yes," she responded. "There are so many loose ends ..."

"Good," he said. "We'll do something special."

"Absolutely," Karen chimed in. "Something at my place."

"I want to thank all of you," Gabby began.

I shook my head. "There's no need."

"Yes, but there is a need. Sometime we take friends for granted. I think ... no ... I know there have been times I've taken you guys for granted. But without each and every one of you, I don't know that I would've made it through. Alicia and Gary, you've become like a sisters to me." Alicia dabbed her eyes in response; Gary's eyeliner ran.

"Raheem, whenever we've asked, whenever we needed you, you were there." Raheem gave her a shy smile. She gave them each a hug. "Chris, where would I be if you hadn't been there that night? You and Jordan, like knights in shining armor." Lastly, she turned and hugged me. The squeeze was hard on my bruised ribs but I wouldn't have traded it for the world. I felt a bit like the scarecrow when Dorothy whispers, "I think I'll miss you the most of all ..." We watched as she worked her way through security, we waved as she went toward her gate, and then we walked quietly to our cars.

"Do you mind if I get Alicia's number?" Chris asked me. The timing was odd and Alicia's number wasn't mine to give. "Sure," I said. I watched as he asked for her number and then Alicia and Karen got in my car and I drove them home.

Chapter 104

Nov 7th (Friday)

Chris decided not to call Alicia. He wanted to know if Peter had overdosed. But he didn't even know his last name. So broaching Alicia was silly. Instead, he went to David's. The smug look on David's face said he had been waiting for Chris's return.

"Well," David said as he opened the door widely, "the prodigal son has returned."

Chris ignored the comment. He had avoided more than his share of calls from David in the past three weeks. "I need to know what happened that night."

"What happened to you?" David asked as Chris stepped inside. "Who gave you a black eye?" He reached for Chris's face but Chris shrank away. "You need a painkiller?"

"Don't worry about it. I want to know what happened that night."

David followed Chris into the living room. "Like I said, I fell asleep and the guy was fine." He strolled past him and poured himself a glass of wine. "Care for one?"

"The guy," Chris said, "has a name. He's your ex. And no thanks."

"Peter. Peter was fine," David said with forced coolness.

"Bullshit."

"What?"

"Bullshit. You're lying. He wasn't fine. What happened?"

"Why do you even care? You don't even know the guy." David sat on his couch and turned on his TV. "You see my new toy?" He pointed the remote at his new seventy inch screen. "Got it this weekend."

"I care because I do."

David snapped the TV back off. "If I tell you what happened, will you let this go?"

"Yes," Chris assured him as he walked around to the couch.

"Everything? You'll let it all go? We can go back to the way it was before?"

"I promise." Chris sat down.

"Okay, okay," David placed his wine on the coffee table. "Peter was strung out. I couldn't wake him. I really thought he was gone this time. His eyes were glazed over, he was drooling and shit. So I dragged his ass to my car. I drove him back to his house. I still have a key. I unlocked the door, put him on the couch, and called 911. There. You have it."

"You just dropped him off at his house?"

"I drove a couple blocks and waited for them to come. I didn't need that shit coming down on me. They took him to the hospital. He was there for a couple days. End of story. Happy ending."

"Dude, you are a fucking doctor! You dropped him off at his house?"

"I'm a pharmacist. And the last thing I need is some drug addict overdosing in my house. Peter and his stupid ass. Besides, I was fucked up too. You want me to lose my license?"

"Got'cha." Chris stood to leave.

"Wh-where are you going?"

"I'm going home."

"I thought you said that if I told you, you would let it go."

"I am letting it go. I'm letting it all go."

"What?"

"You asked me where I got this black eye. I'll tell you. I got it from this maniac who was attacking my two best friends. The guy jumped me and cold-cocked me while I was downstairs. Then he crept up the stairs and tried to kill my two friends. You know what I had forgotten? That my friend Jordan would take a bullet for any of us. He is ride-or-die. You don't find those friendships anywhere. And I've been shitting on it too long. Kinda like the way you shit on Peter and me. Like you shit on me every friggin' time I come over here. You're not my friend. They are."

"Whoa daddy," David said coolly. "No one forced

you to do anything. Everything you did," he beamed when he said it, "you did because you wanted to."

The words were more painful to hear than Chris could've imagined. "You're right," he said quietly. He gave David a small smile and then he stood to leave.

"You're still leaving?" David's coolness gave way to confusion. "Don't go, please. Chris, we can work this out."

"Yes. Because I want to. And I need to."

"Fuck you," David hurled at him. "You leave and I promise you I will find you at one of those stupid ass happy hours. No joke. I will come to one of those happy hours and tell all your friends that you like boys."

"Do what you have to do. But it'll change nothing at all."

Chapter 105

Nov 8th (Saturday)

"Did Chris call you?" I asked Alicia over dinner.

She shook her head no as she dipped a piece of bread in olive oil.

"He asked for your number. I just thought … " my voice trailed off.

"You thought what?"

"I dunno, I thought …I think Chris may be getting high to avoid dealing with his issues."

"Are you going to talk to him about it?"

"I am," I said.

"It's funny the things we'll do to avoid dealing with our issues," she said as the waiter served her chicken lasagna.

"So true," I said. "I once knew a guy who would take physical intimacy over emotional intimacy instead of dealing with his issues. But he recognized that."

She smiled. "Then you know a man who has matured tremendously." She raised her wine glass. "To him," she said.

"To him."

Chapter 106

Nov 10th (Monday)

The phone flashed Gabby's number around midnight. I snatched it up.

"Hey you," she said.

"Hey you."

"How are you doing?"

"Shouldn't I be asking you that question? The ribs are a little sore, I won't be boxing for a while. But otherwise, I'm good."

"You know I'm so sorry ..."

"Don't say it. You know if you need me, I'll always be around. Regardless of what happens. Speaking of, what's happening? Are you moving home?"

"No. But I have to tell you, it feels good to be here."

"To be away from the craziness and the memories?"

"More than that. For the first time it feels warm to be here. I ... I apologized to my mom last night."

"You did?"

"Yes, I apologized to her and I apologized to my brother. I feel like I've held them hostage with all of the misplaced anger I had toward her. She was trying to protect us and I thought she was weak."

"How did she respond?"

"The way she has always responded. With love and kindness. She's been a far better mother than I've been a daughter."

"You haven't been a bad daughter, Gabby. You've been on your journey."

"Thanks, Jordan ..."

"Anytime, beautiful."

"Yes, well, I'll probably be flying back and forth between here and Dallas for a little while."

"Trying to catch up?"

"Trying to catch up, trying to get to know my mom better, trying to build a bridge ..."

"I think that's great."

"I'd love for you to come out here on a visit."

"I'd love to come."

She changed the subject. "How's Chris?"

"Still shifting through his own shit, unfortunately."

"Are you going to talk to him?" *Everybody asks me that.*

"I am."

"Good. Let me know."

"I will," I said. "By the way, when are you coming back?"

"Monday."

"Do you need me to pick you up at the airport?"

"That would be great."

"Cool. Text me the info."

We talked for a few more minutes and then got off the phone.

Chapter 107

Nov 12th (Wednesday)

They say that admittance is half the battle. That's a lie, Chris thought.

He stood in his bathroom staring into the mirror.

The journey to admittance is the long road, but it's not the hard one. The hard one is remaining on the road when the self-pity, or the yearning, or the fear threatens to make you exit.

Exiting is easy. Any negative emotion can trigger it and suddenly you're journeying back to where you started. How often was he going to journey back, he wondered.

He continued staring when his phone rang. David was calling. He called incessantly. And finally Chris had begun to wonder who really needed who. .

David's tone faded and the phone immediately sang again. This time it was Jordan calling. Jordan Spencer – a loyal friend, who looked out for everybody's emotions even more than he did his own.

Jordan would offer his support. That's what Jordan did. But he let Jordan's call go to voicemail, and then he picked up his phone and dialed a few numbers of his own.

Chapter 108

Nov 14th (Thursday)

"How do you dispose of a gun?" Gabby asked. We were at Hibiscus.

Chris looked a bit mortified. "What? You're going to

get rid of your gun?" He turned his astonished gaze to me and I grinned happily.

"I don't think I need it," she said.

"Are you kidding me? You could be the poster child for the NRA." Chris looked positively baffled.

"You aren't even in the NRA," I said.

"Stay outta this," he said to me. "I'm so tired of you liberal New Yorkers always trying to tell the rest of the world what to do."

"Whatever," I said with a hearty laugh.

"You do realize," he added, "that as part of the Texas Constitution, we can secede. As a matter of fact, we are the only state in the union with that ability."

"And I believe the other states in your so-called-union, would be happy if Texas did."

He hit me.

"Look at Jordan," Gabby said in her Latina homegirl voice. "He's finally got an opinion on something."

"A worthless one," Chris said. "Go back to waffling, it suits you better."

"I never waffle .." I began.

"You do waffle," Gabby said.

"I don't waffle, I process."

"Whatever," Chris said.

"As much as I'm enjoying you two catfight," Gabby said, "can we get back to the subject of gun disposal?"

"Chris has never disposed of a gun," I said. "He has no idea how to ..."

"Shut it," he said.

"But if he does tell you, lemme know. I'll tweet about it ..."

"Tweet?" Chris said. "Bro, you can barely spell tweet."

"You, tweet?" Gabby declared. "You aren't social

enough to tweet. Space issues ..."

"Closing my spaces ..." I said deliberately.

Yeah, Hibiscus is for special occasions, so it was the right place to be.

"I think we should have the crab dip," I said.

"We always have the crab dip," Chris replied.

"Always? We haven't been here once this year. And it's dungeness crab. The only place in Dallas that serves dungeness crab."

"Have you ever thought about being a food critic?" Gabby asked.

"We're not ordering the crab dip," Chris put his foot down. "You have got to start stepping out your box."

I opened my mouth to disagree.

"Just order two appetizers," Gabby said with mock exasperation. "That's what you two do every time we come here. And ... can we please get back to the business of my gun."

"Are you sure you don't want it?" Chris asked.

"Absolutely."

"Well then I'll buy it from you."

"You're a regular Charlton Heston, aren't ya now?" I said.

He replied by giving me my second punch of the day.

"You don't have to buy it," Gabby said. "You can have it."

"If you're sure. We'll have to change the registration ..." he began.

"Whatever you need me to do or sign," she replied.

Our waiter stopped and asked us about drinks.

"The Hibiscus Martini," Gabby said.

I asked for a glass of Riesling. Chris asked for iced tea.

"Iced tea?" I said. "This is a celebration and you are having iced tea?"

"I know, I know," he said bashfully. "I drank too much last night ..."

I refrained from asking with whom.

"And by the way," he said, "I will probably miss the next few happy hours."

"Why is that?" I asked.

"I have my reasons," he simply said. I knew Chris well enough to know this was going to go someplace. So I waited.

"Well," I said, "I don't know that happy hour is so important anyway. I mean, it was just an ..."

"An excuse?" Gabby offered.

"Yes. An excuse for us to get together. I'm sure we can find a lot of other things to do aside from sitting around getting buzzed on Mondays. Not that I'm against a good Monday buzz," I added. "But you get what I mean."

Chapter 109

Nov 17th (Monday)

"So I know you kids kept me out the loop with that Brad situation," Karen said as she plopped another large dollop of macaroni and cheese on Raheem's plate, "but I want to know what's going on with him now. Don't keep me in the dark." It was the closest Karen had ever come to being stern.

This was our early Thanksgiving. Next week Karen's kids would be in town and everybody else would be going home to see family. Gabby was going to be in DC, Raheem to Atlanta, Chris to Baton Rouge, and Alicia to Kansas City.

Karen had blessed us with more of her cooking: fried turkey, macaroni and cheese, candied yams, stuffing, mashed potatoes, string bean casserole, homemade rolls, sweet potato pie, peach cobbler, and an apple pie. It was an area where she could do no wrong.

I looked at Raheem. "Um … no carbs after six, remember?"

"I got an eight-pack, baby boy," he replied. "I can spare one for the night."

"Uh, the vanity," Gabby rolled her eyes.

Raheem shot her his signature smile.

"I'm serious," Karen said as she loaded Chris's plate with a fried turkey leg, a side of mashed potatoes, and more string bean casserole.

"Well he spent about two days in the hospital," Gabby said. "But none in jail. He's got a great attorney."

"He's also got some serious charges against him," I added.

"And a bevy of people who are planning on testifying against him," Chris added.

"Are you scared?" Karen asked.

"I was," Gabby said. "But that's no way to live life." She looked at Jordan. "That's what my friends have taught me."

Karen's voice was a mixture of empathy and admiration. "I can't believe what you went through, doll. You're a strong lady. How are you feeling these days?"

"Better every day. I've learned a lot, about myself. I'm not afraid anymore. I don't want to run and hide. I'm not sure if

I'm strong but I'm definitely stronger."

"You're strong," I said.

"Here, here," Karen added. She uncorked a bottle of wine. "Anybody want a glass?"

"Would you excuse me?" Chris stood, took out his phone, and walked into the other room. My eyes met Alicia's.

"Did you ever look up Roger Guenvar Smith," Karen said as she poured my glass. "You look just like him, you know?"

"I did. And I do not look ..."

"A much younger version, of course. But you do ..."

"I've always thought he looked like The Rock," Alicia said.

"Oh no, dear," Karen said. "The Rock is so muscular. No, much more like Roger ..."

"I've always thought Vin Diesel," Gabby added.

They do this, you know. My friends talk about me like I'm not in the room.

"I don't look like ..." I began.

"Wow," Raheem said. "And I thought white people thought all black people look alike. I didn't know they did the same with their own."

"Whatever," I said. "Besides I'm not ..."

"But I can kinda see Vin now that Gabby mentions it ..." he continued.

" ... white," I finished.

"According to the 2007 census, I think you are technically filed under bi-racial," Chris said as he stepped back into the room.

"Really?" Karen said as she took a box of Breyer's Vanilla Bean ice cream from the freezer. "And here I thought you were Italian."

Chapter 110

Nov 24th (Monday)

      I spent Monday playing taxi shuttle. I took Alicia and Chris to DFW and Gabby to Lovefield.

Everyone had invited me to come home with them, including Raheem.

I appreciated the invites but I decided to go the week alone. It had been a while since I had crawled into my shell and refueled.

Interestingly enough, I didn't require as much solo time as I needed before. Don't get me wrong, I still needed it. I doubt that would ever change. But I didn't need as much. As a matter-of-fact, by Thursday I was feeling a bit lonesome. Which wasn't good as that was the day I got a text from Nicole. Go figure. Three months after my nonperformance, three months after she told me to lose her number, she texted me.

Do you want to come over?

I had a vision of Nicole, standing at the door, looking like a model on the cover of Essence. The image of her brown skin against mine raced into my head and I got a bit of a boner. I took a long minute and then picked up the phone and texted back: **No, I don't. Thanks, though. And please lose my number.**

I got an instant – **Fuck you** – in return.

Yeah, fuck me. Whatever. I got up, called down to the shelter, and found out they needed me to come by at four pm. Cool. That gave me two hours. I threw on some shorts and went jogging.

Chapter 111

November 29th (Saturday)

The West Village is the center of all that's hip in Dallas. While it's no more than four city blocks and sixty or so stores and restaurants, its magic pulls people from all over the metroplex for a drink, a stroll, or a movie.

November in Texas is still a warm month, and as expected, the West Village was packed with the young, the old, the sexy and the not-quite-but-trying-hard-to-be-sexy. Chris and I were sitting on the patio of Taco Diner, carefully positioned to see as many people as possible. Raheem was on his way.

"Do you remember that girl?" Chris asked.

I took a chip and dipped it in some queso. "Of course, I remember all your girls," I said sarcastically.

"I'm serious," he said. "The girl from Gloria's."

"The blonde? You two still in contact?" I asked.

"More like friends … but yes."

I nodded. It was time. *We had to talk.* "Look Chris we need to talk about …"

"Yeah," he said as if he'd been reading my mind. "We do." He proceeded cautiously. "I have an addiction. I don't know if I'm hiding behind the addiction or if the addiction itself has led me down some of the paths I've taken. I have to figure that out. Although, I believe it's a bit of both.

"Remember that night at Karen's? I got up and made a phone call. I was tempted to have a drink. But I'm trying to let it all go … including the drinking … at least for a while. So I called my sponsor. I needed someone to keep me on track.

"I go to a meeting every Monday where we talk about our addictions. That's the reason I can't make happy hour, aside from the obvious," he laughed self-consciously. "That's the reason I was drinking iced tea the night we went out to Hibiscus. I know I lied. I wasn't ready to tell you guys. But I need to be honest with you guys if this is going to work."

I was at a loss for words and beside myself with admiration. "Chris, I'm so proud of you. You know I would be your sponsor …"

He cut me off. "I know, Jordan. I gotta tell you, you

are the only cynic I know hellbent on saving the world. But I had to take this step solo. I had do this first step on my own. Don't worry, though. I have no doubt there will be times I call you."

"Good for you. Good for you." I was so proud of him I could've stood on the tabletop and shouted. "I'm so excited," I said. "I feel like ordering a round of water for everyone."

He laughed. "You're stupid. There is one other thing." His smile faltered.

"What is it?"

"David. Has been calling like crazy. Sometimes thirty times a day. I haven't talked to him. But he said he was going to drop by happy hour one day and tell everybody that ..."

"That you two had a threesome?"

"We had more than a threesome," he admitted.

"Do you think he would?"

"I dunno. I realize he's terribly manipulative and terribly unhappy. But I don't think he has any real backbone."

"Well, if he does," I said, "I'll just reach over and grab your hand. Pretend like you're mine."

Chris's eyes widened. "You would do that? Mr-Don't-Touch-Me?"

"Of course, you're my boy. Besides," I added. "Everybody has a little … bi in them."

"You do?" He asked.

"Oh hell no," I said. "Not me. That's *nasty*," I laughed. "But a lot of people do."

"What about Raheem?"

"Fuck no. He'd beat both our asses for suggesting it."

"Then who?"

"You see that guy over there," I pointed to the skinny white dude with over-sized Gucci sunglasses on his face and the coach bag flung over his shoulder. "He does."

"Fuck you," he said with a laugh. He punctuated the statement by flipping me off.

Good times.

Chapter 112

November 30th (Sunday)

"I need to tell you something," Alicia said into the phone.

Her voice was earnest; I turned down my music and stopped my multi-tasking. "Sure," I said. "Anything."

She hesitated. "Um ... there was a guy ... no, there is a guy at work who asked me out." She paused. "I said yes."

I would have preferred for Brad to have kicked me in the ribs ten times over than to hear that statement.

"I know that we are just friends," she continued. "But I felt like I needed to tell you. That I needed to be honest. It's just a date," she said. "But still ..." her voice trailed off. "Are you there?"

"I'm just ..."

"Processing?"

"Yes," I said. "I'm processing."

"I'm sorry, Jordan."

"Oh, you don't owe me any apology. I appreciate your being so forthright and honest. It's one of the many qualities that I like about you. I want to share something with you. But before I do, please understand my intent in telling you this. I'm not trying to persuade you from this guy, I'm just being authentic and honest, like I should've been in the beginning. You said to me once that I was afraid of commitment. That's not what it really is. I'm afraid of losing the people I love, like I lost my family. The idea scares me shitless sometimes, so I pull people in, because I need the closeness, then get afraid and push them away. I've done it over and over again. I thought I was saving myself from pain. But I wasn't."

"I didn't .." she began. "I'm so sorry."

"There's nothing for you to be sorry about. You made me face that demon, Alicia. I want to believe I'm a better man because of it. In the spirit of authenticity, let me say that I'm jealous. I'm insanely jealous. But I'm sure this guy is a great guy."

"I don't know him well. But he seems nice."

"Well you have impeccable judgment, present company not included."

"Impeccable? I only wish." Then she added, "Let's not let this hurt our friendship."

I wanted to say it won't but it already had. "You're friendship is very important to me, Alicia Farmer. You know that."

"Jordan, you know you're a great guy."

But not great enough. "If you ever need me, you know where to find me. In the meantime, I really hope you and this guy click."

"You do?"

"No, not really," I laughed. "But it was the mature thing to say." She laughed. "So let's catch up later. Let me know how the date goes," I said. Then I made my excuses and got off the phone. The truth is sometimes we lose, right? Sometimes we learn too late. Sometimes the best things are right under our nose and we don't appreciate them. We live, we learn, we deal. No emotional eating. No emotional sexing. Even when it hurts so bad.

I pulled on some shorts and headed out for a jog. One of the nice things about Dallas is that sometimes winter feels like spring.

Chapter 113

My Month of December

In case you ever come to Dallas, let me make a few recommendations. Food: Dallas does an exquisite job on Steak, Mexican, New American (which is a fancy way of saying southern eating), and surprisingly enough, sushi. Dallas has some sushi that rivals some East Coast spots. On the other hand, stay away from Italian. If you ask for a recommendation, someone is liable to send you to Olive Garden and praise the freshness of their bread. So don't do it. And, of course, Tex-Mex. It will pack the pounds on you, but you can't leave the state without trying it.

I'd like to make a recommendation for a club or a place to dance. But like I said earlier, I'm not in good with whoever establishes where the "it" places are. By the time you got here, the places would have changed. Pick up a copy of *D magazine.*

If you're looking for sites to see, skip it. No wait, I don't mean that. Just don't think you're coming to NYC. Dallas isn't "site-laden". But there is Southfork, and the stockyard, and the memorial to JFK and some other cool things to do.

Avoid coming during the summer, it's a beast.

What I'd suggest is going to Greenville ave. and listening to some music, finding a spot in Uptown and watching the beautiful people, or sliding down to Deep Ellum and hobnobbing with the artistic.

For me, things are a little different. Happy hour is mostly a thing of the past. It's not the best scene for Chris and Gabby has been flying back and forth between DC and Dallas a lot. She hasn't decided if she's going to stay in Dallas. I hope she does. But I understand if she doesn't. What's most important is that she is in a good place and that she's rebuilding a relationship with her family.

She will be back the last two weeks of December and I'm looking forward to that.

Chris has been substance-free. I want to say that he seems like the old Chris. But he doesn't. He seems more mature than the old Chris. I'm not sure if he's gay, bi, or straight. I think he's still hammering that part of his life out. But I know Chris and I know him well enough to know to wait for it. He'll tell me when he's ready. It's his journey.

And I'm reading, writing, boxing, running, and volunteering at the homeless shelter. Yeah, knowing your personal demons doesn't make them go away. But it makes them easier to battle. So I'll continue battling mine. I owe that to any and everybody who has tried to have a positive impact on my world – my parents, my little sister, Alicia.

I owe it to myself.

December 24th (Wednesday)

"So are you going to Glenn's party this year?" Alicia asked.

I switched the phone from one ear to the other. "No, not this year. Gabby's having a get together at her house. Something very small. Intimate. I don't think we need that party anymore. Didn't Gabby tell you?"

"She did," Alicia admitted.

"Are you coming?" I asked her. "It won't be a nice as Glenn's. No valet. But it'll be fun all the same. And if you need someone to park your car, I'm happy to oblige."

"Yes, I'm coming. I just know how much you enjoy Glenn's party."

"Whatever," I replied. "So ..." I began, "Are you going to bring the guy you're seeing. Gabby won't mind and I'd love to meet him. I'm sure everybody would."

"No, he won't be coming."

"Why not?"

She laughed. "He was a very nice guy. But there wasn't any really chemistry. And I'm not talking physical chemistry. Although he was a lousy kisser. We just didn't connect."

"Oh," I said. "Too bad."

"Is it?"

Alicia Farmer had caught me in a lie. I felt compelled to make it right. "Actually, it isn't. It's quite good." Neither of us spoke. "Um … I'm a pretty good kisser."

"I know," she said.

"I have a suggestion," I started.

"And that is?"

"Stick with me here," I said. "You could be … wait for it … *my* date."

"I could," she said.

"We could cuddle on Gabby's couch and drink champagne."

"We could," she said.

"You could come back to my place," I continued.

"I doubt that," she said teasingly.

"And you could make eggs in the morning."

"Really?"

"Oh yes, definitely. Scrambled eggs. With cheese."

And then we both laughed. Because sometimes ya gotta.

www.ingramcontent.com/pod-product-compliance
Lightning Source LLC
Chambersburg PA
CBHW070557260626
47161CB00002B/633